# DIARY OF A
## Blues Goddess

D1039212

## ERICA ORLOFF

resides in south Florida, where she enjoys spending
her free time with her extended "family" of friends and
relatives, as well as several unruly pets. She confesses
to being virtually tone-deaf, but does adore jazz music
and the blues, particularly the music of Django Reinhardt.

Erica is also the author of *Spanish Disco*, as well as the
upcoming *Divas Don't Fake It*. She can be reached at her
Web site, www.ericaorloff.com.

# DIARY OF A
## *Blues Goddess*

### ERICA ORLOFF

**RED
DRESS
INK**
™

If you purchased this book without a cover you should be aware
that this book is stolen property. It was reported as "unsold and
destroyed" to the publisher, and neither the author nor the
publisher has received any payment for this "stripped book."

First edition August 2003

DIARY OF A BLUES GODDESS

A Red Dress Ink novel

ISBN 0-373-25032-0

© 2003 by Erica Orloff.

All rights reserved. The reproduction, transmission or utilization
of this work in whole or in part in any form by any electronic, mechanical
or other means, now known or hereafter invented, including xerography,
photocopying and recording, or in any information storage or retrieval
system, is forbidden without written permission. For permission please
contact Red Dress Ink, Editorial Office, 225 Duncan Mill Road,
Don Mills, Ontario, Canada M3B 3K9.

All characters in this book have no existence outside the imagination of
the author and have no relation whatsoever to anyone bearing the same
name or names. They are not even distantly inspired by any individual
known or unknown to the author, and all incidents are pure invention.
Any resemblance to actual persons, living or dead, is entirely coincidental.

® and TM are trademarks. Trademarks indicated with ® are registered in
the United States Patent and Trademark Office, the Canadian Trade Marks
Office and/or other countries.

Visit Red Dress Ink at www.reddressink.com

**Printed in U.S.A.**

Dedicated to my father, Walter Orloff,
who taught me about jazz

## ACKNOWLEDGMENTS

I'd like to, first and foremost,
thank my father, Walter Orloff, who provided advice,
ideas and historical background about jazz and the blues.
As far as I am concerned, he is the world's greatest jazz expert,
and his extensive—some would say exhaustive—record
and book collection helped greatly, as did our e-mails and
conversations. I'd especially like to thank him for reluctantly
giving up several of his Django Reinhardt albums.

I must, as always, acknowledge my wonderful agent,
Jay Poynor, who remains my greatest supporter.
We talk daily, and it truly helps to know he is in my corner
at all times. "Darlin', you're my Luv."

Thank you to Margaret Marbury,
the best editor I could imagine. When I decided
to take the tone of this novel in a different direction,
she was not only supportive but excited. Thank you. I look
forward to our collaboration for many years to come.

What would I do without Writer's Cramp?
Pam, Gina and Jon. Thank you for giving me discipline
as a writer—and wine. Let's not forget the wine.

Thanks to my friends Pam, Nancy, Cleo and Kathy
for being such totally cool women. In the immortal words
of Miss Bella: "You rock."

I acknowledge the late Viktor Frankl
for giving my life philosophical meaning.

Thanks to my mother.
Whenever I felt like procrastinating on finishing this book,
I called her, which was daily. And she happily obliged.
But then would tell me to get back to work.

Finally, to Alexa, Nicholas and Isabella. You can't possibly
imagine what inspiration you are. To J.D., for *everything*.
Always.

*"All I know is when I sing the blues,
the notes are like tiny shards...
proclaiming how my heart is broke in a million pieces."*
—Irene "Honey" Walker

chapter 1

I live in a house with a dead prostitute.

More precisely, I live in a house with her spirit. At least that's what my grandmother, Nan, thinks.

New Orleans is filled with spirits. We're so used to them, we don't give them a thought. Mist-filled cemeteries are tourist attractions, and houses on St. Charles have ghosts. Halloween is more important than Christmas—at least to the drag queens. Voodoo priestesses still practice their art, and superstition is interwoven through our lives as much as the bayou and crawfish.

Our house in New Orleans used to be a brothel and has been in my family since 1890. My grandmother ran the brothel briefly, until Sadie Jones was murdered over sixty years ago. A customer with an obsession for the redheaded whore with the alabaster skin and green eyes stabbed her in an upstairs bedroom. He'd been wordless, with the vacant-eyed look of a man possessed, and my grandmother has never forgiven herself for not turning him away. Another customer, a senator with a handlebar mustache, who enjoyed the brothel every Friday night, shot the murderer dead with a pistol and a single bullet as the man ran outside. My grandmother cradled Sadie's head in her lap as the young woman took her last breath. After that, Nan closed the brothel, married my grandfather, who'd been her most faithful customer, and set about becoming one of the more colorful characters in New Orleans, a city known for colorful characters.

When I was eighteen, I came to live with my grandmother in this house with twenty bedrooms. I soon found out that the spirit of Sadie had opinions on the opposite sex. According to Nan, if she felt you were making a big mistake with a man, she would slam the door of the bedroom in which she'd been murdered. If she approved, the house was at peace.

Considering my track record over the last ten years, there's been a whole lot of door-slamming in New Orleans.

*chapter*

2

"Oh my God, why'd she have to die!" Dominique wailed like a Greek woman throwing herself on the casket of a loved one. "Why? Tell me why?"

"Here's a tissue," I said, calmly passing her one as we sat up against huge pillows, side by side on her bed. We were watching *Steel Magnolias* for the *third* time in two days, huddled beneath Dominique's pink Laura Ashley quilt, with a bowl of popcorn swimming in a tidal pool of melted butter and a pitcher of Sex on the Beach on the nightstand—Dominique likes any drink with sex or genitals in the name.

"I don't understand how you can just sit there, stone-faced like that, Georgia Ray Miller. It's unnatural," she sniffled at me.

"Dominique, you *know* Shelby dies in the end. You've

known this since the first time we watched this video together in high school, and through every single solitary fucking time we've watched it since then. I just can't cry anymore. I cried myself out five years ago."

"But the cemetery scene…" She hiccuped, and with that, she started blowing her nose.

Drag queens are rarely subtle. Give Dominique a feather boa, platform shoes and a new platinum-colored wig, and watch her strut her stuff. But *believe* me, a drag queen with a nightclub act—and Dominique has a sellout one—doesn't *begin* to hold a candle to the sight of a drag queen with a broken heart.

Dominique was actually our only lonely heart at the moment. Good thing, since she was practically a full-time job. One of the benefits of having a house with twenty bedrooms is providing refuge for the lost and lonely. Nan rarely turns anyone away. She has two rules: no weapons and no drugs. Beyond that, if someone's a friend of mine, he or she is welcome to stay as long as necessary. Rent is minimal. And everyone contributes to meals and kitchen cleanup. We've had as many as six lonely hearts at one time following Mardi Gras two years ago when it seemed as if nearly everyone I knew, including myself, walked in on his or her lover in the arms of someone else. That's Mardi Gras. Getting blind drunk, flashing your tits in the street and fucking up your life.

Dominique sighed, flinging her head against her pillow like Gloria Swanson in *Sunset Boulevard*. I stared at her cocoa-skin and her long jet-black lashes curled slightly and framing eyes such a dark brown you couldn't see the pupils in the irises, just coal black. She was beautiful, her cheekbones so high they seemed to carve out cavernous hollows beneath them, like a runway model's, her chin a dainty point with a tiny dimple in its center. She was stunning, even without her usual Velvet Mac lipstick and eyes made up like two wings of a butterfly. "I'm swearing off closeted men, Georgia. I am." She looked at me. "And closeted white men are the worst."

"No, married men are the worst. What am I saying? They're *all* bad, Dominique. It's men. Straight, gay… Of course, I don't include you in that category, Dominique. You're a woman even if…parts of you aren't."

"Thanks…I think." She clutched her tissue, then dabbed her eyes. "Is my mascara running?"

"Running? Honey, you cried it off a half hour ago during the kidney transplant scene. Look, two days in bed is enough, Dominique. Come on…you've left Terrence before."

"But this time there's no going back, Georgia."

"Don't say that."

She lifted her head from the pillow and shook it vigorously. "I am saying it."

"But this moping, this…" I waved my hand at the television. "Endless watching of Julia Roberts on her deathbed…isn't helping, Dominique. You've got to get back out there. You don't see me moping around in my nightie, do you?"

She stared at me. I was wearing a Victoria's Secret black peignoir set. "As a matter of fact, I *do* see you in a nightie."

"This is sympathy nightgown wear. For movie watching. I meant that as a figure of speech. I mean, you don't see me moaning and groaning over my love life. In a nightgown or otherwise."

"Uh-huh." She rolled her eyes at me. "Georgie, you are the original magnet for bad men. Might as well hang a sign on the front door. Married men and mama's boys apply here."

"Yes, but that was the *old* me. Now I have a system."

She snorted. "System? You call what you have a system?"

She was referring to Sadie's ghost.

"Yes, it's a system."

"A door slams, and you take that as a sign. Baby Girl, that's no system. That's plain crazy-talk."

"Yeah, well, you just moved in. You'll see. She'll be slamming doors for you, too. Anyway, at least I *have* a system. I'm not the one who went through two boxes of tissues this afternoon." I stared at the wastepaper basket overflowing with crumpled tissues.

"That's the point. What don't you understand here? This is Heartbreak 101. *Steel Magnolias* is our four-hankie movie. I was *supposed* to have a good cry. We both were. But you didn't so much as shed a tear. You are one cold-blooded woman, Georgia Ray. *Cold.*" She pretended to shiver. "I might have to call you the b word."

"I am the b word." I stroked Dominique's white Persian cat, Judy Garland. "Dominique, there's nothing wrong with me. I sing at weddings every weekend, and before long, I'll sing at the weddings of the second marriages of the very people who were so madly in love with someone else not a year or two before. If I stay in this business long enough, I'll start singing at their third and fourth weddings."

"Sugarplum, if you're trying to cheer me up, you're doing a pathetic job of it."

"That's what best friends are for." I winked at her. "But it's true. Just look at the conventions. Every weekend a new group descends on the city—dentists, insurance salesmen, stockbrokers, engineers, proctologists. I see these guys with gold wedding bands—or telltale tan lines where the wedding band *should* be—and I just know they've got a wife, 2.2 children, a dog named Spike, a picket fence and a minivan at home somewhere, yet they're making a play for every woman at the convention—including the entertainment. It's not a ringing endorsement of the power of love."

"Well, I still believe in love," Dominique said. "And even if you're too damn cynical and stubborn to admit it, you do, too."

Judy rolled over on her back and stretched, demanding, in her regal cat way, that I stroke her belly. This was Dominique's second stay in our house, nicknamed the Heartbreak Hotel. Last time she went back to Terrence again, and I was pretty sure if he turned up at her show tonight with a dozen mauve roses—her favorite—she'd go back to him this time, too.

"I do not," I said rather unconvincingly.

"Yeah right. How is it that I remain best friends with such a liar?"

"Look, you've got a show to think about. You've had your cry. Now it's time to get out of this room and do what you do best, my dear." I stood up and went to her trunk at the foot of the bed that was full of her stage accessories. I pulled out a purple feather boa and flung it around my neck, sending several feathers floating through the air. I sang the first line of Gloria Gaynor's classic, "I Will Survive," the headlining song of Dominique's act.

"That's *my* song, girlfriend."

"Then belt it out yourself." I spun around. "Or maybe you've lost your falsetto."

She gasped as if I'd slapped her.

Never challenge a drag queen to a sing-off. Even without her wig, false eyelashes or makeup, Dominique leaped off the bed, grabbed her own feather boa from her trunk and started singing, transforming before my eyes into her stage persona.

"Get her off the stage," I mock shouted. "She's got five o'clock shadow."

Dominique finally broke into a grin, revealing her dimples. "Thanks, Georgia Ray. Love you." She hugged me, my head against her chest. "Girl, you are so cute, you're lickable."

"Well, I love you, too. Even if your chest does need waxing."

She stepped back in panic. "God! I'm on in *six hours.* A girl's got a lot of waxing and shaving to do." She dashed out of the room toward the shower across the hall. Before she went in, she turned to me and blew me a kiss.

I smiled at her, then lifted Judy the cat and kissed her nose. I left Dominique's room and went into mine and opened the French doors to my balcony. Stretching the length of my room, it has an intricate black wrought-iron railing and a chaise lounge for nights when I want to look at the moon and drink a glass of wine. From this vantage point, I have tossed down beads on the screaming crowds of Mardi Gras. But today I leaned over the railing and saw just a few clusters of tourists and a couple of college kids walking around the French Quarter; otherwise the street was surprisingly quiet. The day was stifling hot, and it was only May. New Orleans has an oppressive humidity. It contributes to the general insanity around here.

I shut the doors to keep the cool air in and went and flopped down on my bed, the goose-down comforter fluffing up on either side of me and letting me sink down into it. With the return of Dominique, the Heartbreak Hotel was officially open.

Heartbreaks seem to come in sets of three. That's another bit of superstition from Nan. I looked up at my ceiling fan spinning slowly around and around. It wasn't a question of when, around this place. It was just a question of who was next.

*chapter*

3

I didn't have to wait long. The next morning, Jack, my band's guitarist, arrived on my doorstep, suitcase in one hand, Fender guitar case in the other.

"It's over," he sighed, setting down his suitcase. "Is my old room still available?"

I rushed forward and hugged him, my hand instinctively brushing back one of his blond curls from his cheek. "You know the Heartbreak Hotel is always open," I said, stepping aside and sweeping my arm up toward the staircase in a gesture of welcome. He hefted his suitcase again, which bulged at the seams and apparently contained everything he owned, and walked through the frosted-glass front door. Following behind him, I silently clapped my hands and shook my hips back and forth in a sort of we-hate-Sara-and-we're-so-glad-she's-gone dance.

"She was cheating on me," he called over his shoulder, looking at me as he mounted the carpeted staircase. "With her cousin's husband. And you don't have to look so positively ecstatic that we broke up."

"I'm not ecstatic." I widened my brown eyes to look innocent. "Just mildly pleased," I muttered under my breath.

He turned around as he reached the landing. "I heard that." He faced forward and walked down the hall, continuing, "I know I was an idiot for putting up with her. I know it. But let's leave the I-could-have-told-you-so-Jack looks alone."

I contorted my face into my best effort at looking appropriately sad and nodded. I tried to refrain from taking the remaining stairs two at a time and skipping down the hall to his old room, two doors down from mine. He opened the door and set his suitcase and guitar on the Oriental rug one of Nan's old lovers, the mysterious Mr. Punjab, had shipped her from India, with a letter professing his undying devotion.

I sat down on the bed, and Jack came over and sat next to me, exhaling slowly. "Just like old times. Two years ago, was it? The Mardi Gras I found Leigh in bed with her old boyfriend?"

"Yeah. That was the year we all took leave of our senses."

"Well, I can't say I like finding out my girlfriend was fooling around on me, but I do love this place. I was almost relieved to move out, knowing I was coming here. Knowing you were here. And Nan."

"And Dominique."

"She's here? God help us all. Yes…even Dominique. Though if she comes at me with any of her mud masks or aromatherapy treatments, I'm going to lock her in the room with Sadie's ghost."

"She doesn't believe in Sadie."

"Yeah, well, wait until she's home alone some night and hears the door slam." Jack draped an arm around my shoulders and pulled me closer to him. "Did everyone know except me?"

"Know what?"

"Don't play dumb with me, Georgie. About Sara."

I shrugged. "I don't know, Jack. You always seemed more in love with her than she was with you, but it wasn't my place to tell you. Or any of the guys'."

"Hey, next time…if there is a next time…I give you permission to stop me. Between you, Gary, Tony and Mike, someone in that band had better talk some sense into me. You guys are my best friends. You're supposed to prevent me from dating women like her."

"And what exactly is a woman like her?"

"Trouble. Two-timing trouble. I don't know. See…I'm not even sure I can spot them when I see them. But you can. You knew. It's that women's intuition."

"Women's intuition. Bullshit. Look…she flirted with every guy in the room. But even if we had all tried to say something, it wouldn't have mattered. People in love don't listen—especially men. You go on autopilot. And the pilot is your penis."

He grinned at me mischievously. "Then you better talk to Jack Junior down there and stop me from making another mistake."

"I make it a point not to be on a first-name basis with my friends' penises. As far as I'm concerned, Jack Junior is on his own."

"That's not very nice, leaving Jack Junior with no sense of direction."

"His direction is up—and hard. Jack, you—and Jack Junior—always go for the blond-haired, blue-eyed beauty queen with ice water in her veins. Do you not see a pattern?" I shook my head. "Why is it up to me to point out your woefully bad taste in women?"

"Because I'm a man. We're stupid. It's a genetic failing in our chromosomes. I admit it."

"Thank God. It's about time."

Jack and I have been friends ever since he joined Georgia's Saints, our band, replacing our old guitarist, Elvis, who got into channeling "The King." Shortly thereafter, Elvis showed up at a society wedding in a sequined polyester jumpsuit instead of the requisite tuxedo. We were sad to see Elvis head for fame and fortune in Vegas—or at least a gig singing "Love Me Tender" at this little wedding chapel. But Jack fell into a groove with us, as if he'd always been part of our group.

I flopped back on the bed. "I am sorry about Sara. I never liked her, but that doesn't mean I'm happy that you caught the little bitch with someone else."

He fell back next to me. "You're practically oozing with sentimentality, Georgia."

"Yeah. I know. It's one of my many shortcomings."

"I don't know that you have as many as you think. Anyway, I figure a night blinded by tequila, a few clubs, some R and R at the Heartbreak Hotel, and I'll be over her in no time."

I rolled over and kissed his decidedly stubbly cheek. "That's the spirit.... You're face is all scratchy. You need a shower and a shave. I'm going to go take a nap before the wedding tonight."

"Didn't you *just* get up?"

"Yeah. But that means nothing to us creatures of the night." I feigned a Transylvanian accent.

He stretched. "Sara and I fought all night long. A little shut-eye sounds good to me, too."

I got up and walked to the door. "Sleep tight. Watch out for Sadie."

"I'm more afraid of the wandering drag queen and her mud masks."

Hours later, Jack frantically knocked on my door. "You ready to go?"

"Of course not."

He opened my door, handsome in his black tux. "Jesus Christ, you're not even *dressed?*"

"You know I am genetically incapable of being on time."

That is my stock answer. I also blame it on pantyhose. And sequins. They're a deadly combination.

Sequins are unforgiving. If you want to wear something that screams out that you've indulged in a chocolate binge of epic proportions, including Junior Mints, followed by a pint of Heavenly Hash ice cream, wear sequins. If you want to remind the world—no, flaunt to the world—that you use the treadmill in your bedroom as a coatrack, wear sequins. If you want proof that God in heaven, indeed, has a fucking sense of humor, then look in my closet. In the colossal cosmic joke that is my life, I wear sequins every weekend. I live in sequins.

And so there I was, in my best bra—which simply means my two cats haven't chewed it—and a body shaper, staring at six sequined dresses like a sparkling, spangled rainbow, and dreading putting any of them on.

"Gary's going to kill us," Jack said, his hair still wet from the shower.

"You shaved. Very baby-faced now. Cute."

"Sara liked that whole slightly edgy musician look, complete with perpetual five o'clock shadow, so it's outta here. She also hated the earring—" he pointed to the small diamond stud in his left ear "—so it's back. Now stop talking, Georgie, and start dressing."

"I *hate* these dresses. Every damn one of them," I moaned. "Sure, you all get to wear classy black tuxedos, but I have to look like a refugee from the 1970s."

"And you would rather wear…what? Your bra on-stage?"

"No. But not this." I held up a silver-sequined gown. Being in a wedding band is like being stuck in the disco era. Think of every song you've ever heard by ABBA, and imagine singing them each and every weekend while grandmas and aunties, often in sequins themselves, take to the floor, usually dancing with prepubescent nephews and grandsons who roll their eyes and wish their private-junior-high hell would end. Playing conventions is worse. Imagine two thousand dentists converged on one dance floor in the grand ballroom doing the 'gator. That's a lot of bicuspids you're looking at. Now picture that you have no time for a personal life because you're singing for *other* people's personal lives, and you get the idea.

Georgia's Saints is the most popular wedding band in New Orleans. We do a set of zydeco at conventions. However, most white men can't dance, and they sure as *hell* can't dance to zydeco, no matter how generic we play it, so truthfully, what we do is pretty basic, though the guys are excellent musicians and my voice can even make a ballroom full of funeral directors get up and dance. I've been friends with Gary, the keyboardist, since my freshman year of college, and we formed the band seven years ago while we were still in school—first for extra money, then, as we started getting booked even a year in advance, we devoted ourselves to it full-time. Gary is stuck in another dimension. He actually *likes* ABBA. He also likes leading the hokey-pokey, singing to grandmas in sequins and getting a room full of computer geeks from Silicon Valley to do the electric slide. He was positively giddy when the macarena craze began. Gary is balding, and probably all of five foot four, married now with three kids born in four years—like he doesn't know what causes that?—always short on money so he accepts any job that comes our way. He's also a great keyboardist and gifted arranger—even if what he arranges are KC and the Sunshine Band songs. I forgive him his eccentricities, like the fact that he refuses to believe disco is dead, and the hippest he gets is listening to vintage Madonna, and he forgives me mine.

He accepts that I am always late, always have a run in my pantyhose, crave Junior Mints, often have chipped nail polish and, to cap it off, lipstick on my teeth, and that I always cry, no…sob…at weddings. Something comes over me, and so I keep a tissue tucked in my cleavage just in case. I also wear waterproof mascara. Dominique is wrong. First of all, she wears mascara that runs despite my arguments for waterproof. Second, though she accuses me otherwise, I also still believe in love. I don't know whether I cry because I think the love between two people taking to the dance floor for the first time as husband and wife is so beautiful, or because I'm not sure I believe it ever really lasts. Or because some of the greatest guys in my life prefer wearing pantyhose and mascara, just like me, and want to borrow my clothes. Or because no one's ever asked me to marry him.

I want to get married someday. But after all I've seen as a wedding singer—grooms making out with maids of honor in upstairs hallways, the bride's side ending up in a massive brawl with the groom's side, and even a couple of no-show grooms on the big day—I picture, instead, me growing old like Nan. Still in this house surrounded by my friends and a few cats. I'll be the Crazy Cat Woman of New Orleans. Though, with all the eccentric characters in this town, I'm sure that coveted title is already taken.

"Georgie! Decide already!…Come on! What about the red sequins?" Jack pulled me back to the immediate crisis of what I was going to wear at the wedding we should have left for twenty minutes before. He grabbed the red dress on its hanger and thrust it toward me.

"Convention-wear." I hung it back up. "Stuffy parents of the bride do not want their wedding singer dressed in red. They prefer silver, pale blue…lavender, even."

"Then wear the silver. The silver is fine."

"Well, I have a slight problem with that."

"What?"

"Guess?"

"Your fucking pantyhose."

I nodded. "The silver's got a thigh-high slit." Pantyhose is the bane of my existence. They can put a man on the goddamn moon, land a probe on Mars, but they can't make a pair of pantyhose that are runproof? If men wore pantyhose, I can assure you they'd have an entire Pentagon division devoted to finding a way to make them. I know that it's oh-so-sexy to go without pantyhose, but I rather like my control tops. It's the runs that kill me.

"Georgie…honest to God, we don't have time to stop at the drugstore to buy a pair."

"I know." I shook my head. My hair was amassing into ringlets, thanks to the fact that I hadn't left enough time to blow-dry it straight. My hair has a life of its own. I look white—sort of. People ask if I am Spanish or "something." The "something" is pretty accurate. Nan's mother was black, my father had some Cuban on his mother's side, and my paternal grandfather was half-Cherokee. Down through the generations what I have from the maternal side of my family, besides a love of New Orleans and music, and great pride and a pretty strong stubborn streak is willful hair.

"Come on, Georgie," Jack urged. "Just wear the silver, and we'll worry about the pantyhose on the way." Jack, quite possibly, knows more about pantyhose than the CEO of Hanes or L'eggs. In fact, every single member of the band has at one time or the other raced out on break to buy me a pair. And Jack and Gary have also bought me tampons in an emergency. Being in a band with four guys is like having four very tolerant brothers.

I threw the silver dress over my head, Jack zipped me, snagging my hair in the zipper and causing me to shriek in pain. After extricating my curls, and Jack pulling the snagged hair out of the zipper, I grabbed my makeup bag and the one pair of hose I did have that had a small-ish run that might be stopped in its tracks by Wite-Out. Yes, clear nail polish works better, but when none is available, Wite-Out will do. It sort of glues the run to your leg. Elmer's is a close second. I've even tried Crazy Glue in a pinch, though I very nearly glued my fingers to my leg.

Jack and I flew down the stairs, blowing kisses and waving to Nan as she sat on her balcony, watching us pile into Jack's old Buick. If I have willful hair, he has a willful car. I settled into the passenger seat and started putting on my makeup, while he put the key in the ignition. We both crossed ourselves simultaneously in prayer that the car would start. It did. A testament to the power of miracles and the Patron Saint of Jack's Car, whom we'd named Saint Mary Emmanuel of the Buick. Jack drove us out of the city of New Orleans toward the plantation where the wedding was to be held.

In the tiny little mirror on the visor, I watched my crimson lipstick smear on my chin as I applied it at the precise moment we hit a bump. I sighed. What the hell was I doing? How did I get to be a wedding singer in sequin dresses, pantyhose and cat-chewed bras? What I really want to do has nothing in common with dental conventions or weddings. Or leading a roomful of thirteen-year-old bar mitzvah boys on the make in the limbo (which inspires them to try to look up my dress). Or the macarena.

I want be a blues singer.

But I'm a prisoner of a fear so cold it wakes me up in the middle of the night—when I find myself talking to the spirit of Sadie. If you sing at a wedding, you have a captive audience. A roomful of people are probably so drunk they wouldn't know an off-key C from an A-flat. They're happy with disco and cheesy standards. Conventions are more of the same. People pretending to be single for the weekend grope each other in grand ballrooms. But blues and jazz enthusiasts are a breed apart. They're obsessed with jazz, with what makes one instrumentalist a wedding-band player, and another John Coltrane. And the great ladies who have sung the blues are legends who cast a very long shadow. So I've been taking the easy way for a long time—so long that I sometimes tell myself I don't mind being where I am. Singing ABBA instead of Billie Holiday.

Sometimes I think I haven't earned the right to sing the blues. I've had a dozen relationships go up in flames, but I've never met The One. I haven't loved a man so much I thought I would rip my own soul out for the chance to see him once again. I haven't suffered enough.

I'm also not like Michelle Pfeiffer in *The Fabulous Baker Boys,* writhing around on top of the piano without being so klutzy that she rolls *off* the piano. Nor am I like Nicole Kidman in *Moulin Rouge,* hanging from a swing and inspiring a roomful of men to sigh. Yes, singing bubblegum pop is one thing, standing in a spotlight like a true chanteuse is something else entirely.

So while I bide my time, waiting to evolve into a blues goddess, waiting to get the nerve to stand in that hot light and belt out a song that speaks to other people, in the way that static electricity can send a shock through one person's hand to another, I sing the words to every song I wish I didn't know.

"Get Into the Groove," by Madonna. Know it.

"My Heart Will Go On," by Celine Dion. Know it.

"Oops! I Did It Again," by Britney Spears (know it and particularly hate it).

"Celebration," by Kool & the Gang. Can sing it blindfolded.

Unless, of course, it's at the Wedding of the Year, and I get the shock of my young life.

Cammie Winthrop was to marry Dr. Robert Carrington III, the plastic surgeon who can liposuction your Heavenly Hash-enhanced thighs away, on this particular beautiful sunny day in May—with no humidity—as if her father had ordered up the weather from God himself, which he might have because if God can be bought, Roger Winthrop is buying. He is the king of New Orleans real estate, and the reception Jack and I were racing to in his Buick was to be held in the ballroom of the Winthrop family's very own plantation. That's another side of New Orleans for you. Plantations and Greek Revival mansions surrounded by moss-draped oaks. You feel as if any moment someone's going to hog-tie you into a corset and a hoop skirt.

Jack and I arrived at the Winthrop plantation. Gary was pacing as we entered the ballroom.

"Do you live to torture me?" he asked. Then he put up his hands. "Don't answer that. I know…the Four Horsemen of the Apocalypse will ride through the French Quarter before you're ever on time." He looked at my leg. "Wite-Out? Please….please, I am begging you, tell me that's not Wite-Out. Georgia…when you go to *buy* pantyhose and tampons, can you not just make a mental note to purchase enough for a few months? Like pantyhose—buy every last pair in your size. I mean, why do *I* know more about your preference for control tops than you do? Why? Tell me why!"

Gary was clearly panicked, and his voice was rising into a falsetto range usually hit only by Dominique. Did I mention, the Winthrop wedding was *the* social event of the year? If we played well, which, after years together, we did effortlessly, we would have weddings and functions filling our schedule for the next two years. But Gary thrived on panic. That and ABBA made him tick. Just like antagonizing him brought me small comfort and wrought revenge for the sequins.

"You need to *seriously* take a Valium. Go to the bar and have a shot of something."

"Georgie, you are the reason I live on Tums," Gary whined. "See these?" He pointed to beads of moisture accumulating near his receding hairline. "You cause these."

"Fine. But I'm the only person in the band who can fill out a sequin dress."

Endgame.

Soon, I was singing my heart out, hoping, as I often and ridiculously do, that there among the tables-for-ten surrounding the dance floor was some record executive waiting to discover me—the easy way. All right, so this isn't exactly a formula for being discovered, but I tell myself it's possible. Like run-proof pantyhose being invented.

I was, this day, quite specifically, singing the infamous, crowd-pleasing, no-wedding-will-be-complete-without-it song, "Celebration." Ever notice how few words it has? It's pretty much just endless repeating of "Celebrate good times" and "Come on." Doesn't take Billie Holiday to sing it. But Cammie Winthrop wanted to dance to it with all her blond sorority sisters (not a brunette in the bunch, though the band and I had a betting pool on the number of *natural* blondes, which was likely considerably smaller). And whatever Cammie wanted, Cammie got. Including a five-thousand-dollar muted oyster-colored Vera Wang dress and a diamond tiara.

I was on the small stage that had been built by the dance floor, sparkling in my silver gown, with not one but *two* pairs of pantyhose on. Well, not exactly. I had one leg each of two separate pairs. I arrived at the wedding in the Wite-Out pair, which I had put on while Jack screeched his way onto the plantation's grounds, me wriggling into them on the front seat, and which had a run in the left leg—held in check by a smear of white. Gary, obviously tired of my ruining a pair of hose at every wedding, and always in the leg visible through the slit of my dress, almost always keeps an extra pair of my size B's in nude, *with* control top, in his keyboard case. I had counted on that all along. I had grabbed them from him as he mopped at his forehead, and I raced to the bathroom, sweating all the while, making my hair frizz and curl faster than ever. Putting on the new pair, my nail made a run in the opposite leg. Again, I cursed the geniuses who could send a probe to Mars but not make a run-proof formula. However, with some creative cutting with a steak knife borrowed from the kitchen, I had, ostensibly, one full pair of pantyhose. One of each leg, with a double set of control tops. I was feeling very tight-tummied.

And I was singing the aforementioned simple-to-remember words to "Celebration."

And I glanced across the dance floor.

And the words to "Celebration" left my mind.

Gone. Like a giant black hole had sucked them from my brain. Nothing in my mind but "la, la, la." Gary looked at me imploringly. Jack stared at me desperately, as if willing the words into my brain. But it was hopeless. Because there, across the dance floor, standing on the perimeter, looking slightly older but still confident and handsome, was Casanova Jones.

The only man I'd ever, even briefly, thought might be The One.

*chapter* 4

It was the shriek heard round the world. Or at least round the French Quarter.

The day after the Wedding of the Year and my momentary attack of amnesia, my friend Maggie came over to cut my hair and dye Dominique's eyebrows to match her new platinum look. As soon as I told them that I had run into Casanova Jones, Dominique shrieked and began hugging me and jumping up and down.

"Did you fuck him in the men's room?" Dominique squealed.

"No, I did not!"

"The ladies' room?"

"Give me a break."

"You thought about it though." She stepped back and wagged her finger as if scolding a child.

"God help me, you're impossible."

"This guy must be something if he's a possible bathroom screw," Maggie said, directing me toward the sink. "I need details. Like who is he? And what the hell kind of name is Casanova Jones?"

"I can't tell you yet. I'm in hair shock. What, exactly, are you doing with your hair?"

Maggie works at a trendy salon near the Garden District. She makes a ton of money—in cash. She makes a whole lot more than a wedding singer, I can tell you—though I guess that isn't really saying a whole hell of a lot. Still, she doesn't have to wear sequins to do it. She's considered one of the best stylists in the city and even does the hair of a couple of well-known actresses when they are in the Big Easy shooting movies. But somehow, despite knowing everything there is to know about cutting hair, and highlights, and foils and all of that, her own hair is what I would gently term "experimental." It's art. What kind of art, I can't tell you. This particular Sunday, I would *perhaps* call her hair color raspberry, though it was more accurately some strange hybrid of red and purple. And the cut was lopsided. As in uneven.

"It's asymmetrical. That's very in this season."

"It's lopsided."

"*You* call it lopsided." Her hazel eyes played peekaboo as her hair fell in front of her face as she moved. She has a smattering of freckles across the bridge of her nose, and though her skin is very pale, she never wears makeup—which drives Dominique insane. "My clients call it asymmetrical and pay a hundred and fifty bucks to have it cut this way."

"Fine, but while you've got sharp scissors in your

hands, remember that I'm still in favor of both sides being even."

"You can *carry* the asymmetrical look."

"I don't want to carry it."

"Why are we even talking about hair? Tell me about this guy you two are screeching about."

"All right. He was my one unrequited love. The *one* guy that if I could go back and do it all over again, go back to high school knowing what I know now, I would have fucked him. More precisely, I would have lost my virginity to him instead of the asshole I finally did lose it to my freshman year of college." I liked to pretend my entire two-month relationship with Dan What's-his-name, Virginity Bandit, never occurred.

"So what happened between you?"

"Nothing much. A lot of flirting. I don't know. We just never acted on it. Maybe it was timing. That and he was one of the 'beautiful people.'"

"I know you'll find this impossible to believe," Dominique interjected. "But Georgia, despite being one smokin'-hot, overwhelmingly sexy thing now, and me, being the delectable creature standing before you…we were outcasts in high school. For God's sake, I was a *boy* in high school." She shuddered.

"You—" Maggie raised an eyebrow and playfully stared up and down at Dominique "—I could see. But Georgia?"

I nodded. "And he was…I can't really explain how I couldn't even speak every time I was within five feet of him. Total lust."

I knew Maggie would understand. Maggie had wanted Jack from the first moment she laid eyes on him five years ago. He was her one unrequited lust. Jack, on the other hand, gravitated toward magnolia queens, not a Goth, pale-skinned, raspberry-haired woman with a pierced belly button and tribal tattoos encircling her arms.

"We just called him Casanova Jones because he was such a damn slut," Dominique added. "His real name was…what the hell *is* his real name, Georgia?"

"Rick."

The night before, Rick had approached me between sets, raising the eyebrows of my bandmates. Certainly, I was their lead singer, but to them, I was the woman with panty lines and lingerie-obsessed cats. I was the woman who spilled cocktail sauce down the front of her one white gown—which no dry cleaner could salvage. In short, to them, I was Georgie, the woman least likely to attract a guy who owned—didn't rent—a custom-fitted black Armani tuxedo.

"I thought it was you." Rick had smiled, leaning in to kiss my cheek, and allowing his lips to stay there for that fraction of a second too long. He took my hand and held it, his index finger stroking the inside of my wrist ever so slightly. "You're still as beautiful as ever, Georgia."

"Thanks. You look the same. Shorter hair… A little more corporate, but other than that…" His eyes still crinkled in the corners when he smiled, and his teeth were toothpaste-commercial perfect. His hair was still thick and a deep black; he had a strong jawline and very broad, former football-player shoulders.

"You know…you were the *one* girl I've wondered

about…. Have you stayed in New Orleans this whole time?"

"Can't get beignets anywhere else."

"I never left either. Even went to law school here. New Orleans is my town. Must be destiny that we ran into each other finally."

Yeah. Destiny. Or another cosmic mind-fuck.

"And then what?" Maggie asked.

Dominique held up her hand. "Wait…was the kiss on the lips or the cheek? There are more important things to discuss first."

"Cheek," I said firmly. "Ladies, he was there with a date. A *gorgeous* date, I might add. She looked like a Swedish supermodel. And she was perched on these four-inch stilettos and walked around in them like she was in sneakers. Effortlessly."

"Don't you *hate* women like that?" Maggie asked as she stuck my head under the faucet and started washing my hair.

"Hold on, girls." Dominique sashayed over to the counter and hopped up on it, sitting there, legs crossed and fluffing her hair. "*I* walk effortlessly in stilettos—you can't judge a woman for that."

"Yes, we can," Maggie said.

I have never seen Maggie in a pair of heels. She always wears black boots, even in the dead of summer. If she dresses up, it is only to wear her black boots with a black skirt, topped with a black jacket. She saves all her color for her hair.

Maggie lathered me up with her secret shampoo. I talked loudly over the water, my voice kind of echoing in the sink. "So his date was hovering in the background, a few feet away, trying to look disinterested but giving me the evil eye. And he asked if he could take me to dinner on Friday. For old time's sake. To catch up."

"Once a male whore, always a male whore," Dominique called out over the sound of the faucet.

"I don't know. I didn't get the feeling she was his girlfriend. But I barely know him. I don't even know if we could figure out enough things to talk about over dinner."

"Oh please," Dominique clucked. "I thought he would bend you right over a desk and take you from behind the way you two talked in homeroom. I remember wishing someone would talk to me that way." She sighed. "If things go right, you won't be doing very much *talking* at all."

Maggie finished rinsing and piled my hair into a towel, which she did up into a turban.

"Shut up, Dominique! I don't usually have sex on the first date."

"You don't usually date, period," she countered. "You're always busy with the band. You should take up sleeping with one of them—not Gary. One of the other ones. Not Jack—Maggie has dibs. That leaves Mike or Tony. And Tony has a British accent, so I vote for him."

"Irish."

"Irish what?"

"It's an Irish accent."

"Fine. I mean, if you're going to spend every weekend with those guys, you might as well."

Maggie sat me down in a chair and started trying to pull a comb through my hair, which is akin to pulling a comb through Brillo. My hair falls to the middle of my back, though with the curl in it, when it's dry, it's usually just past my shoulders.

"Ouch! What are you *doing?*" My eyes teared up from the tugging.

"Sorry," she muttered. "Listen, you *have* to go out with him. Come on. I'd go out with Jack in a heartbeat."

"And I'd go out with George Clooney if he asked," Dominique said. "Well, if he *begged.*"

Dominique takes her Clooney obsession very seriously. And she firmly believes if he just for a moment put aside his rampant heterosexuality, he would, indeed, go for a six-foot-two-inch drag queen with platinum hair and a collection of vintage transvestite go-go boots.

"Look, dating is hard enough without being with a guy so good-looking that all the women in the room want to sleep with him."

"Is that what this is all about? Personally, I *want* to date a man everyone wants to fuck because I'm so *deliciously* fuckable myself," Dominique said, pushing her fake tits together and admiring them. "You know, Georgia Ray Miller, you have had some ridiculous theories before. And this from the woman who takes advice from a ghost."

"Fine. Don't come screaming into *my* room in the middle of the night when you hear her footsteps in the hallway and her slamming doors."

"Uh-huh, girlfriend." She hopped from the counter and wiggled her hips. "Let's put aside the ghost for a minute, and consider Casanova Jones. First of all, I don't know what it's going to take for you to realize how beautiful you are. I have to *work* for *my* beauty! You think all this waxing and dyeing and primping and plucking is easy? Hmm? Georgia Ray, I remember Casanova, and he *was* one of the fuckable gods of high school. But you—" she came over and stood directly in front of me "—you are an equally fuckable goddess. A beautiful, sexy, voluptuous goddess. I have breast envy. I mean, yours are perfect." She reached out and squeezed one of my breasts. I didn't even blink. She's had breast envy since I got my first padded bra in seventh grade, and feeling me like an overripe cantaloupe was just typically Dominique.

"Well, you've slept with your quota of men since high school, so I'd say it's time to consummate things with this Casanova guy," Maggie said. "Most of us would do anything to be with that one guy we crave."

Maggie is fearless enough to wear lopsided hair and not care about it. She gets her tattoos without getting drunk first, and she doesn't even flinch. She will speak her mind to anyone—from a drunken Mardi Gras reveler, to a snobbish customer, to her very formidable father. She was the first person I knew to pierce her belly button. And the only person I knew who pierced her nose—and her tongue. She eventually took out the stud in her tongue, but a tiny diamond in her nose remains. Maggie never cares what anyone thinks about her. Not when her hair is pink, not when her tattoos are displayed in all their glory when she's wearing a tank top.

Dominique is also fearless—though not about spiders or scary movies or any one of a dozen things she's ordinarily terrified by. Still, she was a he—Damon— in high school. After we graduated, Damon told his father, a retired captain in the army, that he was gay. When his dad promptly threw him out of the house, he came to live with Nan and me, heartbroken, with a black eye, but grateful our door was open. Three years later, he was Dominique, and the beautiful voice he had raised to the rafters in his gospel choir was now used to belt out show tunes and disco hits onstage. His father has refused to see him all these years, yet Dominique will not change who she is, not even for her family. She volunteers at an AIDS crisis center, and instead of beads, she hurls silver-foiled packages of condoms at Mardi Gras. She's vocal and in-your-face sometimes. And she tells everyone she's not gay—but queer. And proud of it.

Maggie finished combing my hair, and the three of us went out on the side porch so we could sweep up my hair cuttings when we were done.

I continued, "But you should have *seen* this girl he was with. She had cheekbones to die for and perfect hair. Shampoo-commercial perfect. You know, like the one with the blonde who's acting like she's having an orgasm while she's getting shampooed by young, hunky men."

"I *love* that commercial," Dominique cooed.

Maggie began snipping. "He obviously hasn't forgotten you, so go for it. What's the worst that could happen? A bad date. Big deal. You've had plenty of those."

"Amen." Dominique chimed in.

I looked up at Maggie, hearing the metal snip-snip of the scissors clicking away. "Remember…I want a *trim*— not lopsided hair."

"What about a bob? A sort of European, angular thing?"

"If you cut my hair in a bob, I'll look like a troll doll. I like it longer, and I like to go with my natural curls.

For God's sake, you've been cutting my hair for four years now. You know what I want."

This was true—after much trial and bad-hair error. Dominique and I were Maggie's guinea pigs. This fact itself was a mark of our friendship, because long before she was cutting her own hair lopsided and dyeing it raspberry, she was doing all kinds of things to ours. I've had bobs and pixie cuts, punky spikes and Madonna-like platinum. Dominique has had fades that make Grace Jones's hair look conservative. She once even ended up bald thanks to a chemical straightening process gone awry.

"So…you're finally going out with the love of your life." Dominique clapped her hands.

"He's not the love of my life." I shot her a glance.

"Then the lust of your life," Maggie offered as she bent over and cut angled pieces near my face.

"Well—" Dominique put her manicured hands on her hips "—I say go for it."

"I'm not even positive I'm going."

Maggie picked up a pair of clippers from her "house call" bag of scissors and combs. "If you don't go I'm buzz-cutting you right now."

"Georgia's-gonna-get-some," Dominique singsonged, waggling her hips. "A little sucking. A little fucking."

"Why is it queens don't know the meaning of the word *understated?*" In Dominique's case, I'd settle for mildly dignified.

"I'm going to ignore Her Royal Bitchiness. Maggie, you should have seen the stare-downs between them." Dominique twirled. A pair of tourists walked by, and she waved at them and struck a pose, daring them to take her picture, which they obligingly did.

"Seize the moment," Maggie said, moving around to my left side and trimming away.

Dominique leaned over and grabbed her own rear end. "Seize some *ass,* honey. Some tight little ass."

I shook my head; she was on a roll. There was no stopping her.

"Stop moving!" Maggie shouted at me. She finished my cut and we went back inside so she could blow out my hair. When she was finished, it looked shiny, straight and perfect. Of course, with my luck it would rain the minute I stepped out the door.

Next up was Dominique, with bleach across her eyebrows. She looks beautiful in platinum hair. When I see how striking she is, I just know occasionally the heavens screw up and send a girl down in a boy's body.

Jack came into the kitchen, stretching, bare-chested, in a pair of plaid-flannel pajama bottoms.

"Hello, ladies."

"Hey, Jack." Maggie smiled. For a chance to be near him, she joins us at gigs every opportunity she gets. We tell the management she's our manager. Maggie has partied with morticians, the national gathering of Kappa Alpha Phi fraternity, the New Orleans Fire Department (when, despite her love for Jack, she went home with a sexy captain who was Mr. November in a firemen calendar), orthodontists, the navy (when, again, despite her love for Jack, she went upstairs with a sailor who looked a lot like Tom Cruise) and the gathering of a Scottish Highland clan—who partied with us afterward and made us all drink single-malt scotch until we were sick.

"Mags." Jack smiled back. "I love Georgie's hair. You did a great job. Georgie, you look very sexy."

"As opposed to my usual appearance?" I was getting tired of my band thinking I was little more than sequins and pantyhose.

"Give me a break. You always look hot, but this cut shows off your eyes, and how exotic-looking you are. Don't tell me all this is for that guy last night."

"Casanova Jones?" Dominique crossed her arms, waiting for the bleach Maggie applied to her eyebrows to work. "So tell us how he looked, Jack."

"Nothing great. Not as beautiful as Georgia."

"Get off it, Jack," I muttered.

"I'm not. He just looked like any average on-the-make guy. In a penguin suit."

"I'm not listening to this. I've got to go. I have a date."

"Not with that guy, I hope." Jack's brotherly protective side took over.

"A certain piano player. Ta-ta, gang," I said, brushing my shirt. "I'm off to get depressed or drunk enough to sing the blues."

"Tell Red I said hi." Dominique waved.

"I will." I left the house and headed down the street. Whatever weather Cammie's father had paid for the previous day was gone. New Orleans humidity hung as thick as Spanish moss. I tried to soak in the Crescent City's native moodiness. If I was ever to become a blues goddess, it had to happen here, in the city I called home.

*chapter*

**5**

Red Watson *is* the blues. We found each other a couple of years ago when I kept returning to Mississippi Mudslide to hear him play the piano and sing. He won't tell me how old he is—well, he does, but the number often changes—but I would say he is pushing eighty.

When I first heard him play, I felt a strange sense of déjà vu, as if all my life I'd had a tune in my head I hadn't been able to quite remember, to give voice to. And then I heard his song, and it was as if it was already a part of me. As if the blues were in my blood. As if the song was mine.

I had finally grown the nerve to ask him to teach me the blues, to work with me. I'd been listening to jazz since I was born. Before that even, in my mother's womb. But Red wasn't interested. Not only wasn't he interested, he brushed me off like a buzzing fly. So Tony, the band's sometime-bass player and my partner in scouting out jazz music, and I went back to the Mudslide again and again. And again. We were tireless. Tony and I had always stayed through the last set to talk to Red, no matter how late it got.

"Now, you two here *again?*" Red had asked us.

Tony had just smiled and lifted his beer in salute.

"The Irishman and the lady." Red sat down at our table. It was almost three in the morning.

"Incredible second set," Tony said, his brogue made thicker by the beers he'd had.

"Now how'd a man from clear across the ocean—you told me you're from Dublin—come to know so much about the Delta blues is what I want to know." Red smiled.

Tony shrugged, always somewhat taciturn until you got to know him.

"Come on, now, how come you're here most every night I play…when you two ain't playing?" By now he knew we were in a band. Albeit one that played ABBA.

"I may be an Irishman, but in another life I must have been a Delta bluesman. Since I was this high—" Tony stuck out his hand "—they're all I've wanted to play." Tony's black eyes had a faraway look.

"Another life? You a Buddhist, man?" Red asked.

Tony laughed, his smile always having the ability to change his face from incredibly serious and tough-looking to something childlike. He shook his head. "Maybe I am…maybe I am."

"And you?" Red turned his head to me. "You still got some fool idea you want to sing the blues?"

I nodded.

Red just laughed. More like a hoot. "Child, now

singin' the blues isn't like singing wedding songs. You gots to feel it, here." He tapped by his collarbone. "Inside."

"You ought to let her sing you one," Tony said almost inaudibly, staring into his beer bottle, the little vein on his forehead throbbing.

Red looked at me. "But do you have it? Inside. See…I used to travel this country in a bus with ten other stinkin', sweatin' men and a blues goddess or two. We'd play in club after club until we was so worn-out. Hungry sometimes. Laughing and good times, too. But half the guys, they're into reefer and sometimes worse. Sometimes a lot worse. And 'cause we're black, we play the biggest shitholes this side of the Mississippi. We play the chitlin' circuit. We *know* the blues, ya see."

"Let her sing," Tony said simply, with authority. Something about Tony made people take him seriously. Then he leaned over to me. "Just sing a few lines of 'At Last.' Go on, gorgeous."

So it wasn't an audition. Not really. Just the three of us in a club still smelling of lingering smoke as the bartenders and barbacks were breaking the place down for the night, glasses clinking, the place sort of echoing now that nearly everyone had left. Half the houselights were up, the floors were sticky with spilled alcohol. I sang the first verse of the Etta James classic, my voice echoing. I had nothing to lose. Red had been telling me for months I was too much of a kid to sing the blues. I wasn't hardened by the road. I had no right to sing the blues. Not like the first ladies of the blues who all did time in jail, or got hooked on heroin, or went through five and six marriages, unable to find lasting love.

I sang the lines, thankful I'd had four black Russians

to give me some extra nerve. And when I was done, Red leaned back in his chair, mouth open. Tony looked smug and bemused. Red didn't say anything for a good minute. Finally, eyes twinkling, he leaned forward and said, "Now, child, how come you never told me you could sing the blues before?"

I knocked on the door of apartment 1A, the ground floor of an old Southern courtyard home. Red rents it for a song, literally, from an eccentric dot-com million-aire (there are still a few of them left) who trades cheaper rent for weekly piano lessons—even though the guy's still struggling with "Twinkle, Twinkle, Little Star."

"Is that my girlfriend?" Red smiled and opened the door, enveloping me in a hug and pulling me inside.

His apartment is nirvana to me. Original posters of Ella Fitzgerald, Nina Simone, Sidney Bechet, Billie Holiday, Mildred Bailey and Duke Ellington hang in frames covering every square inch of wall. It's a shrine to all things blues and jazz. Each week I walk in and knock on the framed Mildred Bailey picture for luck. Though I don't know how much luck poor Mildred had. She had an unbelievable voice, a way of singing that made you feel it deep down. But she was sort of homely and overweight, consequently overshadowed by the blues singers who would be packaged and powdered like sex.

"Drink, sugar?" Red winked at me and pulled out a bottle of Chivas. It's our Sunday ritual. We each have half a glass—all his doctors will allow him each day now—and toast to life, the blues, sometimes even to death. Whenever a blues or jazz legend dies, we observe a moment of silence. On those days, we cheat and have a full glass.

He poured me a scotch, which I drink out of deference to him, but which feels like hot fire sliding down my throat. It used to make me want to retch. I don't know if it's an acquired taste or what, but now I don't cringe when I drink it. Because I am always striving for a more raw blues voice, I pray before each glass that it's doing the trick.

"To Ma Rainey and Mildred, and all the jazz and blues goddesses, including this one right here in my livin' room, Lord." He poked a bony finger gently into the hollow between my collarbones. We clinked and swallowed.

"Mighty fine." He smiled.

I blinked away the tears hard liquor always brings to my eyes. "Yeah, Red. This stuff is gonna kill me."

"Ain't killed *me* yet, and I'll be eighty my next birthday."

"I thought you were going to be seventy-nine."

"Truth is, I got no idea." He shrugged his shoulders, staring into his now-empty glass. I waited patiently to see if he might say more. He was often closemouthed about all he had seen and done, even about what his given name was, certainly not Red. But sometimes, a fragment of memory, maybe even a single chord on the piano, a song, a note…would carry him away to another time, playing piano with blues legends, riding in a bus in the Deep South during segregation. During times when he might have looked out a bus window at the countryside and seen a lynched black man hanging from a tree in the distance. Billie Holiday sang about that sight in a song entitled "Strange Fruit."

"My mama died in childbirth, and I was sent off to live with my grandma," he said softly. "My pa was always traveling in search of work. Then Grandma died…had to be when I was maybe ten. And I struck out on my own, but I never did know for sure how old I was because there wasn't much fuss over birthdays in our house. Always too worried about feeding me, keeping warm in the winter…stuff like that. That was a long time ago. Different times, Georgia. Of course, my grandma was a good woman. She meant nothin' by it— we just didn't put too much stock in birthdays."

His face was the color of pale coffee, and his eyes were coal-black and, with age, seemed to be perpetually teary, rheumy, the whites turning a yellowish color. He wore a pair of gold wire-rimmed glasses, and his hair was now a soft silver-and-black Afro, with a bald spot the size of a small saucer on the crown of his head. What fascinated me most were his hands. His fingers were long and graceful, wrinkled, the nail beds wide and pale. The tops of his hands were crisscrossed with raised veins, and when he put them to the keys of a piano, magic happened.

He stood up and went to the shiny black baby grand—a Steinway—by the window. He said it had taken him ten years to pay it off. Closing his eyes, he sat down and rocked back and forth a few times, hearing something in his head, some melody. Then he began to play, humming along to the tune he envisioned while playing complex harmonies and bebops I could only hope to one day come up with on my own.

Each Sunday was the same; he would start playing, and I would wait. He told me you can't rush the blues. You have to hear the blues in your soul first. Actually, *feel* them first. So he would play and hum, and when I felt that my voice could be quiet no longer, I sang. Sometimes I sang old songs from the 1920s, 1930s and 1940s, sometimes newer arrangements, maybe some Diana Krall or Norah Jones. Sometimes I would just scat, which means singing nonsense syllables in a way that imitates a trumpet or maybe a tenor sax. With Red, I sang from deep inside, the place that was just instrument and soul. The place I shared with no one. Not even Maggie or Dominique. Most definitely not with Gary or Jack. Sometimes Tony, I guess. But only if we were both drunk. We all have that space. Maybe for some it comes out in prayer; for me it comes from my song.

I started singing, but Red stopped me, sighing with frustration.

"Dig deeper. You call that the blues?"

I gritted my teeth. He never questioned my voice. I hit every note. I came in on the right beat. I got the tempo. He questioned my soul.

"Red…I'm singing the song as best I can."

"I heard better blues from a goddamn alley cat."

I exhaled loudly. He started in on the piano. Again, I sang. I shut my eyes and tried to get lost in the song. Soon I realized I was singing without the piano. He had abruptly lifted his hands from the keys.

"Georgia…you got your mind someplace else. Now when I say go to that place, you got to go there! Think why you sing the blues. Why? To sing to some roomful of fancy-assed people? No, you sing the blues 'cause you got the blues. Now sing 'em right or go on home today."

Again, he moved his fingers on the keys, his feet on

the piano's pedals. I tried again. He'd made me angry. Sometimes I think he does it on purpose. But sure enough, with the anger came the blues.

That Sunday, I sang of a man lost, then found. I sang of mothers gone forever…for both Red and me. An hour went by while he and I made music, while we shared something that others only felt in a place of worship, if they were lucky. I sang in a way that was raw and naked and sacred. When we were done—determined by some indefinable moment when we both sensed we were finished—Red stopped playing and came over to me. I was sweating and spent. Where had that voice come from?

"Sweetheart…you are gettin' it. You sing from that same spot each time, and you will be a blues goddess like her." He nodded toward a poster of Bessie Smith.

I looked away. "I'm not sure where that came from. I can't find it every time, Red. That's what made her great and me…me." I still mentally pictured me rolling off a baby grand piano.

He shook his head.

"The blues and jazz are just a part of you. When you come to believe that, your life will change, Georgia."

He offered me a glass of water. "So how's your nana?"

"Fine, Red. You should come by and pay her a visit. It's Sunday. Why don't you come to dinner tonight? She's been asking after you."

We played this game every Sunday. He was, of course, always invited to Sunday supper. I had introduced him to my grandmother shortly after I started singing with Red. Tony and I dragged Nan to a club to hear Red play with a trio. Nan loved the music, and I think she's grown pretty fond of the man, too. Red played along with me, looking pleased at the invite. "I'd like that very much, sugar. What time shall I call on your nan?"

"You know we eat at eight o'clock. Don't play too hard to get with me." I winked and set my glass down. He walked me to the door, and I spontaneously kissed him goodbye on the cheek. I started down the little path to the sidewalk. He called out to me.

"Georgia?"

"Yes, Red?" I turned around.

"I think today your mama and my grandma were sittin' up in heaven together clappin' their hands."

"Thanks, Red," I whispered, and started toward the Heartbreak Hotel, the New Orleans humidity pressing in on me and making me feel claustrophobic.

*chapter*

6

Walking home from Red's, I thought back to high school, when I was the helpless victim of a mother who believed fashion can be bought at places with bright fluorescent lights, wide aisles and endless rows of sales racks—much of it polyester-laden. While the princesses and prom queens of my high school wore designer jeans and carried purses with labels on the outside tipping off others to their two-hundred-and-fifty-dollar price tag, I was relegated to wearing no-name jeans and no-name sneakers, and slinging my shiny pink lip gloss in a worn-out denim purse. My mother refused to believe this mattered in the social feeding frenzy that is high school.

"Georgia, who cares what you wear? It's what's inside that counts," she'd tell me, while she calmly folded socks or cooked her tuna casserole. Easy for her to say. Mom lived in a Carol Brady bubble. She didn't have to sit in lunchroom no-man's-land, with only Damon for company. My mother didn't have to face down Casanova Jones in social studies as he undressed me with his eyes and flirted shamelessly, while I felt hopelessly clumsy, embarrassed by a chest that had unexpectedly grown out of control, as far as I was concerned. Damon and I did our stupid "We must, we must, we must improve our busts" exercises. But I guess my body took that mantra too much to heart. As a woman's body replaced my baby one, as I developed into this curvaceous 1960s *Playboy* ideal when the rage was waiflike, I felt even more like an outsider.

My mother, on the other hand, lived her life like a television show. She bought the perfect laundry detergent for the whitest whites and the brightest colors. She whipped up meals she meticulously cut from the back of Campbell's soup can labels and mounted on recipe cards. She knew one hundred and one ways to prepare Jell-O. She entered bake-offs. She ironed my *underwear.* She made every one of my childhood Halloween costumes, including a lobster complete with giant claws the year I was obsessed with crustaceans. In short, she was the picture-perfect mother, right down to her hair, which she had washed and set every Friday afternoon at the beauty salon. All she wanted was the perfect daughter. What she got was me.

I pierced my ears five times before I was thirteen, doing them at home with a cork, a needle and Damon's pep talk to steady my shaking hand. I was hell-bent on being a singer, living my life in rebellion, being like Nan. My father was a jazzman; he played the bass, and from what I remembered of his playing, he was very talented. He was also an alcoholic. Sundays were spent tiptoeing around the house while he slept off his hangovers. Mom pretended he was just "tired."

I adored him anyway.

Dad taught me how to "phrase" a song by playing endless records, he and I together in the den, the stereo spinning old 45s and 78s and ancient albums with dust all over them. He never seemed happy to me, except when we were playing music—especially Gene Krupa and Jess Stacy, Duke Ellington and Etta James.

He left my mother and me when one of his old musician pals came to New Orleans with a moderately successful jazz quartet, in need of a new bassist. He departed, first for the Chicago blues scene, and then for the Blue Note in New York City, with the Buster Keys Quartet, promising to return home "soon," and sending money along the way. He wrote me postcards, which I still have in an old shoe box in my room. He was the only person who made me feel beautiful:

Angel, I'm doin' fine in NYC. When you come visit, we'll go to the Empire State Building and touch the sky.
   Stay beautiful and keep on singing,
                                        Love, Your Father,
                                                    Dad

He signed each card that way. He was a dreamer who believed we could touch the sky and talk to God. We could speak to heaven and listen for ghosts in the attic.

He was everything imaginative. He was the blues. He was the music. He was everything my mother wasn't.

But after a while, both the postcards and the money stopped.

My mother's reaction to this wasn't anger or rage, hurt or tears of abandonment. Instead, she focused all her energies on creating this fantasy of perfection—and making sure I didn't become a singer. That I didn't abandon her, too. And my reaction to her reaction was to try my hardest to infuriate her.

My father had left behind his blues record collection, which was enormous and still lines special shelves I had built for them in my room. I played his music over and over and over again. Sometimes the same song tirelessly. I did it to feel close to him. I did it to hurt her for driving him away with her picture-perfect ways. Etta James's "At Last" was their song. So what else would an angry adolescent do but play that song morning, noon and night. Music has always been my weapon and my refuge.

At first, I was certain Dad was going to come back. When he didn't, the blues were already part of me. I played them, then, because they reflected how I felt about adolescence—it was like one long, angst-ridden blues song.

I was never quite sure if I succeeded in hurting her. Besides piercing my ears, I wore dark black eyeliner and bleached my hair blond, though it fried to a vague orange. I stayed out past my curfew every weekend night. I was sullen from the moment I woke up, staring through hostile eyes as she cooked me pancakes with raisins set in them to make little happy faces. Yet she never yelled

at me, never grounded me. She kept smiling and cooking and cleaning and ironing, refusing to show how
much I was breaking her heart—just like he did. As long
as I wasn't hanging out with musicians, she seemed content that it was all "a phase." She didn't want to risk pushing me away. She even let Damon sleep over at our
house, knowing, I think, he was my only friend. A lot
of the time, I convinced myself the only person holding me back from going to New York City and finding
my father was Damon. Later, Damon and I had an elaborate fantasy about going to New York together. He'd
be a top fashion designer, and I'd sing with my father's
band.

When I was almost seventeen, my mother was diag-
nosed with breast cancer. It was late-stage before they
found it because she was too busy tending to me to take
care of herself. Suddenly, hating her for her decidedly
bad taste in clothes and bedspreads (mine was still Bar-
bie in high school) was pointless.

I read to her while she was sick in bed. She liked ro-
mances with happy endings, and that's what she got,
though I was at an age when I didn't believe in happy
endings. I still don't. "I can see you rolling your eyes,
Georgia," she weakly said one afternoon.

"Mom, happy endings are bullshit."

"Georgia Ray, the language."

"Fine. But they're still bullshit. Happy endings aren't
for people like me."

"What exactly is a person like you?" she asked, breathless. Everything, every word, took so much effort.

"An outsider. Different."

"You're New Orleans born and bred. How does that make you an outsider, Georgia?"

"No father, for one." As soon as I said it, I regretted it. Now that she was sick, I was trying so hard not to wound her, but sometimes my resentments were right there on the surface.

I tried to explain to her that happy endings were for the popular girls, not for me with my kinky hair that I never quite accepted, and my exotic looks in the southern state of Louisiana, the social scene in high school dominated by Magnolia Queens and blond debutantes with beautiful drawls. Happy endings weren't for Damon either, with his lust for the homecoming *king*—not queen. His desire to *be* the homecoming queen. Yet complaining about my hair seemed selfish, when my mother's own perfect coiffure fell out in clumps in the shower one day, swirling down the tub and clogging the drain. I dropped the subject and kept reading to her.

Damon used to come over and give her makeovers, drawing on eyebrows and tying up colorful turbans out of silk scarves. One time, he did her eyes and eyebrows like Elizabeth Taylor in *Cleopatra*.

"You look just like Liz, Mrs. Miller," Damon said, painting on the last of her new eyebrows.

"Hand me a mirror."

I went to get a hand mirror, knowing she would freak out the second she saw herself.

"Now, you just have to go with it." Damon stood and surveyed his handiwork.

I handed her the mirror, bracing myself for her reaction. But it wasn't what I expected. She howled with laughter until tears rolled down her face, all the while

Damon was begging her, "Don't cry, don't cry. It'll all run." Soon, she had black tear stains tracing a path down her now-thin face. Then Damon and I started laughing, too. After that, for the first time, my mother started to relax a little, to laugh with us. Maybe she was trying to leave some good memories for me.

Surrounded by death at home, I tried to be a normal teenager knowing my mother was slipping away and my father had stopped sending postcards when I was in the tenth grade. I tried to eat lunch with Damon and study about the Civil War with Mr. Hoffman, my favorite teacher, and learn about sines, cosines and tangents in math class. I tried to carry my lunch tray without tripping and open my locker without getting crushed by the crowds in the hallway.

We eventually moved in with Nan, selling our two-bedroom house in a parish outside New Orleans and coming into the city to live with my grandmother and her ghost. Nan had always been more like Auntie Mame than a grandmother. Strong, adventurous, feminist, stubborn, she tried to will my mother into getting well. But my mother had always wilted in the face of her mother, just as I wilted in the shade of my own mother's shadow, and so Nan's will aside, my mother was gone before winter was out. She died in a hospital, something she never wanted to do. Nan and I were there. It was the first time I ever saw a dead body.

That night, I cried until my stomach ached, and then I cried more but without any tears. I had never been perfect for her, and now I wouldn't have the chance to lose the adolescent brooding and be nice to her, and maybe get a prom date while she was alive. I wouldn't be able to prove to her that I wasn't the rebellious girl she thought I was, with the messy room that drove her crazy. "Georgia, I can't see the floor in here," was her mantra. I had been angry for so many years, and she had loved me when I didn't deserve it, and now she was gone.

Casanova Jones came to the wake. I remember sitting in the front of the muffled and velvet funeral parlor, my mother in her best dress—the one she'd been saving for a "special occasion." She looked serene, but most definitely not like my mother. She was thin and bony and looked as if she was made of wax. Damon was wailing in the bathroom, unable to even come in to view her body. Nan sat next to me, patting my hand and accepting my used tissues, which she discreetly shoved into her vintage clutch purse.

I looked up, face blotchy and red, and mascara-streaked, my hair an unkempt mass of curls, and saw Casanova Jones heading straight toward me. He even had on a tie. His black curly hair fell past the collar of his white shirt, and his swagger, half man, half boy, was still evident, but as my grandmother whispered to me, "He cleans up good." Rick, aka Casanova, mumbled an "I'm sorry" in the awkward way of high-school kids unsure of what to say when thrust into an adult situation. I loved him in that moment. Actually, I'd been in love with him all of high school. Something about how he pushed his hands through his luxurious head of curls—curls that behaved, unlike my own—and sort of shook his hair into place, about his pale blue eyes, or how he played with a lock of my hair while flirting with me threw me right over the edge. He was my crush. He was my obsession. And he picked my mother's funeral to show he really cared and wasn't just toying with me. I was too numb to care.

The last few months of high school passed in a blur of grief. I had originally planned to go far away from my mother after I graduated. I wanted to go to college in Manhattan, rooming with Damon, who longed to go to the Fashion Institute of Technology. Instead, I chose to go to the Newcomb Department of Music at Tulane. That way I could live with Nan. She possessed the spirit I wanted. She could bring out the Georgia who was buried beneath wild hair, hateful adolescence, and all that eyeliner. In Nan, I had a kindred spirit. She saw something in me—a spark of life she called it. I don't think she ever forgave my mother for living an ordinary life, for being a homemaker and not burning her bra and changing the world.

Nan was the first person to encourage me to sing. My mother said I had a pretty voice as a child, before my father left, but she was the kind of person who didn't believe in showing off or attracting attention. I remember once being invited to a birthday party when I was a little girl. More than anything, I wanted to wear my new pink dress with the ruffles and crinoline—okay, so what did I know about fashion then? What I didn't realize, until years later, was that the birthday girl was poor. If I wore my new party dress, I would outshine her at her own party. So my mother made me wear something old and, to my eyes, ugly. This was another of a thousand misunderstandings that only made sense after she had died.

With the wisdom of hindsight, now I see that she

couldn't risk me leaving New Orleans to follow my fortunes as a musician or a singer. I needed to do something "steady"; I had to have "something to fall back on" when I failed, as she was certain I would. The odds of succeeding as a jazz singer or musician are a million to one. For every Harry Connick Jr., every Wynton Marsalis, every Diana Krall, there are ten thousand men like my father, broken down and tormented by their music just as much as they desire it. Some blues singers, like Billie Holiday, embodied both success and destruction. Strung out on heroin, she was a poster child for how the music business can destroy you. My mother wasn't about to let me risk *anything*. Least of all my life.

Now, Nan is a different story. I'm not sure how the two of them were even related. My mother occasionally used to sigh at her own mother and mutter something about "baby-switching" at the hospital. Nan was a rebel and risk-taker all her life. She was the kind of woman who wore flaming-red lipstick and kept her hair short, in the latest "Parisian" styles, as a young woman. She had a sense of self that stares back at you in the black-and-white photos in her albums, her high cheekbones and dark eyes commanding attention. She rode in a motorcycle sidecar across the United States with one of her boyfriends, and she danced on a bar with Ernest Hemingway in Key West. She ran the brothel until Sadie died, and even after she married my grandfather, a professional gambler and whiskey importer, she threw parties that made the newspapers. She also never let her racial heritage define her, even down here where sometimes you step off the St. Charles streetcar and swear it's another era.

Nan was the one to sneak me off to R-rated movies

before I was even thirteen. She bought me Junior Mints and filled my head with talk of love affairs and Paris, and the way a man loves a woman with a "bosom." My mother couldn't even say the word *bra* to me. She couldn't look me in the eyes when I told her I got my first period. Everything about womanhood embarrassed my mother, while Nan encouraged me to embrace it all. Nan was velvet and lipstick. Mom was a buttoned-up oxford shirt and Ivory soap.

Nan pushed me into voice lessons in high school, and then in college she was always there behind me nudging me into the spotlight, telling me that's where I belonged, "Out where people can see and *hear* you, for God's sake, Georgie. Anybody can stand in the shadows. It takes courage to shine."

Yes, Nan is a character all her own. And I knew on the pressing issue of Casanova Jones her advice would be quite simple. Nan believes approaching summer drives all of us in New Orleans mad. It has its roots in Mardi Gras, whose long finger extends madness throughout the year. But deeper than that, it has its roots in the bayou and the mist.

When summer comes, she believes we all need romance, because, as she puts it, "Georgia, there's nothing to do in the Crescent City heat but drink mint juleps, make passionate love, lay naked afterward underneath the ceiling fan and listen to the blues."

*chapter*

7

Arriving home, I stood in front of our house, its ancient brick weathered and elegant. The house did seem to be alive. Some nights, Nan and I would hear a woman walking upstairs, her heels clicking across old floorboards. Occasionally, I smelled perfume in my room, a complex mix of jasmine and lily of the valley. Not my perfume, yet an intoxicatingly familiar scent. The way I could smell it just in one spot in the room as I crossed my floor made me feel as if I was being watched by someone. I wanted to whisper to Sadie's ghost, *What is it you want from me?* But I think I was afraid of the answer.

I stepped inside the house and found Nan in the kitchen preparing a feast. All the members of Georgia's

Saints would be attending Sunday Saints Supper, along
with Dominique, Gary's wife, Annie, Maggie—and Red.

"Smells good, Nan. What're you making?"

"Georgia, for goodness' sake, you've lived in New
Orleans since the day you were born. Can't you smell
it?"

"Jambalaya?"

"Mmm, hmm. Mighty spicy, too."

"Red's coming. I hope that's all right."

She looked genuinely pleased—as she did every Sunday we went through this little charade. "Of course
that's fine, Georgia. You set another place at the dining-
room table."

Thank God my grandfather left Nan "loaded," as
they say, because she likes to entertain with style.
Every Sunday bottles of good red wine are uncorked
to breathe, champagne chills in the refrigerator, and
delicious smells emanate from brewing pots and pans.
Our dining-room table could fit twenty, its cherry-
wood surface polished to a brilliant sheen. The house
recalls the grandeur of New Orleans, and the antiques
give it character. At any moment, you half expect a
Southern belle with a hoop skirt, or a flapper from
the 1920s, to walk down the stairs…or Sadie to return to life.

I pulled another plate out of the china cabinet. The
plates had been imported from France at the turn of the
twentieth century by my great-great-grandmother. It
made me nervous serving on them. Each of them, hand-
painted with a pattern of tea roses, was probably worth
more than the band pulled in on a Friday night, but my
grandmother doesn't believe in saving the good china

for fancy occasions. Her motto is: "Having your friends gathered around your table is occasion enough." We'd lost a plate and a saucer or two, as well as several teacups—three when we opened our house to a Christmastime historic-homes tour—but we still had most of the pieces, and the table did look spectacular each Sunday, with ivory-colored linen napkins and stemware sparkling beneath a chandelier dangling with Austrian crystals.

After setting the table, I went up to my room to wait for Tony.

Tony lives for the blues. Every Sunday he and I listen to music for hours before dinner. This Sunday, he arrived disheveled as always, his shirt crumpled. He wears his hair close to bald, shaven down, which makes him look like a tough guy. His black eyes twinkling as he poked his head into my room, he gave me a crooked grin. He has a pair of dimples, pale Irish skin, near-perpetual five-o'clock shadow and a small, ragged white scar over his right eye. He's our bass player, and he moonlights as a limo driver—mostly airport runs. He doesn't say very much in a crowd, but he clearly loves Nan, as he always brings her a bouquet of magnolias or jasmine when he comes. He's an amateur horticulturist, and beyond that, we don't know much about him. I tell Jack I think he's in the witness protection program. He never misses a Sunday Saints Supper—and occasionally, after several glasses of wine, his brogue considerably thickens as he sings ballads for us. He's closemouthed about how he got from Dublin to Louisiana, of all places, or even when he came to the United States. This has led Jack and me to a new conclusion that he's actually an IRA gunrunner hiding from Interpol.

"Brought you something." He walked in and put a flat, square package in my hand.

"Hmm…what could this be?" I joked, though it could only be a record. Tony haunts a used-CD and record store, always digging up rare finds. I pulled the album out of the bag. "A Mildred Bailey…"

"I hope you don't have it." He said, his brogue a lilt that made every sentence, even those that weren't questions, end on a rising note.

"No…I don't. But then again, I think you know my record collection better than I do. Thanks, Tony." I jumped up and kissed him. He flushed, the pink almost translucent on his skin, and moved away.

"Put it on."

I went over to my old stereo, a Philco that had belonged to my Dad. I know CDs are scratch-free and sound…perfect, but I like listening to old albums. They take me back in time. Mildred came on singing, a true blues goddess. Tony came over closer to me.

"What a voice."

I nodded.

"You're just as good. One of these days, you're going to have to leave the band and go sing what you feel, Georgia."

I shrugged. "I know."

"We could go to Ireland."

I turned to face him. "What?"

"Go to Ireland. Play the blues…. I miss Ireland. Dreary sort of place sometimes. But I'm homesick, Georgia.

Miss the green grass. Really is emerald. Leprechauns, too."

"Sure. Four-leaf clovers. Pots of gold."

"You're talking now. And ale. Very good ale."

"You would go back there?" I had gotten used to Tony. He was, besides Red, the only person who understood the blues. We didn't have to speak, just shut our eyes and listen.

"Someday."

"And what do you mean *we?*"

He stammered. "Nothing…. Nothing. I didn't mean a thing. I guess I meant you could come and visit." He walked over to the far wall of my bedroom, standing and staring at the photos I had hung there, his back to me. His shoulders moved slightly to the music. If he had a few "pints" in him, he was an amazing dancer, raw and sexual. "Who's this bloke?"

"Who?" I came and stood behind him as he pointed. "Oh…that's my dad."

"Played the bass?"

"Yeah. That's him and his old quintet. He was good."

"And you never hear from him?"

"No."

"My father's dead."

"I'm sorry."

"Don't be. He was a bit of a bastard, really, love."

I waited for him to share more, but that was all he said. We both retreated into our own worlds and listened to Mildred, separate but together. Every Sunday was some variation of the same, separate but somehow one. I looked at Tony, his eyes completely blank now, not twinkling, far away. In Ireland maybe. An ocean away from me.

★ ★ ★

About ten to eight, the doorbell rang. Tony and I went downstairs, greeted Jack as he descended the stairs, too, and found Nan letting Gary and Annie in. Kissing Nan and me, Annie is positively adorable. If Gary is five foot four in shoes, she can't be but five foot tall. Next to Dominique and her high heels, she's an elf. Or, as Tony teases her, a leprechaun. It never ceases to amaze me that Annie has popped out three babies from that tiny belly and those narrow hips of hers. Gary and Annie hold hands constantly, and somehow, she makes balding, slightly potbellied Gary seem like a sex symbol. They prove the adage that there's someone for everyone. Around her, Gary doesn't pace, let alone break out in a cold sweat. He's funny and charming. Sundays are a date night for them. Her mother watches the kids, and Gary and Annie come to supper and then go out in the city for cocktails—alone. Gary says he falls in love with her all over again each Sunday night. She even likes ABBA, too, scary as that is.

Mike was the last of the Saints to arrive. He plays the drums, and he drinks way too much. He shows up for our gigs sober, or sober enough to play, but he's still trying to get over his wife, Delilah, who deserted him two years ago for a guy who flew in for a convention. She was a dealer on a gambling riverboat and left Mike cold without even trying to work things out. Understandably, Mike is bitter. He says Gary and Annie make him gag.

Red arrived shortly after Mike. He brought Nan a perfect yellow single rose he picked from a neighbor's garden he passed on the way over. It was just beginning to open its petals. Red kissed Nan's hand, and she just smiled and looked into his eyes. She's had a couple of boyfriends since Grandpa died when I was five, but Red was the first "gentleman caller," as she put it, who made her blush.

And finally, in walked Maggie, in her black boots, black miniskirt and tight black T-shirt. She smiled at Jack and winked at me. I blinked hard. Her hair was now even, and I swear it was a slightly different shade of red than earlier in the afternoon. She has hair schizophrenia.

After a round of cocktails—Nan makes these fabulous champagne cocktails with sugar cubes and bitters—in the living room, we all went into the dining room. Sitting down, Nan asked Red to say grace.

"May the music move us, and the spirit guide us. And thank you for this fine New Orleans meal. Amen."

Mike never said amen. He let it be known ages ago that he was an atheist and an existentialist. I just think because Delilah had gone to church every Sunday morning, he wasn't having any of it. But Annie crossed herself, and Dominique bowed her head piously. She has a rosary bead collection, thinking of them as some sort of talisman against bad luck.

We all dug in. Then the waterworks started.

Two bites into the jambalaya, my eyes were tearing and my nose was running. Nan knows how to make it right. If tears aren't running down your face, it ain't New Orleans jambalaya. More likely it's jambalaya from some chain restaurant where the cooks don't know how to sling the cayenne.

Gathered around the table, we laughed, we toasted New Orleans, we drank. We drank a lot more. We wiped at our tearing eyes and runny noses with our napkins. We emptied eleven bottles of champagne and wine. And then, in the midst of all the chattering, Tony's brogue emerged, thicker than ever, and he began to sing, in a simple, poignant voice, a Celtic song about a sailor and a lost love who died on the sea. When he finished, we whistled and applauded.

Red spoke when the clapping died down, "That's like the Irish blues, isn't it? See, don't matter where you're from, as long as there's love, there'll be the blues. No use pretendin' otherwise. A beautiful song, Tony. Georgia, you should sing the one from last week." He snapped his fingers, trying to recall the title. " 'Give Me Back My Dead Daughter's Child.'"

"What the hell kind of song title is that?" Dominique sputtered. "What's with you blues people? Tony's got a woman drowning with saltwater in her lungs and now a dead daughter's child? What's next? Suicide? Murder? War? Is this song going to make me cry?"

Red smiled. "If Georgia sings it right, it will."

Dominique stared at me. "What's wrong with 'We Are Family' by Sister Sledge? Something upbeat?"

"You wait there, Dominique, before you pass judgment. Go on, Georgia, sing it," Red urged.

The song was a very old one, maybe first sung at the birth of the blues. Jelly Roll Morton, one of the old kings of blues, loved it. It made him cry. I'd had some champagne. And Red had put me on the spot. So I began to sing the blues. I mean, the title says it all. Could there be anything happy in a song like that? People think country music is full of clichéd old sadness: "I Shot My Brother's Hunting Dog with a Rifle after a Quart of Jack Daniel's." But the blues were inventing grief in song long before any cowboy twanged a guitar. I started singing quietly at first but found my range and shut my eyes. I really didn't want to see everyone looking at me, even if they were my friends. I felt my cheeks flush, but I kept on singing this mournful song. And when I was done, no one said a word. Not exactly the response I was looking for.

I opened my eyes, and they were all staring at me. Then Dominique leaped to her feet and began screaming and hooting and clapping. Everyone else started clapping, and Maggie banged her silver spoon on the table and then began clinking her crystal champagne flute with her spoon. Jack and Red followed suit. I cringed. The glasses were nearly as old as Nan.

I stood and took a bow. "Thank you... Now it's someone else's turn to sing."

But they didn't stop. All except Tony, who hadn't clapped at all actually but had raised his glass in a silent toast to me.

"One more clinking glass, and I'll force you all to sit through my rendition of 'Dancing Queen.'"

"Ditch the fuckin' disco. We could be a damn good blues band," Tony said. "That was great. Bloody 'ell, that was fuckin' amazin'."

"We'd starve as a jazz band," Mike chimed in.

"Maybe," said Red, smiling, "but you all'd be makin' real music."

Gary stared at me from across the table. "Georgia...that was great, but you wouldn't leave the band, would you?"

Jack elbowed him, staring at me as if I'd never sung

before. "With pipes like those and a song like that we *could* be a blues and jazz band."

Gary shook his head. "But we've worked so hard to get to the point where we can actually make a *living* doing what we're doing. A *living.* You know…that which pays the bills."

Annie bit her lip and bowed her head.

I raised my hands. "Hey…I need to earn a living just as much as the rest of you. It was a song. One song." Out of the corner of my eye I saw Red exchange a look with Nan. I hate when no matter what you do, you're not going to make everyone happy.

No one else was going to do any singing, and certainly no one wanted to hear "Dancing Queen" (except maybe Dominique and Gary), so we cleared the table and Dominique, Red and Nan did the dishes. Dominique insisted on wearing her apron. It's permanently in our linen closet, especially for her. It has ruffles, and it's pink. Nan, all five foot two inches of her, stood at the kitchen sink and washed. Red stood next to her, not much taller, and dried. And Dominique, towering at six foot two, put the dishes and glassware away. I was tempted to get my camera and snap a picture.

Everyone started to head home. Tony kissed me good-bye and whispered in my ear, his breath hot and sending a tingle down my spine, "You were fuckin' brilliant, Georgia." I stepped back and looked him in the eye. Coming from Tony, that was a high compliment.

Mike, who'd brought a bottle of Wild Turkey and drank most of it, stumbled out the door. Annie and Gary waved and headed out on their date. Red and Nan went up to her sitting room to play gin rummy. Maggie lingered, and she, Jack and I opened another bottle of champagne. I knew I'd pay for it with a hangover the next day, but I was hoping to get the two of them together. About halfway through the bottle, Jack yawned.

"I'm going up to bed."

Maggie looked at me in "do-something" panic.

"Can you walk Maggie home?" I hurriedly asked him. She lived about eight blocks away, renting a one-bedroom in an old house that had been divided up into apartments, but we never let her walk it alone at night. Usually she just crashed in an upstairs bedroom, but this seemed like a good ploy to get them alone.

He shrugged. "Sure." He helped her up from her chair, and she kissed me good-night.

"Have fun," I whispered. We'd tried every ruse we could think of in the last couple of years to throw those two together, but you never know.

I went upstairs and washed up in my bathroom, put on an old T-shirt and looked around my room. It used to be my great-aunt Irene's room when she visited. She was Nan's sister, a diva, and insisted on the best room in the house, with a view of the street below, and a fireplace. My room is spacious, unlike some of the other bedrooms, and we think it was probably the master bedroom when the house was first built. Dominique had moved to New York City for a little while, fine-tuning her act. After she moved back here a few years ago, she said my room was the size of her entire apartment there.

The room, filled with antiques and pictures of my mother, father, Nan and my ancestors on the fireplace mantel, made me feel connected to the past. I walked over to my father's record collection. I never called it "my" collection, maybe because that would mean I was sure he wasn't ever coming back to claim it. I pulled out an old LP and put it on the turntable of my stereo. I listened to a song called "Glad To Be Unhappy." Only the blues and jazz have song titles like that.

I sauntered or half danced over to the wall where I have family pictures, old black and whites, in frames. I stared at the picture of my father that had caught Tony's eye. My family was a mixture of black and white, some Spanish and Native American on my father's side, down through the years. We were a melting pot all on our own, and I was the result of all those lineages mixing together. My room, the house, was a place where it was safe to grieve, to feel joy, to be with the ghosts of the past and the extended family of the present. I longed for Casanova Jones as the song stirred emotions in my drunken heart. I finished playing the record and then turned off the stereo. The house was silent, but I almost always feel as if the house itself breathes, alive.

Quickly, I fell asleep…or passed out. That was a matter of definition. But I was awakened at three-thirty in the morning by the loudest slam I'd ever heard. So, apparently, were Nan, Dominique and Jack. We all converged in the upstairs hallway, groggy, clutching robes (Dominique and Nan) and pulling on T-shirts and sweatpants (Jack and I), but very clear that we'd all heard something.

Dominique grabbed my hand and whispered, "Remember when I mocked your *system,* Georgia?"

I nodded, undecided whether to be terrified or fascinated by our resident ghost.

"Well…I didn't mean to make fun of you."

"Yes, you did. But now you heard her yourself."

Jack whispered, "Nan? You heard it, too?"

"Stop whispering," she commanded. "We can't let her think we're afraid of her."

Jack, who, out of instinct, had been hunched over as if he expected a demon to come popping out of a closet or something, pulled himself up to his full height. "Of course we're not afraid," he said out loud.

I rolled my eyes. "Men! You're so big and brave. And full of shit."

Dominique grabbed Jack's arm. "Well, I for one am glad he's here," she said. "Which room was Sadie's?"

"That one." I pointed to a bedroom we never used down on the right-hand side of the long hallway.

"Are you sure?" Jack asked.

Nan spoke up, "Of course Georgia's sure. That was Sadie's room. I remember it because I was there the night she was murdered. We closed up that room and have never used it."

Jack ran his hand through his messy bed-hair. "But I swear to you the slam came from my side of the hallway."

Dominique agreed, "Me, too. Actually, if I was going to guess, I'd say it was *that* room." She pointed to a back room Nan and I used for storage.

"Well," I said with bravery I didn't feel, "let's go down and take a look."

Dominique wasn't thrilled with the idea. "Now, Georgia, there's a reason *The Exorcist* and *The Omen* and *Rosemary's Baby* only happened to white people. Because black people are too smart and too chicken to go investigating ghosts and—" she dropped her voice and whispered "—the devil."

Nan clutched her green silk robe tighter around her. "Well, I'm half-black, and I'm not afraid. Now…there's four of us. And you two—" she eyed Dominique and Jack "—are big enough to handle just about anything. This is *my* home, and enough is enough. Come on."

Like a bad *Friday the 13th* movie (were there any good ones?), the four of us, half afraid, half brave, edged our way toward the door to which Dominique had pointed. Inch by inch, we crept down the hallway, holding hands, silent. My heart was beating fast as a rabbit's, and my mouth was dry. I'd heard Sadie slam doors before, but never this angrily, this loudly. And no, I'd never had the nerve to investigate before. We just accepted the ethereal life that seemed to reside in the house with us. In a way, Nan liked the company. And maybe I was just a little bit frightened to go challenging Sadie. Nan once held a séance with a guy who turned out to be a major fraud, and Sadie didn't make an appearance. After that, I almost told myself it was all the wind.

The four of us, holding hands, stood in front of the wooden, eight-paneled door.

"Open it," Dominique whispered.

"You!" I elbowed her. Finally, Nan took the worn brass knob in her hand and turned it. We'd been in the storage room a hundred times before—mostly in daylight. Nan flicked on the light. The room was filled with boxes, most of them mine and containing my mother's things. An old, nonworking fireplace. Built-in shelves lined with old books. An ancient push-pedal sewing machine. Boxes of vintage clothes I occasionally raided for an outfit when I hated everything in my closet. Old lamps. Even a box of stuffed animals from my girlhood room, with names like CoCo the Bunny, Miss Prunella the Monkey, and Belinda Bear.

I surveyed the room. "Nothing very interesting," I said aloud, trying to sound confident and walking deeper into the room. "And no ghost."

The four of us looked around. Jack opened a closet. Just more junk. But it was Dominique who stepped on it. Literally.

"My *heel!*" she squealed. We all looked down at her silver-feathered mules, one of which had its heel caught in the floorboard. "Will you look at this?"

There by the fireplace, the floorboard was loose. It didn't align properly, and if you looked closely at it, clearly someone had taken a screwdriver or a knife to it.

I knelt on the floor. "It's a secret compartment, Dominique. Pull up your slipper and see if it will loosen the board," I urged her.

She removed her foot from her heeled slipper and tried to pry up the board. It wouldn't fully budge, so she used her fingernail—for about two seconds. "All right. I love you all, but I'm not breaking my nail over a ghost, Georgia Ray. These are a fresh acrylic set, girlfriend."

"I'll go get a nail file," I said and rushed down the hall to my room, grabbing one from my basket of manicure supplies and racing back, not wanting to be in the hallway alone.

I pried up the board, with Nan, Jack and Dominique leaning over me. In the hole in the floor, I saw what looked like dusty papers. After shuddering about sticking my hand down into cobwebs, I pulled out two old photos of Nan and her sister, Irene.

"Nan...it's you," I whispered, handing her the pictures.

"Will you look at this?" Nan said in amazement, staring at the pictures tenderly.

"Who'd hide them in here?" I looked down into the dusty hole. "And there's something else." I reached in and pulled out a small package in brown paper and wrapped with twine. I handed it to Nan. She blew the dust off it, unwound the twine and opened the package. Inside was a leather-bound book. She opened it up, and her eyes immediately filled with tears.

"I can't, Georgia." She handed it to me. "I can't look at this."

A cold chill fell over me, like a January breeze had whooshed through the room. I opened the front cover. In a woman's tiny handwriting were the words:

*The Journal of Honey Walker, year of 1939*

"Who's Honey Walker?" Jack asked.

"My great-aunt Irene. Nan's sister. Honey Walker was her stage name. This was her journal? Did you know she kept one?" I looked at Nan, who shook her head sadly.

"Georgia, I had no idea."

"What happened to her?" Dominique asked. She was kneeling. I plopped down on the floor cross-legged next to Jack. Nan sat down in a brocade-covered rocking chair.

"Irene was five years older than I. We were as close as two sisters could be. But she always had...a sadness about her. Maybe it was that I could pass for white, and she couldn't. Her skin was your color, Dominique. She was just beautiful, but at a time when black *wasn't* beautiful. Far from it. Especially in this city. Everything was measured by how much black you had in you. Octoroon. Quadroon. For just how much of a fraction of you were black, and how black your mama or your grandma was. We both had the same mama, the same father. Just how we came out, I guess.

"Honey was a singer. A blues singer. Very good." Nan rocked back, remembering. "She just had a way about her that…she was magnificent." Nan looked down at us, her brown eyes grief-filled. "Irene had always been out on the road. Singing. She just up and left when she was of age, left with a man who claimed he could make her a star. Then one year, she came here for the holidays. Just showed up on the doorstep, thin as a rail and tired. Well, of course, I took her in and we just picked up where we left off. She was here for New Year's, 1939, and several months of that year. Then she just disappeared."

"What do you mean, disappeared?" I asked.

"One morning I woke up and her bedroom—that was your room, of course, Georgia Ray—was empty. All her things gone. Packed up in the middle of the night and left. And she didn't even leave me a note. Nothing. I never heard from her again."

"You never told me that, Nan."

"It still breaks my heart, Georgia. It wasn't but some time after Sadie died. It was a very difficult year for me. When I look back on my life, that year and the months after your grandfather died and then…of course, when your mother died were the hardest times of my life— and I've lived a long time."

"So whatever happened to her?" Dominique asked.

"I got word a few years later that she had died. It was all very vague. She passed in her sleep, and I never knew whether it was suicide or just tiredness with life. Maybe a weak heart. But we were never reconciled. Her lover at the time had her buried in New York, not here with the rest of the family. I didn't even find out until a musician friend of hers passed through town and stopped by to tell me. I think Irene left here hating me, and I never knew why."

"But maybe this journal will explain why she left," Jack offered. "Maybe it will…give you closure."

"Maybe." She stood up. "But I just can't read it. I can't…. I loved my sister. She was so dear to me, and I grieved her leaving here a long time. But the real grief never goes away. It just gets hard, like a little scar, and then something happens, and it opens it up again. You read the diary, Georgia. You read it and tell me what it says." Her eyes were moist as she looked at me. "I'm going to bed. There's been more than enough excitement for one night." She kissed the top of my head and then shuffled off to her bedroom, the ballet slippers she wore almost silent on the wooden floor.

"Well?" Dominique looked at me.

"We're going to read it, right?" Jack asked, rising.

"Hell, yeah. Come on!" I stood up, and we turned off the light and hurried down the hall to my bed, where the three of us flopped down on our stomachs and opened the diary.

chapter 8

*January 1, 1939*

*Happy New Year.*

   *Here I am…at home, after bein' a wanderer for a long time. I've left Joe for good and come to my sister's house—of course, this used to be my house, too. When I was a girl. But I've come home.*

   *We had a party last night until all hours, and I slept in. It's nearly supper time, and I'm just gettin' up. That's pretty typical in this house. Always something goin' on all hours. But it is January first—even if it is late in the day. A time for new beginnings. Is that possible for me?*

   *Arrived at Myra's sportin' house two days ago. Always when I return to New Orleans, I feel the music. Here it seems as if the entire world converges. Like four corners of the earth meet-*

*ing in one spot. Here. This one city. Spanish, Creole, French, American, colored, white, music spilling into the streets and out of windows. Music in the graveyards, and music in the houses. Jazz from every corner. Trumpets and pianos. Trombones playin' the backbeat. Drums and the deep sounds of the bass. Singers. Such singers. Jazz, blues, music that comes from the Gypsies. Music that comes from the churches. Music. Converging here… Only New Orleans embodies this. I think of New Orleans as Mother Music. She is my city, my home, my birthplace. She gave my music life. She gave my voice a life.*

*I'm tired. Just rode a bus a long, long time, touring for seems like nickels and dimes while white singers play in fine places where they are treated right. Might as well put me back on the plantations. Bend and pick cotton.*

*Makes me just plain mad. 'Cause I can wear a fine dress specially made. I can put a flower in my hair and wear perfume from France. But still places don't want no Negro woman…most especially mingling out front. Fine to sing, but don't sit down and talk with the customers afterward. Some nights I just played shacks, that's all they was. Shacks with a piano inside that catered to the colored folk. Dirty, ragged…but full of life, I can tell you. Like Mother Music herself, you can't quiet us forever. We will not be silenced.*

*I'm so, so tired. Myra, she is full of laughter, full of life. I can scarcely remember when we was little girls, little girls holding hands and singing songs. She and I used to learn all spiritual-type songs that our grandmama sang. Sad songs. Cotton-field songs. Songs about hard times. Songs about Jesus. But that seems so long ago. That little girl, holding hands with her sister. One hand colored, one hand white. I can't remember that joy. It's why I sing the blues, I think. That and this never-ending tiredness. Sometimes I think I'm tired because I* am sad. Other times I think I am sad because I am tired. Now I know that doesn't seem to make a lick o' sense, but it's how I feel inside.

Happy New Year, I say to myself, tonight. I whisper those words. Happy...New Year. Here, nestled in the arms of Mother Music, I am determined to find happiness. For this year, I say I am going to have a happy year, a new year, a happy new year. I'm going to live those words.

I've made a decision. Maybe I just made it now, this moment, as I write.

I'm going to stay here with Myra for a while. I'll sing downstairs. The piano player, Harold, he is talented. I'll stay here and sing. I will sing the songs of Mother Music, the songs of this city, the songs of the South, of the blues. Jazz songs.

I will sing...and I will rest. I will try to find out why it is I am so tired. And cure myself. And maybe, in this momentous year, I'll remember what it's like to laugh.

# chapter

9

I stopped reading, feeling my great-aunt's very tiredness coming through the page and into me.

"She really wrote this." I ran my fingers over the page. Her handwriting was thin and delicate. For someone whose mother died and father took off for parts unknown, holding a piece of my family history filled me with a sense of awe.

Dominique, Jack and I were all still nestled across my bed; I was in the middle. I had read the words aloud. Then I read a second entry. She wrote about a club she played—or was going to play—but she and a largely white band were turned away because she was black. Her reaction was a mixture of fury, humiliation and weariness.

Dominique looked at me, and said, "The South's strange legacy, sweet cheeks."

"Could you ever call me by just my regular old name?"

"I could, but that wouldn't be half as much fun, honey bun."

I held the diary reverently. "It's as if she's right here when I read this. I just can't believe she hid the journal in the house. Some nights I swear this house is alive with spirits. Not Sadie slamming doors, just a feeling, instead, like we're all being watched."

"Let's hope not," Dominique said. "'Cause what I don't want is any ghosts watching *me*."

"Read more," Jack urged.

I shook my head. "I want to savor it. I…I don't know. Want to read a little bit each day."

"I never knew your nan's name was Myra," Dominique said. "I would have figured it was Mitzi or Cha-Cha or something wild."

"Cha-Cha? That's a drag-queen name." I rolled my eyes. "It's Myra May." I climbed out from between the two of them and went over to the fireplace. I had a faded black-and-white photo of Nan and Irene when they were seventeen and twenty-two, respectively. They both wore hats and gloves, Sunday-church dresses. They clutched hands and grinned at the camera with exuberance, as if the photographer had just caught them sharing a private joke while they stood in front of this very house. The frame was ornate silver and tarnished.

"Here." I brought the picture over to them. "Here they are. Right about the time Irene wrote in her journal, too. Give or take a year or so."

Jack and Dominique looked at the two sisters. "Nan was beautiful," Jack said.

"Still is," Dominique mused. "Red sure thinks so. He was moonstruck all night. And Irene was beautiful, too. Look at those eyes. They're kind of like yours, Georgie. Like a cat's. You look more like her than Nan. And you sure don't look like your mother. Or your father, what I remember of him, and pictures."

"They don't look like sisters, do they?" Jack asked.

"No. Not really. The happiest stories Nan tells, though, are of when they were girls. She said they shared a secret language. Almost like twins, even though there was that age gap between them." I put the frame on my nightstand. "Irene watched out for Nan. Loved her very much. Nan said it was like she was more a mother, especially when their baby brother died and their mother became depressed. Irene practically raised Nan."

Dominique stretched and yawned. "Well, I love hearing about all this, but thanks to this haunted house, it's now after four o'clock in the morning. I'm going to my room. A girl's got to get her beauty rest!"

She slid off the bed and stood. Pulling herself up to her full height she stared up at the ceiling and said loudly, "Any ghosts…y'all just keep away from me. All this nighttime activity isn't good for the circles under my eyes." She looked over at Jack and me. "I'm going to need a cucumber mask tomorrow. You will, too, Georgie. You look like a wreck. Your hair reminds me of a fur ball my cat spit up the other day."

"It's 4:00 a.m. and I've drunk the better part of two bottles of champagne. Could you cut me some slack?"

I sat down on my bed. Dominique was forever concocting beauty potions in the kitchen. No one escaped. One time Nan came home from church to find me, Maggie, Dominique, Tony and Jack all with some kind of magic mud on our faces. Cucumber masks were Dominique's cure for what ails your face the night after too much drinking and too little sleep. Which is pretty much de rigueur around here every weekend.

"Precisely. Hot-oil treatment for your hair, cucumber for the face. I don't even know whether that will be enough, but at least it's a start."

She blew kisses at Jack and me, turned and shut my door, and went off down the hall. Jack scooted up on one of my pillows. He patted the other pillow. "Come on and lie down, Georgie. Between all the champagne earlier, and then…I don't know what you'd call it…a haunting? You must be wiped out."

I nodded, yawning. Moving up to my pillow, I faced the fireplace, my back to Jack. He curled up around me, spooning me. Call it the tiredness, or maybe the lingering effects of the champagne, but I found myself leaning back against him.

We'd lain in a hundred beds together before. On the road, we always chose each other as hotel roomies. We occasionally played a more far-flung wedding. We've even played on riverboats a few times, though I get seasick. Mike, Gary and Tony—when he is on the road with us—always share a second room. Their slovenliness dictated my roommate choice. Mike is the worst offender. Underwear on the floor, socks strung across the tops of lamps, crushed beer cans, cigarette butts. Tony's a little neater, but still, in their bathroom, whiskers sprinkle the sink and counter. Wet towels on the floor. Gary, though fastidious, roomed with them because he snored, and I tried one night with him on the road and nearly smothered him with a pillow. Jack, both neat and a quiet sleeper, became my buddy. Yet tonight, I scooted my hips against him, finding a place to nestle as if I'd been there all my life. In the past, he'd held me when I broke up with boyfriends. Like Mr. Married-but-I-forgot-to-mention-it. I held him when his brother Tom nearly died in a motorcycle accident before Tom went to rehab and sobered up. This was different.

Jack brushed my hair away from my ear and whispered, "You sang tonight like I've never heard you before."

"You've heard me sing the blues."

"Not like tonight. You sounded like Billie Holiday. You had this edge to your voice. It was like you were channeling your aunt Irene or something."

"It's the Chivas that Red feeds me every Sunday," I murmured. I wanted to go to sleep, and my body ached with tiredness. But my heart was beating as though a bird had taken up residence in my rib cage and was flapping its wings faster and faster.

He was raised up on one elbow, his hand now reaching over and touching my face. "You know…I've always loved your hair. Don't listen to Dominique," he whispered.

"It does look like a fur ball."

"It doesn't." His fingers traced my cheekbone. "And I love your face. And your voice."

He nuzzled my neck. "I think you should let your hair go wild. It's sexy that way."

"Easy for you to say, he of perfect white-boy blond hair."

He didn't say anything, just kept stroking my hair softly. I let myself relax a little, but still my breath was shallow. He kissed the back of my neck again.

"Jack…" I murmured.

"Hmm?"

"Let's go to sleep. This may not seem like such a good idea in the morning."

"Roll over and look at me."

"No."

"Please?"

I rolled over, as I had a hundred times before. This time he took my face in his hands and kissed me. Then he pulled back, and his tongue traced its way down to the hollow of my neck.

"Jack…don't," I said, though my body wasn't thinking *stop.*

"Why?"

"Because we have to work together, and if we make a mistake it puts the entire band in jeopardy."

His hand slid under my T-shirt and played with my nipples, first one, then the other, his thumb circling them. "We won't make a mistake. We're best friends. We'd never hurt each other."

"Have you paid attention to all my other relationships? My haircuts last longer than my typical relationship."

Jack's hand traveled down and was now stroking my stomach, giving me butterflies.

"But this is different. This is you and me." He slid closer to me, so our stomachs were touching. He pulled up his shirt, letting me feel his skin against my skin.

And so I did what any blues goddess would do in my position. I ignored every bit of good sense I had in my head.

I kissed him back.

We went from kissing, to making love. It wasn't crazy love, but slow, sexy and tender. Then we fell asleep like all our nights on the road. Only this time, we were naked.

# chapter 10

Musicians aren't like other people.

We don't live in the nine-to-five world full of gray flannel suits. We live in the nighttime world of neon colors.

We are a breed apart. We sleep in. We eat breakfast at noon and supper on the run. We drink mint juleps and champagne cocktails and spend lazy days doing nothing and then work our asses off on weekends. We party until we drop. And we wouldn't be caught dead behind a desk.

Consequently, I use the word *morning* liberally. When morning came, it was close to noon, and I was distinctly aware that I had a stiff neck from sleeping in the crook of Jack's arm. I got up to go to the bathroom and brush my teeth. I had that postsex maybe-we've-made-a-*huge*-mistake, Georgie-what-were-you-*thinking* panic. The face staring back at me in the mirror was not pretty. I had neglected to take off my makeup the night before. Or I had, but just not enough to remove all my mascara, which had given me raccoon eyes. My hair, merely fur-ball wild not a few hours before, had taken over like a Chia Pet on steroids.

I had never really worried about how I looked in front of Jack before. When we shared a hotel room, Jack could be in the shower and I'd also be in the bathroom, brushing my teeth, removing my makeup…peeing. We were roomies. I'd seen his penis, aka Jack Junior. But I'd never *touched* it. Touching it meant it was now, officially, a *cock,* something sexual, and not a penis, as in Jack's penis that I'd seen in the shower and hadn't given a thought to before.

Jack, for his part, had seen me stepping out of my dress. He'd seen me right after a shower. Without makeup. In my underwear. Fighting to put on my bra. (I always hook it in front first and then slide it around.) Even vomiting, the time I'd gotten food poisoning from a bad batch of crawfish. He'd cleaned up after me without a word, and he'd gone out in the middle of the night in search of Gatorade and ginger ale, the only thing my stomach would tolerate. A relationship of vomiting and peeing, seeing each other at best and worst, friendship and laughter, destroyed by a nuclear explosion of hormones—a night of sex.

After brushing my teeth and washing my face, I pulled on a T-shirt and returned to bed. Jack was opening his eyes.

"Hey, beautiful," he said, smiling, his voice raspy.

"Hey, Jack."

"No regrets this morning, I hope."

I shrugged. "Not really."

"Not really isn't exactly a 'No, Jack, last night was fantastic. You are a sex god.'"

"It was and you are, but in the light of day this may not be the most intelligent thing we've ever done."

He sat up. "We fit, Georgie. We always have."

"I know. But let's just figure this out on our own before we tell anyone. This could get really complicated with the band. Really complicated…period."

"Our secret then." He slid out from bed. There was his cock again. Cock, not penis, at half-mast. He pulled on his sweatpants. Picking up his T-shirt from the floor, he smiled at me. "But I've thought about this for a long time."

"That makes one of us…. Remember, my last boyfriend was married. Though he neglected to tell me that little detail *before* we got involved. The one before that was gay. It took sleeping with me for him to really get in touch with that. Before last night, I was considering joining a convent."

He kissed my cheek. "No convent for you, I'm afraid. Sister Georgia, Patron Saint of All Things Blues, I'm off to shower. Then I'm going to practice in my room awhile."

He left, and I snuggled down into the blankets. It was only noon, for God's sake. I could sleep more.

I have always had an uncanny ability to ignore my treadmill, my laundry, and even, on occasion, the chaos of Mardi Gras for a nice long nap. So I dozed, reveling in lazy sleep until my phone rang. I had forgotten to turn off the ringer. Caller ID told me it was Maggie. If I wasn't panicked before about sleeping with Jack, I was overwhelmed now. Ordinarily, I dish with Maggie about everything. Everything. Our periods are even in sync. We've spilled all there was to tell about lovers. From cock size and oral-sex techniques to heartaches and butterfly kisses, I don't think I've ever held anything back from her—not even the night I got drunk and kissed a woman who turned out to be a man…but that was another story—however, if Maggie knew about Jack, she'd be crushed. What the hell had I just done *to* one of my best friends *with* one of my best friends? Guilt stabbing me in my gut, I picked up the phone.

"Hey, Mags." My voice was gravelly.

"Not so much as a hint of a pass."

"Hmm?"

"Jack. He didn't kiss me good-night. He didn't hold my hand. Didn't even hug me. Nothing."

I had forgotten he'd walked her home. "Well…he's just been burned by Sara. Big-time. He's not ready for another relationship." The irony of this was not lost on me.

"Who said anything about a relationship? I'll take a two-week fling. He knows I like him. He has to. I've dropped every hint under the sun. Short of showing up naked in his bed—"

"I wouldn't recommend that." By now I was sitting up. "Maggie…I don't even know that he's your type. Not when it comes right down to it. He's pretty conservative. Neat. If he walked into your apartment he'd faint."

"I can be neat."

"No, you can't. Nor can you be on time. Neither can I. And it drives him crazy."

"He drives me crazy. God…he is so fucking hot."

Jack was the band member voted "most likely to go home with a bridesmaid." Women fell for those soulful eyes, and guitarist's biceps and forearms. In a tuxedo, he looked like a model, and because he was a touch on the neat-freak side, his tux was always perfectly pressed and crisp.

"Tony is just as hot." I thought about how he had blushed the night before, how his grin was slightly lopsided and impish. "So's Mike."

"Mike is an alcoholic. Or almost one. And Tony's cute," Maggie mused, "but he's not Jack."

"Well…you can pine for Jack, but I think it's a waste of time. Look at Sara. She is one of those down-home Southern belles you and I can't stand. Perfect highlights. Perfect smile. Perfect everything. And you, my dear, are the total antithesis of that."

"And proud of it."

"Exactly. But Jack has a long pattern of going for blondes." Of course, last night ruined that theory.

"What are you doing today?"

"Sleeping. Sadie was door slamming last night. Long story. We were all up until four o'clock in the morning."

"Does anyone ever sleep over there?" she asked. More irony.

"Margaritas later?" I changed the subject.

"Sure." Maggie's salon was closed on Mondays.

I ran my hand through my hair. It was a mass of knots. "But I have to tell you… Dominique is breaking out cucumber masks today."

"Gross."

"Consider yourself warned."

I hung up the phone but couldn't fall back to sleep. My relationships with Maggie and Dominique had buoyed me through more bad dates, bad-hair days and much darker moments than I could count. I had now committed a sin of omission, which was the same as lying in my book. Sadie would surely slam a few doors over this one.

*chapter*

11

That night, over margaritas, Dominique gave us all cucumber masks—including Jack. She painted my nails a fire-engine red. She also got two dozen mauve roses from Terrence but was holding firm on not seeing him. I think she also guessed about Jack and me, but for a change she kept her big mouth shut—probably because she knew it would kill Maggie if she found out, too.

"Margaritas and Mayhem" was our name for violent action movies washed down with margaritas and take-out that we sometimes planned for Mondays. Georgia's Saints got the occasional convention gig on Mondays, but few people marry during the week, so we were often free.

When Maggie had arrived, despite sitting down on the couch practically in Jack's lap, he remained oblivious to her. I spent the night feeling guilty and drinking enough margaritas to slow down the Terminator, which was our flick of choice.

"Let's go out," Dominique said after the movie. Every time she broke up with Terrence, once she got over her initial crying jag, she liked to go out seven nights a week.

"Where?" Maggie brightened.

"What about House of Blues?" Dominique suggested.

"Great. I'll call Tony and see if he wants to meet us there." I was anxious for any reason to avoid being alone with Jack.

I ran upstairs to my room and called Tony's cell phone. He answered on the first ring.

"Wanna go to House of Blues?" I asked him. I knew he liked smaller, intimate clubs, but Dominique favored loud, boisterous places with crowds. The better to make a scene.

"Who's going?"

"Me, Dominique, Jack, Maggie."

"Sure. Meet you there." He hung up.

Typical Tony. Say it in as few words as possible. He was an enigma to me. Something about him was wounded, but he had a way about him, like a tiger in a cage, that made me afraid to ask him what it was.

I opened my closet door and tried to figure out what to change into, when Jack knocked on my door.

"Come in."

He made a beeline for me and kissed me. "I've wanted to do that all night. I just wanted to hold your hand during the movie. Touch you."

"Jack—" I tried to keep the panic out of my voice "—I told you…this is something *very* new for us, and

I don't want the whole world knowing until we're sure this is right. And you may think it is right, but I'm not so positive. Not to mention—you're on the rebound."

"Fine…" He backed away from me. "I'll be discreet. But you can't blame me for sneaking in a kiss now and then."

"Go get dressed. I'll meet you downstairs."

My head swimming with margaritas, we all climbed into Jack's Buick—Maggie in the front seat—and set out for the House of Blues. As soon as we arrived, found a place to park—easier said than done in New Orleans, like any city I guess—and entered the club, I scoped the crowd for Tony. He spotted us first—not hard to miss a six-foot-something drag queen.

We scored a table and settled in to hear a local acoustic band. They weren't bad, sort of a rock/blues feel, with an excellent guitarist and a lead male vocalist reminiscent of Bob Dylan, scraggly long hair, droopy eyes and all. In between sets, blues standards blared out. Tony asked me to dance and spun me out on the floor.

"Can I ask you something?"

"Sure," I said over the music.

"What's keepin' you here? Your grandmother? Dominique?"

"What do you mean?"

"Georgie…you're wasting your bloody time with the band. I am, too. I play in between blues gigs, but I really need to be shovin' off."

"You can't 'shove off.' Who else would I go to jazz clubs with?"

"Georgie…I can't take another *NSYNC song. I

can't bloody take it every weekend. So what's holding you here?"

"I don't know. I think I'd like to pretend it's Nan. But it's really being afraid of finding out I'm not good enough to make it."

"Come off of it. You are good enough, and you know that."

"It's also not the easiest thing in the world to look at four guys who count on you, who you vacation with, eat together with, practice with, and spend more time with than anyone else on earth and say, 'Guess what? I'm ditching you all to follow a pipe dream.'"

"What about your da?"

"What about him?"

"Well…he was this great bluesman. Don't you think he'd want you to go for it?"

"His opinion doesn't much matter, Tony. He's long gone."

"But what if you found him? What if you could ask him?"

"Tony…for all I know, he's dead."

"You'd know if he was."

"How?"

"You'd feel it."

He didn't say anything else, just danced close to me. He was right, of course. About needing to find out once and for all whether I had it or not…and needing to stop hiding behind the band. And Nan. I knew she'd be the first person to push me out the door. I leaned my head on his shoulder. Then I spotted trouble clear across the club.

"Oh shit!" I stopped dancing.

"What?"

"Dominique is handing out condoms to those bikers over there. When she and Terrence are broken up, she has a suicide wish, I swear it."

Tony, Jack and I dashed over to the bar to corral Dominique who was on her Safe Sex Soapbox. Give her a few margaritas and she'll dig through her purse and hand out rubbers to anyone. Even senior citizens. Some people find her endearing. Some sure as hell do not.

"Dominique…come on," Jack urged.

"I'm just talking to my new friends," she slurred.

"We're sorry." I looked at the stone-faced guy she had been lecturing. He had a huge salt-and-pepper mustache and biceps the size of my thighs. "She's had a little too much to drink."

"I have not!" she insisted.

"Keep a leash on her then," the biker said to us.

"Hey…" Tony got up in the guy's face. "That's no way to speak about a lady."

The guy with the mustache stared down Tony, but I think he saw the same tiger-in-a-cage look I did. "I didn't mean anything by it."

"Back the fuck off."

The guy threw his hands up and turned around to get another drink at the bar. We all backed away, all the while Dominique was babbling, "We all need to practice safe sex. We all need to love each other but practice safe sex."

"Shut up!" Jack urged her. "One of these days you'll get us all killed."

We paid our bill, left the bar and poured Dominique into the car.

Tony leaned in to say good-night to her. Standing up, he shut her door, then kissed me on the cheek. "Don't forget what I said."

"I won't." I climbed in with Maggie and Jack in the front seat, and we shut the car door and headed off down the street. Dominique serenaded us with the first four songs of her act, stretched out across the back seat, her huge platform shoes up on the window. We dropped off Maggie, who of course leaned over to kiss Jack, and then headed to the Heartbreak Hotel.

I dragged Dominique upstairs.

"I need to take off my makeup," she whined. "It's not good to sleep in it."

Turning to Jack, I said, "Let me get her to sleep. I'll see you in the morning."

He sighed. "I hear you. Good luck and good night…. 'Night, Dominique."

"'Night, Jack."

I struggled to get Dominique into her room and shut the door. Taking cold cream out of a jar, I smeared it all over her face. "You owe me one, girlfriend," she whispered.

"No. Seems you owe me one. You could have been killed back there. Save the safe-sex speeches for guys who don't drive Harleys."

"Yes. But Jack was getting pissed at Tony. And frankly, I just got you out of having to deal with him."

"You're less drunk than I thought you were," I snapped, and smeared an extra big glob of cold cream across her nose.

"Honey, I can hold *my* liquor."

"You bitch!" I squealed.

"Look, sugar lips…Jack isn't the one for you. Casanova Jones is. Don't be fucking this all up."

"Dominique," I said through gritted teeth. "I haven't even met him for a damn cocktail yet."

"Don't get snappy with me, just 'cause I know what's best for you."

"All right, Miss Know-it-all, if you know what's best for me, do you think I should leave the band permanently? Look for a jazz gig?"

Dominique sat up. "Pass me a tissue. I can't think with all this cold cream on my face."

I handed her the box.

"Baby lamb," she sighed. "I'd love to hold on to you forever…. But remember when I left for New York?"

I nodded. Though, of course, Dominique hadn't left for New York. Damon had.

"I'll be lost without you," I had wailed.

Damon shrugged, sticking his hands deeper down into his pockets.

"I'm suffocating in this city, Georgia. I know I'm gay. But I don't know what that means."

"It means you like men. What kind of a statement is that?"

He wore a loose pair of Levi's and a crisp white oxford, a pair of penny loafers. His father had thrown him out of the house, but Damon still ironed everything as if it was going to be inspected. Every crease was so sharp, they looked as if you'd cut your finger on them. His only rebellion was a single earring in his right ear. Small. A tiny rhinestone stud that I'd bought him—the piercing was courtesy of me, too.

"Georgia, except for knowing I'm gay, I don't know what that means for me. Am I going to live 'out'? Am I going to go crawling back to my father…? I miss my mother. I miss my sister. Of course, they hide behind him. They won't dare go against him."

"So why can't you just stay here with Nan and me?"

"Because it's something I have to figure out alone. As a…gay man. I need to go to New York City. Rob is there."

Rob was Damon's first and only lover. When Rob left for NYU, they'd split up but remained friends.

"What will you do?"

"Get a job. Take some courses. Get laid. A lot." He grinned. "Figure it all out. Every time I drive through town, Georgia, I find myself gripping the steering wheel to keep from driving home to see my sister. I feel like running in there and telling them, 'I was only kidding! Can't you all take a joke?' But I can't do that. It's not a joke."

"Just promise me New York won't change you."

"Cross my heart." He had winked at me.

Two years later, he came back as a drag queen.

"I'd miss you." I looked at Dominique.

"Of course, candy lips. I'd miss you, too."

"I'll muddle through this all."

"You always do. With a little kick in the ass from me."

I kissed her on the forehead. "You know, when you came back, you were just a *little* different. What if we hadn't been able to stay friends?"

"Georgia, a little thing like phony tits on a man wouldn't stand in the way of real friendship. If you leave…we'll all go on. And when you come back, we'll just open our arms and welcome you home. That's how it works."

I stood. "You still have cold cream on your chin."

She reached up with a tissue. "What a woman does for beauty… Now go to bed."

Alone in my room, I put on a blues album. Softly. Nan was right. The blues make you crave someone to love.

*chapter 12*

Tuesday night, Jack came into my room, and we laid in bed and kissed slowly.

"Jack, we can't keep doing this. It's stupid. The band will pick up on it, and it's just not what I want right now."

"You wanted it the other night." He grinned.

I slapped his hand playfully. "Jack, we've been friends a long time now. Let's not fuck it up."

"All right. You win." He rolled over and slipped on his gym shorts. "What were you and Tony talking about last night?"

"Honestly?"

"No, lie to me. I really enjoy that in my relationships."

"You're an ass…. We were talking about getting out of the wedding business. It's not what I want. You know it. Everyone knows it but Gary. He knows it but won't face it. Tony wants out, too."

"Tony plays with that other band some. What are they called? The Blues Exchange?"

"Yeah. But he doesn't want to be playing here and there. He wants to play the blues all the time. Sunday, he even said he wants to go back to Ireland."

"Think he can?"

"What do you mean?"

"We're always joking he's on the run."

"Yeah. I think he can. Maybe under an alias," I kidded.

"I'll see you in the morning." He pulled his T-shirt over his head. "Tomorrow night we have the corporate gig."

I groaned and threw my covers over my head.

Corporate gigs are my least favorite. I don't understand how captains of industry, suits-and-ties, executive men and women who make more money in a year than the entire band does, end up drinking so much they start thinking: a) they can actually dance; and b) they can actually hold their liquor.

Tony didn't play with us that night; he had a conflict with a scheduled limo run. So we were forced to use Dave the Rave. Dave is a surfer, despite the fact that there isn't any surf here in the Crescent City, and he punctuates the end of every sentence with "dude."

This event wasn't different from any other. Except I remembered the words to "Celebration."

That night I slept alone.

And on Thursday morning—*really* morning, an indecent nine-thirty—Casanova Jones called and woke me.

"Georgia?"

I mumbled something incoherent.

"It's Rick."

I had almost forgotten about our date. Not really, but I was steeling myself for the eventuality that he wouldn't call. You know, "Let's do lunch sometime," "I'll respect you in the morning," "Give me your number and I'll call you"—the ultimate male-bullshit lines.

"Hey…Rick."

"You didn't forget about our date, did you?"

"No. It's just early…I'm a little groggy."

"Early? It's nine-thirty. On a Thursday."

"Spoken like a suit."

"Well, what do you say to this suit taking you to Brennan's tonight?"

Brennan's was famous for its bananas Foster, my favorite dessert, and its hefty prices. He didn't have to ask me twice. "Sounds heavenly," I rasped. I needed coffee. Badly. "What time? I'll meet you there."

"No…I'll pick you up. Do you still live in that crazy house of yours? The one with all the bedrooms?"

All of New Orleans knew about our house. Besides being historic, and equipped with enough narrow bedrooms to accommodate a whole slew of prostitutes, the fact that Nan thought it was haunted had also been depicted in local glossy magazines, including one big article on the ghosts of New Orleans, which included an interview with Anne Rice. When people found out I lived in the DuBois house, the ghosts were what they asked about first. However, the idea of explaining Dominique, who was having a preshow gathering of four drag queens to celebrate Angelica's one-year anniversary as a New Orleans resident, not to mention Jack, didn't sound like good first-date material. *Let me give you the tour, Rick. Up here is the haunted bedroom. And over here we have five queens carrying on—and yes, beautiful as Angelica is, she is, indeed, a man—and by the way, this is my guitarist. Did I tell you I slept with him? And he lives here?*

"No…I'll meet you. Really. There might be a party here. It would just be better if I met you at the restaurant."

"Okay, then. I have dinner reservations for eight o'clock. Meet you in the bar at seven-thirty?"

"Sounds perfect."

"See you later, then…. I'm really looking forward to it."

"Me, too."

I knew if Jack saved his money for an entire month he couldn't afford to take me to Brennan's. Between his car, music lessons he still took from his old college professor, and the fact that while we made enough to live on, split five ways it was actually a pathetic pittance of money, he and I—all of Georgia's Saints—were always broke. Hence we often played poker for candy, with a Snickers bar the pinnacle of the candy pyramid—we were too broke to play for money. But we'd honed our betting system over many years, many vacations and many nights on the road. Junior Mints were worth double a Necco wafer. A Snickers bar beat a Nestlé's Crunch. I smiled at the memories…then rolled over and went back to sleep.

Even after I finally woke up, I avoided Jack. When he rapped softly on my door, I pretended to be sleeping. All I could do was pray he would go out before I descended the staircase in my best dress—most decidedly not sequins!

At six o'clock, I put on my red silk dress with its mandarin collar. It's actually a hand-me-down from Nan, who bought it in Hong Kong. When I wear it, I feel exotic. It says "Fuck me"—but says it in a unique way. You know how when you're eighteen, you think fuck-me clothes are all about tits and how high your skirt is? The height of your stilettos? When you get a little older, you realize it's about mystery.

My hair had decided not to cooperate. It didn't say "Fuck me" as much as "I've been fucking all day long and just rolled out of bed"—which wasn't true. The humidity was cloying. The "misery index" was high. The misery index was created, I think, for New Orleans. The weather forecaster on the five o'clock news noted that with the temperature and the humidity it was really a hundred and ten degrees in the shade, therefore misery-inducing, and then some. So my hair was going to overtake my entire head. Nothing I could do short of shaving it off.

I poked my head out of my room and, seeing no sign of Jack, dashed down the hall to Nan's room. I tapped on the door.

"Nan?"

"Come in, Georgia."

I entered her room and twirled around for her.

"My Hong Kong dress!" she said admiringly. "You look stunning, dear. Stunning. That man is not going to be able to eat, looking at you."

"Can I borrow your black shawl in case the restaurant is cold?"

"Sure, honey."

The black shawl was once my great-grandmother's. I love vintage clothes, and I am always grateful my great-grandmother was close to my height, with timeless taste in fashion, just like Nan.

Nan opened an antique armoire and pulled it out, its lacy stitches looking like a delicate fine-spun spiderweb. "Here you go, Georgie."

I wrapped the shawl around my shoulders. "What do you think?"

"Smashing. Have you told Jack you're going yet?"

I looked at her and plopped down on a velvet tufted hassock.

"How did you guess?"

"Please. I'm pushing eighty years old, Georgia. You think I don't know what's going on under my very roof?"

"It just happened, Nan. We didn't plan it. But somehow it doesn't feel right.... Besides, if things fall apart, it will just create problems."

"Sometimes we do that," she said, sitting down in her chair.

"What do you mean?"

"Sometimes we create problems as a way of forcing ourselves out of our own inertia. If things with the band become complicated, you might make some different decisions."

"So what are you saying? That I'm sabotaging the band?"

"No. That you have a destiny you need to fulfill. As my yogi once said to me, 'We create the ripples on our own pond.'"

"You know, Nan—" I stood up "—I adore you, but there are times I wish you were just a polite grandma who drank tea and ate little biscotti and handed me a quarter each time you saw me. Instead of being so wise it's scary."

"Well, come give your polite old grandmother a kiss, and I'll give you a quarter."

I laughed and bent over and kissed her cheek and went back down the hall to my room. I put a dab of Chanel No. 5 on each wrist and in the hollow of my neck. And then for good measure on the back of each knee. I slipped on my best pair of black heels and put on a pearl choker. Placing a few things into a small evening bag, I turned off the light to my room and crept downstairs. Still no sign of Jack.

The queens were in the living room. I walked in and spread my arms wide. "Well, ladies?"

Dominique stood up, "Will you look at you, Miss Sequins. Decked out in…dare I say, vintage?"

"Yes." I twirled.

"On the fuckable scale of one to ten, you're a ten, doll baby. I won't expect you home until after breakfast," she laughed. Dominique cracks herself up. She swept a hand around the room. "You do know the ladies—Angelica, Lady Brett, Monica and Desiree, right?"

I smiled at the ladies, and mused, as I always do, why there are never any drag queens with names like Mary and Doris. Only glamour names. They reinvent themselves completely, and I love them for it.

Lady Brett was in her tiara and a Union Jack tank top with a miniskirt. Actually, with the queens, mystery *isn't* what it's about. They're still concerned with tits and how high their skirts are cut, the height of their stilettos. Lady Brett loves all things British and wears "God Save the Queen" T-shirts and pins. She has a British accent, though Dominique says she was born in New Jersey.

"Lady Brett, love the tiara."

"Isn't it just ducky?"

"Ignore Lady Brit here. She just rented *Emma* with the uber-fake-Brit, Gwyneth Paltrow. She's feeling *very* aristocratic today," Desiree joked. Desiree seems to believe in the why-have-a-36C-chest-when-you-can-have-42DDs theory. I'm not quite sure how she pulls it off, but she does. It's her look.

"Shut up before I say, 'Off with your head,'" Lady Brett commanded.

"Wasn't that a Marie Antoinette thing?" Monica asked. She channels Jacqueline Kennedy of the Camelot era.

"No," I laughed. "She said 'Let them eat cake.' I believe 'Off with your head' is the Queen of Hearts in *Alice in Wonderland*."

"Tell me *that's* not some male's dick fantasy…going down into a black hole," Monica said derisively.

"It was a rabbit hole," I said.

"Still a hole." Desiree nodded.

"Don't pay any attention to these queens. Where are you off to, Georgie?" Angelica asked me. She is easily the most beautiful woman I have ever seen. She wears a honey-colored wig. She's part Cuban, and her skin color is creamy, her makeup always perfect. But her bone structure is exquisite. She really looks like a high-born aristocratic beauty. Her nose, her cheekbones. I find myself unconsciously staring at her every time she comes over.

"I have a date."

"With the love of her life," Dominique chimed in.

"He's not. He's an old friend."

"Don't let her tell you this bullshit, Angelica. This girl *loves* him."

"Does she now?" Jack's voice came from the doorway. Dominique looked first at him, then at me in panic.

"Ladies," she squealed, her voice suddenly an octave higher. "It's time for us to *go.*"

*chapter*

13

Mayhem broke loose.

The queens scurried, grabbing purses and wraps, clicking along in their high heels, collecting their champagne glasses, and making their way to the kitchen to put them in the sink and then out the kitchen door. All the while, Dominique was rushing them. "Come on, girlfriends, let's *go.*" The word *go* had sounded like the high-C of an opera singer.

From the kitchen, Dominique called out, her falsetto still way in her upper range—which she does when she's nervous—"I'll do the dishes when I get home," as she shut the door.

I took a deep breath and faced Jack. "Hi." I smiled.

"You're still going out with this guy tonight?"

I nodded, clearing my throat nervously.

"Why?" he asked, his expression hostile.

"It's not anything, Jack. He's an old friend. And I told you I didn't want whatever this is between us turning into anything just yet. Until we find our bearings. But this is one date."

"From what Maggie told me, he was a cheat years ago, and once a cheat, always a cheat."

"Is that a new blues song, Jack, or your personal take on 'Your Cheatin' Heart' by Hank Williams?"

"Come off it," he snapped.

"Come off it? You're not one to talk, Jack. You told me that years ago you cheated on what's her name—Leigh. With her best friend. And what about the time, when you were with Sara, when you brought that blonde up to our room? On the riverboat. Remember that? I had to drink with Tony in the bar until 3:00 a.m. We ended up strolling on the deck and finding two lounge chairs to sleep on."

"I was drunk."

"That's not an all-purpose excuse."

"You're being unfair, Georgie. That was before we were together. Yes, those things happened, but those things happened when we were just friends."

"We're still just friends, Jack. Until we decide what the hell it is we're doing. Now I'm late."

"Fine…go off on your *date.*" He said *date* like "Go out and commit *murder.*"

"You're being an asshole."

"You're being a bitch."

"Do you see why I didn't want this thing between us to continue? You couldn't just give us some time to figure it out." I glared at him and wrapped the shawl tighter around me and walked out the front door. I shivered, and not from the night air, which was still quite humid and heavy, but from fighting with my favorite roommate. Clutching my shawl, I tried to pull Nan's confidence around me like a hug.

Walking through the French Quarter, passing drunken revelers with Day-Glo Hurricanes in "go-cups," I tried to stay aware. The crime rate in New Orleans is high. But I walk purposefully and confidently with a little don't-fuck-with-me attitude. Nan and I took a self-defense course in kav magra five years ago. It's based on a form of martial arts taught in Israel. Nan was the oldest student and, quite frankly, if a guy tried to mug her, he'd find his balls kneed up into his throat.

My mind drifted back to Jack. My favorite memory was of one of our all-night poker sessions. We'd had a Sunday Saints Supper, and everyone was there except Gary's wife, Annie, who had stayed home with a cold. Dominique was living with Terrence at the time, and Nan had long gone up to bed. We had drunk round after round of mint juleps, which I hate, but Gary likes and claims to have a "secret family recipe." Then we'd switched to straight tequila and lemons.

"Anyone for poker?" Tony had grinned, those Irish eyes of his twinkling. You didn't have to ask us twice. Suddenly, out of jacket pockets spilled piles of candy. They must have had the idea that they'd wanted to play all along.

I had run upstairs to my poker-candy stash, which I keep in an old cookie tin. The night wore on with much candy-eating until I thought I would be sick, mixed with drinking. Finally, it was down to the last hand of the evening. Tony, Jack and I were the only ones still in the hand. In the center of the table was a *pile* of candy you had to see to believe. If I recall correctly, it contained at least a dozen snack-size Snickers bars, over a hundred Necco wafers, three marshmallow Peeps (it was near Easter…these were high in value…by summer, as they grew hard, the value of a marshmallow sugar-coated chick falls below a Necco), two large Hershey bars, sixteen Hershey's Kisses, three Tootsie Roll Pops, and unbelievably, a half pound of real homemade fudge that Tony had bought at a candy shop in the hopes of trouncing all of us.

Seven card stud, deuces wild. Tony had a pair of eights showing. No telling what his hole cards were. Jack had a possible straight, but I thought he was bluffing. It didn't matter anyway. I lucked into a pair of twos in my hand, and a pair of kings on the table. That's four of a kind. Unbeatable except by a royal straight flush (highly statistically improbable). The pile had my name all over it. Jack had been acting so cocky. Tony called, which means we had to show our hands. Jack said, "Read 'em and weep." We burst into hysteria because he had nothing. Not even a straight. Not even a pair. Nothing.

I won, and my candy could barely fit in my tin. "You jackass," I'd said to him. "Why'd you stay in?"

"To egg Tony on to make sure you got the fudge," he had said.

He'd winked at me then. But now the memory, once full of laughter in my mind, made me sad. What if we had wrecked the friendship for a fast fling? A late night after too much champagne.

I had no more time to consider it, having arrived, safely,

on the doorstep of Brennan's. I took a deep breath and walked inside to a blast of air-conditioning. Standing at the bar across the room, I spotted Casanova Jones. And as if time suddenly spun backward, my breath left me.

My obsession...

*chapter*

14

Casanova Jones kissed me on the cheek and pulled me close to him, already laying claim to me the way he used to. He always stood a little closer than he had to. Where Damon and I had groped our way blindly toward sex, he had exuded it, confidently. Being near him brought me back to those moments when I fought to keep from trembling.

He bought me a drink, a flute of Moët champagne, and we clinked glasses. He was drinking scotch and soda. He put his hand to my hair and touched my cheek familiarly. "You look so incredible tonight."

"You're not so bad yourself," I purred. On Dominique's fuckable scale, he was the perfect ten.

The maître d', in a black tuxedo, led us to a romantic, intimate table. Rick and I started talking, not about old

times, but about now. We really had no old times beyond
a couple of teachers and classes in common, but whatever that unmistakable chemistry was, it was still there.

He asked me about my singing career.

"The guys are my family." I halted a minute and took
a sip of champagne, remembering my fight with Jack.
"What I'd like to do most is sing jazz, the blues. But I
have a good thing going."

"What about House of Blues or Mississippi Mudslide?
Couldn't you sing there?"

"I could. But I'd have to leave the band to really
pursue it. I'd maybe have to form a new band or join
an existing one in need of a lead singer. I will…some-
day. I rehearse every Sunday with my mentor, Red
Watson. He's one of the last of the great bluesmen."

"I never even knew you wanted to sing. I remember
you as shy but mysterious."

"I was shy. I don't know about mysterious. I always
sang in church, with my mom. But after she died and I
was living with my grandmother, Nan encouraged me
to sing to help me get over my grief."

"Your band is good. I mean, you guys had that wedding rockin'."

"Gary is obsessed with the electric slide."

"Who's Gary?"

"The keyboard player."

"The little guy?"

"Yup. The little guy. He actually likes that music.
Even ABBA."

"That's scary."

"Devastatingly frightening. So how about you? What
do you do?"

"Lawyer. Partner in my dad's firm…. Don't roll your eyes. Everyone hates lawyers, but we're not all Satan's spawn."

"That's *precisely* what Satan's spawn would say to lull us into complacency."

He laughed, and his dimples became deep crags. He leaned forward, his face illuminated by the candlelight. "Remember how we used to talk about sex?"

"Yes. I remember you came up to me in the hallway once and whispered in my ear, 'What do you like, Georgie. Top or bottom?'"

"Do you remember what you said?"

"No. I was a virgin. What the hell did I know about top or bottom?"

"And now?" He held my gaze.

"Top."

"How compatible," he said slyly.

I thought I would slide off my chair and into a puddle on the floor.

We ordered dinner, and for dessert we did get Brennan's famous bananas Foster prepared and served tableside by our waiter. Bits of caramelized liqueur melted with vanilla ice cream and warm cooked bananas. It was sensual and delicious, and all I could think about was touching Rick.

The waiter brought the check, and Rick looked at me. "Will you think I'm Satan's spawn if I invite you back to my apartment for a nightcap? I promise to drive you back to that haunted house of yours whenever you ask."

"Again, Satan's spawn *would* say that. But…that depends. What do you have to drink?"

"If I don't have what you want, I'll run out and get it. I *have* to get you alone and away from all these people and this crowded restaurant. I want to touch you."

I felt my stomach slip like when you fly down the big hill on a roller coaster. "Champagne."

"What?"

"That's what I want to drink. Champagne."

"That I have."

He paid the bill with a gold American Express card, and we got into his car, a shiny black Lexus. I guess that's what having a daddy who owns a law firm gets you. Leather seats and a shiny new car. Though I had never really wanted for anything my whole life, living with Nan wasn't elegant—it was rebellious. She didn't care if Dominique danced on the dining-room table, or a party lasted two days. She told me during Prohibition my great-grandfather had made bathtub gin. My family, even going back in my lineage, was rebellious and wild and defied social conventions. I had one great-great-great uncle who actually had a duel at New Orleans's famous Dueling Oak. He did not live to continue his lineage, as he lost the duel. But that was my family for you. Creole and black and white and Spanish in a complex, colorful mix. Casanova Jones's family was old Southern guard. He got a Lexus and a law firm; I got a bunch of dusty blues albums and a heartache that never quite goes away.

He grabbed my hand, the radio soft, me chilled from the sexual tension. I didn't feel hot. Nervous, more. Cold. Frightened. I collected men like lost puppy dogs, Nan told me. Men with broken hearts, broken wallets, broken dreams. But Rick wasn't broken as far as I could see. This upped the ante. I felt as if I was playing poker and bluffing with only a pair of threes, while he had a royal straight flush.

"Sing to me?"

"What?" I asked him incredulously.

"Sing to me. One of your blues songs."

"I'm too embarrassed."

"You sang in front of me at Cammie's wedding."

"Yeah. But that was different."

"Please…" He begged in a way that made me wonder what would happen if he begged in bed. He was utterly irresistible.

"No."

"Georgia Ray, please sing for me. I've been thinking of your voice since I saw you at the wedding. I think you owe it to me."

"Owe it to you?"

"Sure, I'm certain my billing went down this week. Every time I was supposed to be working on a case file, I was thinking of the lovely Georgia Ray Miller and that voice of hers."

His own voice was almost a soft growl. I couldn't say no.

I sang "The Man I Love," an old jazz standard that just makes my heart break a tiny bit each time I hear it or sing it. I was embarrassed at first, but then I found that place, that blues goddess place that fills me with a quiet confidence and an old grief that needs to be sung about, and I sang from that place. The place that wondered if my father was alive or if I was an orphan. If he would ever come to get his records or if they were truly mine.

When I was finished, we were stopped by the side of the road. I hadn't noticed.

"Are we at your house?" I looked around and could see nothing in the darkness.

"No," he whispered. "I just couldn't drive anymore. If I was standing, Georgia, you'd have brought me to my fucking knees."

He put the car in drive again, and we went on to his apartment. He lived on the top floor of an old house in the Garden District. Personally, I think calling it an apartment is like calling my house a cottage. When he opened the door, I took in the floor-to-ceiling windows and crown molding, the wainscoting. The rooms echoed as my heels clacked on the parquet floors.

"This place is beautiful." I spun around. Original art, lit by tiny little lamps, lined the walls like in a museum.

I wandered, spellbound by the art. I heard him in the kitchen, heard a cork pop, and he returned with two glasses of champagne. He put them on the dining-room table.

"If I don't kiss you, I'm going to go out of my mind," he whispered. "Come here." But I was rooted to the floor, unable to move, not sure if I could even trust my knees. "I'll come to you, then," he said softly, taking the space between us in three strides.

We didn't so much kiss as consume each other. Never in my life, I thought, if I lived to be an old woman like Nan, would I experience anything like it again. We stopped at some point to stare at each other. In my mind, I couldn't believe that after ten years, whatever it was about him that drove me wild was still there. And that he could feel the same way. Then I realized it was something much more. Yes, there had been a connection ten years ago, but this was like a sexual soul mate. Something about him told me that if we went to bed, I'd never want another lover for as long as I lived.

He walked over to the dining-room table. "Okay...so before I lose my mind completely, here's your champagne, Georgia." He held the glass out to me and took my free hand. "Let me show you the place."

We wandered room to room. He told me about each piece of art he had collected. Some of the pieces were new artists, some New Orleans natives. He had some outsider art, colorful eclectic pieces. But he also had a Miro and a Degas passed down from his family.

I looked at his hand holding mine, brought it up to my lips and kissed it. His hands were very masculine and very strong. He leaned in close to me and kissed my neck. I felt completely torn. If I stayed, I would never be able to stop whatever happened next. If I asked him to take me home, I would go crazy until I saw him again. I would lie awake while all that sexual energy filled me with a nervous sleeplessness.

"Stay the night, Georgia?" he whispered.

"I don't know, Rick. This night has been pretty amazing, but this really isn't my modus operandi. I don't usually hit it off with someone like this. Don't usually do this."

"It's fate that we ran into each other."

"Or after a while, you play enough weddings in this town, you run into everyone you ever knew."

He smiled and then leaned in to kiss me again. "You've gotten just a little cynical there, Georgia Ray. God...I even love your name."

I kissed him and then pulled back. "Not cynical... But

you really can't imagine what we singers get to see from our vantage point."

"Don't be afraid of me. Don't be afraid that I'm full of shit. I think I can, actually, guess at what you see playing weddings and conventions. Our firm handles some old family money, and I get invited to a lot of company Christmas parties—the companies those old families own. I see what they're like. I would guess every guy in the room sees you up on stage and makes a play for you."

"Not exactly, but I see enough to get a little negative."

"I see a lot, too, believe it or not. I see families fight each other over inheritances. I once saw two sisters fight over a set of spoons. Sterling-silver spoons. And both of them came into over two million dollars. To this day, they've never spoken to each other again."

"Doesn't that make you cynical?"

"Honestly…no. I mean, I guess I was always a little jaded. Georgia, my family is one of New Orleans's royalty. My parents have black-tie functions in our dining room and go to Palm Beach for polo season. People like that aren't always the nicest. Trust me, I learned before I was eight years old that money can't buy you happiness. I think that's why you always fascinated me. Your family has been in New Orleans almost as long as mine, but you all are French Quarter. You're on the edge. You in that crazy house of yours. Now *that's* what I wanted. To break out of my stuffy family. So while I think I've seen it all, when it comes to you, lady, I'm not cynical. I refuse to be."

"Yes."

"Yes what?"

"I'll stay the night." He had charmed me completely. As he always had. I said yes without thinking about Jack. Without thinking about anything but how it felt to kiss him.

"I want you," he growled. We put down our champagne glasses and kissed again, our hands pulling each other closer. I felt like a man-eater, like I really wanted to devour him, to make him part of me.

We didn't make love. That was what Jack and I did, mistakenly, now I realized. Rick and I fucked. This was moaning-screaming-wake-the-neighbors-shake-the-ceilings sex. Do we each have a sexual soul mate? Do we have multiple soul mates? Doesn't that defeat the idea of a soul mate? How could this man I didn't know well fuck me when old boyfriends had tried for months to please me, to drive me wild, to take me to the place he took me effortlessly? We fucked and then curled around each other in a comfortableness I didn't know I could have with someone.

I had no shame with him. No embarrassment. I didn't believe in fate, but if Sadie could have seen me that night, naked, on top of him, kissing him, I knew she would approve. I was a sex goddess.

# chapter 15

The next morning I woke up to the enticing smells of bacon and coffee. Rick had laid a cashmere robe out on the bed for me. I put it on; the robe was sinfully luxurious. I could get used to being cared for like this. And like last night. We had topped my personal record of four orgasms in one night.

I went into his bathroom and rinsed my mouth with mouthwash. Taking a glance at myself in the mirror, a night of sleeping in my makeup had not been kind to my face. I washed up and scrubbed at my skin until it was shiny and passable for my "morning after" look. Then I went and found him in the kitchen.

"You make breakfast like this every day?" I grinned, approaching him at the stove. "I could get spoiled, you know."

"That's the whole idea. Get you very used to this. I canceled my first two appointments of the day to cook you breakfast and then take you home." He kissed me then popped a piece of bacon in my mouth.

"Mmm."

"Coffee?"

"Uh-huh."

"You singers really are night owls. I was up by six-thirty, but there was no waking you."

"Well…I know one way you could have." I wrapped my arms around him.

"You—" he hugged me and kissed the top of my head "—are very naughty. And I could get used to *that*."

I nestled against his chest, and for the first time I wished I wasn't a singer. Every Friday and Saturday for as long as I could remember, I had worked. I had worked Christmas Eve and all through the holiday season…putting up the tree on the lone night we weren't playing a party. Now I had someone I wanted to have a weekend life with, only I had no weekend. He was a day creature. I was a night one.

We ate breakfast together, and then he loaned me a pair of sweatpants and an oxford-cloth shirt to go home in.

"Glamorous." I smiled, his shirtsleeves hanging down past my hands.

"Baby, I'd like to see you in my shirts every morning."

He dressed in an expensive suit with a crisp white shirt, starched and pressed by the dry cleaners, and a Jerry Garcia tie. I have a thing for a man in a dark blue suit. And men with black curly hair. And blue eyes. If you went down my mental checklist of what made a man deliciously fuckable, as Dominique would say, Rick had it all, including six-pack abs and a voice like a late-night deejay's, raspy and seductive.

I folded my clothes from the previous night into a shopping bag he gave me, and then off we went. Pulling in front of my haunted house, he said, "All right…you can't get out of this car until you tell me when I'm seeing you next."

"Monday night?" We were working Friday and Saturday, and Sunday was the Saints Supper. I didn't think I was ready to introduce him to the gang yet. What was I thinking? I knew I wasn't ready to introduce him, and I would bet five Snickers bars that he wasn't quite ready for a night with Dominique and my friends.

"That long? I don't know if I can wait."

"Sorry. Don't date wedding singers. We are notoriously unavailable."

He leaned over and kissed me. "I'll call you over the weekend, and Monday I'll cook you jambalaya like you have never had before."

"Doubtful. Remember, I've lived here all my life. That would have to be one hell of a jambalaya recipe," I teased, kissing his cheek, which smelled of shaving cream and Polo cologne.

"But this is my family's recipe handed down through generations. You'll be *begging* me for cold beer."

"You're on."

We lingered on a kiss, and then I walked up the steps to the house and inside. Friday, eleven in the morning. In the Heartbreak Hotel, that might as well be predawn. My normally shy cat, Roxie, came and leaned against my leg. She had been avoiding me since Judy Garland, Dominique's cat, arrived. I think she was jealous. But other than Roxie's purr, the house was still. Dominique was probably still sleeping, as was Jack, because knowing him, he went out drinking after our fight, and when he was angry, he drank too much. And Nan always slept until noon. With eye shades on. She swore by them for her beauty rest and tried to convince me to wear them. It was just a little too Gloria Swanson in *Sunset Boulevard* for me.

I crept up the stairs and into my room. I pulled off Rick's sweatpants and climbed into bed still wearing his oxford. I wanted to feel close to him. I kept telling myself that this wasn't love. It was infatuation. Lust. But I missed him already. I was going through orgasm withdrawal.

My phone rang. Caller ID. Maggie.

"Hello, Mags," I said, assuming she wanted all the dirt on Casanova Jones.

"Don't say anything. Don't tell me how stupid I was…but I slept with Jack last night."

"What?" I couldn't be hearing this.

"I know. It was crazy. Listen, I can't really talk. I have to blow out one of my customers and do a foil job. But he came over. We went out drinking. Hopped from bar to bar and ended up back at my place. We woke up naked with a telltale wet spot on *my* side of the bed. I don't even remember if it was *good*, Georgie."

My head started pounding. I wanted to come clean and tell her everything right then and there. But then she'd be even more upset. Her voice was trembling.

"I've liked him for *so* long, and now this? Sloppy sex I can't remember. This isn't the way I wanted things to go. Now it'll be awkward. I wanted fuck-your-brains-out, rock-your-world sex. Not who's-on-the-wet-spot sex!"

I had fuck-your-brains-out sex last night, but I wasn't going to make Maggie feel worse. I leaned over to my nightstand and grabbed my aspirin bottle. Colossal and sudden headache. And I had to play a funeral directors' convention with Jack tonight. I longed to lay him out in a coffin for size. I popped two aspirin and took a swig of water from a glass I always keep by my bed.

She went on, shouting slightly over the background whir of blow-dryers and the usual hair-salon chatter. "Should I talk to him about it? Pretend I don't remember anything? He ran out of my apartment so fast this morning, Georgie. I'm humiliated."

Not nearly as much as if she knew about Jack and me.

"Maggie, honey, we'll sort this all out."

"Will you talk to him?"

"I don't think that's such a good idea."

"Please?…"

"Maggie—"

"Please. I'm *begging* you. As your closest female friend—and I mean female with actual estrogen. As the woman you bought your first vibrator with."

"Technically, that was Dominique. You were just as embarrassed as I was. We both gave her our money."

"Fine, as the woman who nursed you through your breakup with the married creep. As the woman who—"

"Mags, I know who you are. You're the woman who dyed my hair pink two years ago with a bad batch of henna…. But even so, all right. I'll talk to him." Right after I punch his lights out with my grandmother's favorite punch-to-the-nose technique we learned in self-defense class.

"Promise?"

"Yes."

"How was your date?"

"Very hot."

"Tell me later?"

"We're playing a gig. I'll talk to you tomorrow, Maggie."

"I'll see you tomorrow actually. I'm waxing Angelica's eyebrows."

"She's coming over?"

"Didn't you hear?"

"Hear what?"

"She moved in. To the Heartbreak Hotel. She walked in on Frankie with his ex."

"What is this, Mardi Gras? Has everyone I know lost their fucking minds?"

"I don't know. So I'll see you tomorrow."

"See ya, Mags."

My head pounded, and I took another aspirin. Not that I thought it would help. Jack had made Rick sound like the bastard. Once a cheat, always a cheat. But instead, he had certainly made a fine mess of things.

What is it about New Orleans? The city has a rhythm of sex. It's in the steaminess. You just imagine hot supercharged sex then lazy naps beneath ceiling fans. If you walk through certain neighborhoods, the street corners have full bands playing on them, brass, drums, singers, dancers. Making music that sends a pulse through your veins, a pounding beat that taps sex-sex-

sex against your heart. Music and sex and alcohol. Mother Music as my aunt called it.

And voodoo. Dominique is very superstitious about things like that. The city has a history. Marie Laveau was the most famous voodoo queen of them all. If you go to her grave at St. Louis Cemetery, it's covered with black candles and trinkets that followers of black magic leave behind. Maybe someone had cast a spell over everyone I knew. Made us all blind with lust.

I wondered what my great-aunt Irene would have to say about love's foolish spell.

chapter 16

February 16, 1939

*I am in love. I scarce can write it without trembling. I've never felt this way before. Not ever. Sure…on the road I hear all kinds of talk. I once was at the Apollo Theater and T-Bone Malone was makin' eyes at me. This piano player, that one. This sax man. That one. Musicians. They're all full of the same sort of lines. Trying to get this New Orleans girl to believe they really want her for more than just fun and games. Uh-huh. Like I was just born yesterday, as Myra might say. Now, you go out with a band touring on the road, people look at you a certain way. Like you must be that kind of girl. I tell people I'm not. But I don't think they believe me. They think that I'm all about fun.*

*Musicians are known for the weed we smoke and the drinks*

we drink. 'Specially jazz musicians. See, everyone gets that what's happening in music now is changing music. We're making something new. Something special. And these are wild guys. They know they're makin' some amazin' music, and it gets them all crazy.

Then once people hear me sing, people say to me, "Girl, you sing about love like you really know what you're talking about." So they have these thoughts and ideas about me. They draw some conclusions, though the conclusions are wrong. Love? No, I never knew love before.

New Orleans is the city of love and the city of jazz. Paris the city of lights. I love Paris. But New Orleans is part of me. I forgot that. I forgot that until I came home. When I left, I thought I hated New Orleans. Hated its heat. The way it creeps all over you and makes you sweat. Hated the way Myra was treated better than I was on the streets. People sometimes thought I was Myra's maid! But now that I am here and in love, New Orleans is magical. Everything about it is bright like the sound of a trumpet.

This love is secret. I can barely breathe. I think about…this love and it just sets me on fire. Takes my breath away and then sends me over the moon. I stare at the moon out my window at night and wait, every hair standing on end. Waiting. Waiting. Counting the seconds.

At first I thought, I'm in love so I surely can't be singing the blues and my sad songs. But love sure can give you days you feel sad. I sing the blues…it's like remembering every sadness I ever had. Like the day Pa died. Now, he was about the kindest man you ever met. And Mama, her sickness. I think about them, and I feel sad. I want my love to last forever. To live forever. I know it's too much to ask of God. But I'll do some asking anyway when I say my prayers.

*I've lost my mama, my baby brother, my papa. Let me have this one love, Lord. Let me have it without you stealing it away from me. Don't take it from me. Give me this. This one. Please. Lord. Please.*

*Yes. I can sing the blues. I take this longing I have as I wait. Wait for my beloved. And then I sing it downstairs at the piano. I think my voice is better, richer, finer. I can do anything because I have love. I can fly. I can be free. Really free. In the hours past midnight. I am free.*

chapter 17

Love makes you crazy. Makes us all crazy. After reading about Irene's secret love, I thought of Casanova Jones. Why'd we give him that stupid nickname anyway? He was the most giving lover I had ever had. Then again, he didn't have much to stack up against.

I had a mental checklist of every man I'd ever gone to bed with—a reasonable list, neither too long, nor too short. The list was hardly impressive. Each lover had something about him that didn't fit with me. If music is melody and harmony, bass clef and treble clef, then sex is about fitting together high notes and low ones into its own jazz composition, because certainly sex is about improvisation. The men I have been with either rushed the rhythm or just didn't make me *feel* anything deep down. Not until Rick had anyone made my world spin backward, make the room spin, make me feel a *need* for him the way someone feels hunger or thirst.

I tried to take a nap, but I was nervous. I had, for the first time, that feeling I always assumed I'd one day have that maybe, maybe, Rick was The One. I'd thought it, secretly, in high school. But that was a lifetime ago. This was now, and it seemed so real. I gave up on sleep, picked up my remote and started clicking through daytime television. I ended up settling on an old movie on a classic-movie channel. *Waterloo Bridge*—it's one of Dominique's and my favorites. I watched the love story unfold. About halfway through, I heard a knock on my door.

"Georgie? It's Dominique and Angelica," their voices were singsong.

"Come in, ladies."

They entered in housecoats. Dominique's was pink with large flowers on it. I am sure when she bought it, likely at Kmart or someplace suitably mainstream, the cashier either thought she was nuts, *or* thought she was buying it for her grandmother. But no, here she was like a vision of a housewife on acid. Angelica had on a flowered housecoat—and bunny slippers. And had curlers in her hair. They were like a drag version of *I Love Lucy*: Angelica was Lucy, Dominique was Ethel, though she would have been very insulted if I'd said that.

"Oh my God, it's Vivian Leigh!" Angelica clapped her hands, looking at the television.

"And Robert Taylor." I pretended to swoon.

"My favorite movie," Dominique chimed in as they both climbed into my bed, sandwiching me in the middle.

"But we didn't come here for old movies," Dominique said, taking the clicker from me and pressing mute. "We came to hear about your date. Which, we noticed, lasted until this morning. We want all the most naughty details, and if you don't tell us, we'll spank you."

"Ladies... This is it."

"I *knew* it!" Dominique grabbed my hand. "Tell Aunt Dominique all about it now, Angel."

"It was just perfect. From the first glass of champagne, to sex. Yes, first-date sex—usually a big no-no. But Dominique, this was unbelievable rock-my-world sex. And then this morning he canceled his appointments to cook me breakfast."

"What did he make?" Angelica asked. She always demanded the best from her lovers.

"Bacon and eggs, champagne and strawberries."

"What brand of champagne," Angelica pressed.

"Moët and Chandon."

Dominique and Angelica exchanged glances. "He's a keeper," they said simultaneously.

"Does he have a brother?" Angelica asked. "I'm back on the market. And right down the hall."

"I heard about that. Sorry about your boyfriend, but happy you're here... Yes, I do believe Rick has a sister and a brother. However, the brother is *married*."

"One night with me, honey, and grown men are known to cry. And break off engagements and toss aside wives."

"Old Guard, Angelica. I would venture to say the entire family has never even seen a queen before."

"Uh-huh." She smirked. "You think so, but did I tell you my last boyfriend was Darryl Banning III?"

"No way."

"Yes way," Dominique said. "And he was sending her roses every Friday. A dozen, long-stem, red. With hand-written notes."

Darryl Banning III was the very married, very old Southern guard king of tobacco.

"Well, that's certainly…interesting. I guess it goes to show you that you can never tell."

"And don't assume," Angelica added.

"Yes, that, too." I mentally pictured Darryl Banning III from his gubernatorial run. "But I don't think Rick's brother is up for grabs."

"Too bad," Angelica said ruefully.

I sighed. "I left Rick an hour or so ago, and I ache. I literally can't stand it. I don't know how I'm going to sing tonight."

"Young love." Dominique smiled. "When you're fucked right, darlin', you just go runnin' back for more."

"Please…I need to be fucked right." Angelica pursed her lips and fluffed her hair. "I'm back on the market, Georgie, so if you meet a nice boy looking for a beautiful diva to call his own, you send him my way."

"I'm really sorry about Frankie, Angelica."

"I'm not sorry. He had a tiny little cock, and frankly, he just wasn't doing it for me. Anyway, you know I've always wanted to stay at the Heartbreak Hotel. I like it so much, I may never leave."

"Nothing would make Nan happier." Which was the truth. I used to wonder how Nan felt about her home being invaded by drag queens and brokenhearted young men and women. But she liked being around young people. Period. She never judged. In fact, I can remember a few nights when Dominique and her friends did cabaret right in the living room, and she said they were better than the cabaret in Paris she saw as a young woman. She embraced life. And she liked having people around who embraced it, too. Like Sunday dinners, there was always room for one more plate at the table. One more queen in a bedroom. One more set of fishnets tossed over the shower-curtain rod.

"Well…not to rain on your sexual parade—" Dominique elbowed me "—but what about Jack?"

"Jack is on my shit list."

"Well, you're not exactly princess of his parade either, sex machine."

"He slept with Maggie last night."

Collectively, Angelica and Dominique gasped.

"Exactly!" I said, lightly slapping Dominique's arm. "He's such a jerk. He was just using her. You know, that's not like Jack at all. I don't know what's gotten into him, but now I am really pissed at him. And we have to play a funeral directors' convention tonight."

"Sounds like *loads* of fun. Must be really *lively*," Angelica giggled.

"Actually, they are a wild bunch. I have stories," I said. "But I am just so fucking furious at him. We actually sing a duet. 'Endless Love.' In set three."

Dominique cringed. "The old Lionel Ritchie tune?"

"The very one. Well, you tell me how I'm supposed to sing that to him when I want to take his balls and slam them in his guitar case?"

"Does Maggie know about you and him and your little nocturnal hanky-panky this week?" Dominique asked.

"No. And it's going to stay that way."

"My lips are sealed. So Casanova was really good, huh?" she asked. "Tell me...handcuffs? Vibrators? Sex toys? Positions?"

"It was awesome. Beyond that, I don't kiss and tell."

"Bullshit," Dominique squealed.

"I'll say this...he broke my personal orgasm record."

"See, that is just delicious. But vague. You know I like *details.* I'll worm it all out of you sooner or later. Turn up the movie."

The three of us snuggled and watched the tearjerker on TV. We passed tissues between us for the final death scene. Then the ladies went off to fight over bathroom shower schedules, and I watched old movies and tried to decide just what color sequins one should wear to a convention of funeral directors. Was black too obvious a choice?

*chapter*

18

Funeral directors are an odd bunch. Funeral homes are mostly family-owned businesses. I think if you grow up in a household of funeral directors, it's just expected that you'll go into the "family business"—even if that business involves formaldehyde and corpses. So when the funeral directors get together for a big party, there are a lot of interesting families gathered for the partying. Brothers in dark suits. Dads and sons with the same morbid sense of humor. They tell corny jokes about the dead, or talk about unusual funeral requests, like the woman, one told me, who wanted to be buried with a fifth of bourbon and wearing her lucky bra. People, they tell you, get buried with bowling balls, golf clubs, photos, playing cards, gambling dice, fishing poles, bottles of liquor and even books the person can't very well read. But mostly, funeral directors know how to bust loose. I guess if I spent most of my time around dead people, when I got to a city like New Orleans that *knows* how to show *live* people a good time, I would go crazy, too.

So Georgia's Saints had funeral directors doing the limbo and the macarena. We had them in a conga line during my rendition of "La Bamba," and we had them groping each other during Jack's and my version of "Endless Love," which was sung with us glaring at each other. Gary was not amused and yelled at us during break.

"Has it occurred to you two that during 'Endless Love,' you might want to look like you actually *like* each other? *Love* might be a stretch…I'd settle for mild indifference. What the hell is wrong with you two?"

I snapped, "Today we don't happen to like each other very much, so that was the best we could do."

Gary snapped back, "Look, we're *professionals.* If you two are fighting, it's no reason to take it out on your audience."

"Professionals," I snorted, turning to glare at Gary now. "If I have to sing 'The Electric Slide' one more time, I'm going to puke."

"Her problem is she doesn't know what she wants," Jack said, appealing to the band for sympathy.

"His problem is he does all his thinking with his penis," I fired back.

Gary, Tony and Mike stared at this exchange, slack-jawed.

"Well, she doesn't know what she's getting into with this Casanova guy… You think leopards change their spots?"

"One would hope so or that would mean Jack regularly uses people like my best friend and *sleeps* with them to get back at me."

"Fine. And if she comes crying to me and says this guy broke her heart, I'm going to say 'I told you so.'"

"Glad you got that off your chest," I said. "Now I will tell *you* that if you hurt Maggie I will have your testicles for breakfast." I stormed out of the main ballroom, noticing a run in my stockings, and headed for the bathroom, leaving my four male band members stunned.

I eventually returned for our final set—minus stockings…the run was beyond salvaging. The guys were very solicitous of me. Tony even came up to me and offered me a box of Junior Mints.

"Here, Georgie. I got these from the gift shop. Thought you might need a little chocolate."

"Thanks, Tony." I took them.

"Chin up, lass."

"I can't even stomach the idea of singing Britney Spears in this set."

"It ain't my idea of music either."

"It's like a bad Fellini movie. Funeral directors doing a conga line."

"Cheer up. We still have the limbo to do."

"Shut the fuck up."

"I made you smile."

He had. But I'm sure he thought it was all PMS. The guys always think that any difficult behavior on my part is directly proportional to bloating and hormones. Sometimes they're right, but I never let them know that. Then again, Dominique claims she has PMS once a month, too. What is PMS anyway but an excuse to get away with being a bitch? Regardless, the band spent the rest of the evening treating me with kid gloves, even Jack.

While we were packing up after our gig was over, Jack came over to me. "Ready to go home?"

"If you promise to shut up the whole way and not talk to me about our little disagreement." I had gotten a ride to the Omni with Angelica, who tooled around in a fire-engine red Miata, a gift from her last boyfriend. I had left before Jack did in an effort to avoid a screaming match before singing. I used to own a dream of a late-model Mustang, but it was stolen, and I'd never gotten around to replacing it. If worse came to worse, I would drive Nan's vintage Cadillac. It's like driving a land yacht, but it gets me from point A to point B.

"Fine. I'll shut up. Just don't be asking me to sing 'Endless Love' with you."

I stifled a laugh and rolled my eyes. Still, we rode back to the house in mostly silence. When we pulled up to the curb, he turned to me and said, "I'm sorry, Georgie."

"Me, too."

"Let's just take a breather from this whole thing. And I promise to talk to Maggie. I don't want to hurt her. I've known her as long as I've known you."

"Good. Glad that's settled."

"But I'm still rooting for you to dump Casanova."

"Don't start…"

We mounted the stairs and locked up. Upstairs in the hallway, I could hear soft crying sounds.

"Sadie?" Jack looked at me.

"That's no ghost, that's Dominique." I half ran to her bedroom door and knocked gently. "Dominique, honey?"

She quieted, and then I heard a muffled, "Go away."

"No...let me in."

She came to the door and unlocked it, turning around and slumping back down in her chair. Jack and I sat down on her bed. Now that she was settling in, the room had taken on her personality. She had a pink lampshade on a bedside lamp, and photos of her and her friends taped to the mirror. Boas and hats and wigs sat atop the long dresser. Her collection of plastic snow globes from every city she ever visited were lined up on one shelf. She had a framed photo of Liza Minnelli on the wall. It was inscribed, To Dominique, With Love, Liza. Angelica had gotten it for Dominique the last time she and Terrence broke up and she was morose for a month, though one night when Angelica had too much to drink, she told me she bought the glossy and forged Liza's signature. It was our secret.

"What's wrong, honey?" I asked.

"It's Terrence. He says he wants another chance."

I believed Terrence really did love Dominique. He was an uptight, handsome, closeted computer analyst. He frequently flew all over the country, and even to Europe for his job. He became infatuated with Dominique after seeing her perform, and he sent her roses. More than once. However, when they actually sat down and talked one night over drinks, they discovered a connection, a spark between them. But Dominique most definitely stood out in the world, and Terrence lived in a quiet world, an orderly world. Reconciling that world with Dominique wasn't easy, and they were on their third breakup.

"Dominique...I'm sure he's trying."

She looked up at me, mascara running down her face. "Trying isn't…good enough for me anymore, Georgia." She hiccuped, as if she'd been crying for a long time, her breath ragged. "I want to come home to him at night. I want to build a life together. He owns that damn company…so as far as I'm concerned, let him create his own rules about his private life."

Sometimes it was easy to forget that beneath the "flash and trash" (her words, not mine) of Dominique's appearance, scratching beneath the posing and the theatrics, the condom-flinging AIDS activism, was still the same sensitive person I'd known since high school. Damon was a dream best friend in high school, the perfect confidant. He was very affectionate and kind-hearted. Had a wicked sense of humor. And he was a great listener, always available to nursemaid me through broken hearts and ill-fitting prom dresses, even things like death and an AWOL father.

"Not everyone is ready to be out there, Dominique. Prejudice. Fear."

"I'm not going back in the closet. And I'm not changing who I am. And I'm not going back into men's clothes and bein' a boy just to be with him. He fell in love with me—Dominique—drag-queen show and all. That's who he loves. Or says he loves. When he's not ashamed of me."

Jack took her hand. "If you two are meant to be, Dominique, just let it happen. Let Terrence take his time getting his house in order. You can't deny he loves you."

She took a tissue and wiped at her eyes. "I don't know…"

I got off the bed and kneeled in front of her.

"Love, Dominique, is the hard work once the initial infatuation wears away. Give Terrence a chance."

"I'll think about it."

We sat with her while she cried. I rubbed her back and Jack held her hand. I wondered if Rick would be as understanding. Then I pushed the thought from my mind. Eventually, her sobs trickled off to an occasional sniffle. Then silence. "I'm going to wash up and go to bed." She smiled weakly. "Maybe all this will be clearer in the morning."

Jack looked at me. "Maybe that's not such a bad idea for all of us."

"As long as you all mean noon, not really *morning,*" I said.

Jack went to his bedroom, and I waited for Dominique to come back, looking more like Damon. No makeup, no wig, no mascara streaks.

"Dominique?"

"Yeah, honey."

"I just wanted you to know I love you."

"I love you, too."

"You want me to sleep in here?"

She hesitated. "No…that's okay."

"Do you want to come sleep in my bed? It's a king-size. We could watch an old movie."

"I don't know…" I could tell she wanted to say yes.

"Come on. Grab your robe."

I led her down the hall, and we piled into my bed. I flicked on the television, stuck *The Philadelphia Story* in the VCR, until she fell asleep.

I turned off the television and stared in the darkness at the ceiling, making out the paddle fan twirling as my eyes adjusted to the blackness until it became shades of gray. The house was still. Maybe Sadie would let us rest tonight. Then again, I had slept with Jack, who in turn had slept with Maggie. Then I'd gone and fallen for a man nicknamed Casanova Jones. And the two queens were nursing their own cases of the blues. Maybe the ghost of this old house would let us know we were all really fools for love.

*chapter* 19

That night I dreamed of the blues goddess.

I woke up in my bedroom and looked around. It was my room, and yet not my room. All traces of me had been wiped away. The clothes in the closet weren't mine. The pictures on the wall. Dominique was gone. By the bed was the journal, open to a page, with a pen lying across it.

I got out of bed and could hear music downstairs. The most amazing music I had ever heard. A piano player and a singer. I walked down the staircase, and our house was full of people in vintage clothes. Beautiful people, and women dressed in skimpy outfits. Men…speaking in a patois. I heard Spanish, French, Creole. I couldn't understand what they were saying, but I sensed this was the place to be.

And that piano. I had to find that music.

I walked into the front parlor, where people were drinking and carrying on. The piano player was soaring up and down those keys, his fingers flying so fast at times they were simply blurs. He was sweating, but smiling, lost in the music he was playing, the way someone gets lost in sex or even in prayer. And there I saw her. My aunt Irene.

Leaning against the piano, she sang in the richest voice I had ever heard. Like my voice, but the passion behind it was like the difference between a summer rainstorm and a hurricane. She was dressed in a red-and-black polka-dot dress, and she had on strappy black high heels. Her lips were painted crimson, and her eyes were lined with kohl eyeliner.

As I drifted through the party, no one could see me. It was as if I was the ghost. Until I saw my aunt Irene stretch her arms out toward me. She could see me.

"Come to me, child," she sang. I walked toward her, as if sleepwalking, floating.

"I have a secret to tell you," she whispered as I approached. And then she began to move her lips, but no sound came out. I couldn't tell what she was trying to say to me.

"What?" I asked, my own voice sounding as if I was underwater.

Again her lips moved, but I couldn't understand her. I felt more desperate. What was she trying to tell me?

I looked around the room. Could anyone hear her? The party in full swing, people dancing to the tune the piano player was tickling on the black-and-white keys. No one seemed aware that she was suddenly mute.

I turned my head, and in the corner of the room I

saw Sadie. At least I assumed it was Sadie. Her hair was flaming red, and her eyes were green and catlike. Her alabaster skin looked like milk against the black dress she wore. She was breathtaking…and smiling like the Cheshire cat. *She* understood what my aunt Irene was saying.

I walked toward Sadie, but before I reached the corner, she was gone. I turned around, and my aunt was shaking her head sadly back and forth. Then, again, she beckoned me, arms outstretched, but before I could reach her, we all heard a shot upstairs. Was Sadie's murder taking place?

In the commotion, people screaming, running toward the door, I lost my aunt Irene. I called for her while making my way toward the staircase. I ran up the stairs, breathless, calling my aunt, calling for Sadie, calling for Nan. Then I woke up, sweating and breathless.

I felt across the bed. Dominique was there, breathing heavily. The room was still mine. I could make out my pictures on the walls, my treadmill with shapeless clothes draped over it. In the silence, I felt the house breathing. It was alive.

More than that…

This house was trying to tell me something.

chapter

20

"Oh my *God!*" I squealed, panting.

No…it wasn't an orgasm. It was jambalaya.

"Rick, you weren't kidding. This is the hottest jambalaya I have ever tasted—and Nan makes a pretty mean batch."

"I told you it's an ancient family recipe. See—" Casanova reached across the table and stroked my cheek "—I could never, ever have a girlfriend who wasn't a New Orleans woman born and raised. You know what real food is all about."

Girlfriend? Okay, they just didn't make guys like this anymore.

Monday night we picked up where we left off. As soon as we were alone in his apartment, we tore each other's clothes off. After we made love, I put on an old shirt of his from Harvard and a pair of sweatpants, he put on a robe, and he cooked jambalaya while I drank champagne. While he cooked, I had asked him something I'd wanted to ask for ten years: "Why did you come to my mother's wake?"

He leaned over the pot as he cooked, shut his eyes and seemed to think about his answer. Finally, he turned to look at me. "Honestly, Georgia, I was crazy about you in high school. There was something between us. But you know how when you're younger, you can't open up the way you'd like. I needed to show you, in some way, that I really, *really* liked you. That you weren't alone. So I showed up…in a ridiculous tie."

"I remember that tie."

"I felt so bad for you. The hardest thing I had to deal with was the SATs, for God's sake. You were different, all right."

"Still am."

"And I like that you're different. Listen…I have something to ask you. And you can say no if you want."

"All right," I said cautiously.

"My parents are having their annual garden party. This hopelessly boring afternoon thing on Saturday, and I'd really like you to come with me."

"I have a wedding that night, but I can show up for the afternoon. I'd have to leave by four or four-thirty."

"Trust me. You wouldn't want to stay a minute longer than you have to. It will be *really* dull."

"That's sure talking me into it, Rick."

"I'm just preparing you. And my sister and her fiancé

will be there. My sister is a piece of work. She *is* the Satan's spawn."

"Sounds better every second."

He grinned. "So you'll come."

Meeting the parents. The ultimate fashion crisis.

Of course, Dominique had all kinds of ideas, from sexy silk sarongs to elaborate hats more appropriate for the Ascot races in England.

"Dominique, honey, I am not wearing plumage."

"But this hat will look smashing on you!" She plopped it on my head.

"I don't want to look like Big Bird. I don't want to look like Lady Brett." Lady Brett had a thing for hats and tiaras. "I want to look beautiful but understated."

"What's the fun in that? When summertime comes, young men's fancies turn to sex, Georgia. You want to look good enough to eat. Good enough to fuck. Good enough to make you come *five* times."

"Can we get off the orgasm discussion, please?"

"Isn't that the point?"

"What?"

"Getting off?" She howled with laughter.

"Look…I'm glad you find yourself so terribly amusing, but can we please focus? Plumage is out."

"Suit yourself, Miss Snooty Pants."

I decided on a simple vintage summer dress with tiny roses set on black silk. I picked a vintage bag from Nan's collection. No stockings—not for outdoors. So I was forgoing my control tops. Black strappy heels. Just the right amount of makeup…and a head of curls that was impossible to tame. I tried every gel, hair spray and potion Dominique and I could think of, but the heat index was pushing a hundred and ten degrees. My curls sprung so tight they seemed to stick out of my head like Medusa's snakes.

"I'm going to wilt out in that garden."

"At least you'll look great while wilting. Though I personally wish you would have gone for plumage."

I gave her the evil eye.

She held her hands up in defense. "All right, I'll shut up about it. But—"

"Dominique!"

"Okay…fine. Be conservative. So when do I get to meet Boy Wonder?"

"You've met him before."

She snorted. "Like high school counts? I want to meet the older, wiser, sexier, multiple orgasm-inducing Casanova Jones."

"Please," I begged, "get used to calling him Rick so you don't slip up."

"Fine. When do I get to meet Ricky Ricardo?"

"Don't call him Ricky Ricardo."

"Why not. Plain old 'Rick' is so yawn-inducing. Can I at least call him Dick? Now *that* gets my attention."

"Could you try, for just a moment, to be normal?"

"Hmm…let me think about that." She put a freshly manicured finger to her temple. "Um…no."

I laughed then packed a bag with a sequined dress and the dreaded pantyhose—sure to run. Rick was going to drop me off at the convention center—this week a plethora of gastroenterologists was descending on New Orleans—after the garden party.

I waited by the front door. Timing was going to be

tight. Rick's family lived along River Road, a bit of a drive from the city itself. As soon as his car appeared, I dashed down the steps and into the front seat.

"You look great, Georgia." He leaned over to kiss me. Dominique peered out the door and waved.

"That's Dominique," I said, and waved back at her. "She's very nosy about you."

"So that's Damon, huh?"

"Yup." My radar was up. I'd had breakups before that boiled down to intolerance of either the queens or race or politics.

"She looks…different." He smiled, putting the car in drive.

"That she is."

He said no more, and we were on our way. My radar said defense shields were authorized to come down.

"I'm nervous," I said.

"You should be. They're really all pompous assholes."

"God, you make this day sound like it's going to be so much fun…. If you're nothing like them, why did you become a lawyer and join your father's firm?"

"I'm a spoiled brat. I like my bank account to have a lot of zeros in the balance. I admit it. I like my lifestyle. But I need you to teach me how not to be a brat, okay?"

"Sounds like a very difficult job."

"But it has lots of fringe benefits." He reached over the seat and slid his hand up my dress, his thumb caressing my upper thigh.

"Rick…don't make me crazy before I go to meet your parents!"

"I can't help it…you look great. Feel my hand on your thigh? I wish it was my tongue."

I slapped his arm. "I'm nervous enough."

"I'm sorry, Georgia. Women who don't wear stockings in the heat drive me wild." He slid his hand out from under my dress and grasped my hand and squeezed it.

We rode on toward River Road, lined with old plantations, impeccably restored, magnolias blooming and oaks draped with moss, looking, I used to think as a child, like witches with long, evil hair. Pulling up to his parents' home, I took in the enormous white house, and the hedges, clipped to perfection. To one side, the hedges formed a maze. Ancient brick lined the pathway.

Climbing out of the car, we walked along a camellia-and-rose-lined walkway to the back of the house, where a tuxedo-clad quartet of classical musicians played beneath a wisteria-covered arbor. Long banquet tables were covered in crisp white linen and set with finger foods. Two bartenders manned a long bar, and waitstaff wandered with silver trays with champagne in elegant flutes.

Everyone was dressed conservatively, their voices a murmur, certainly not like gatherings at Nan's and my house where we could wake up Sadie with our carrying on.

A very well-dressed older couple spotted us and worked their way toward us through the garden.

"Is that them?" I whispered.

He squeezed my hand. "They're insufferable. But yes, that's them."

His mother was a vision of Southern gentility. She wore a pink suit and had on understated but very expensive jewelry, starting with a diamond bracelet on the wrist of the hand extended to me. His father was an older version of Rick, only with pompous bearing.

"Georgia, these are my parents, Charlene and Richard…. Mom and Dad, this is Georgia Ray Miller."

"Pleased to meet you." I shook hands with his mother first, then father.

His mother's face was a disapprovingly chilly one, with a frozen smile meant to appear warm and Southern. "How lovely that you could make it."

"Yes," his father intoned. "Hot as blazes today, though…. Rick, how do you two know each other again?"

"Georgia and I went to high school together. And we ran into each other at Cammie's wedding. The Winthrop wedding. I told you this."

"Oh." His mother seemed to warm. "Are you a friend of Cammie's?"

"Not exactly," I demurred. "I was the singer in the wedding band."

Her blue eyes perceptibly froze, but Rick put his arm around my waist and drew me to him.

"You wouldn't believe her voice. One of these days I'll talk her into singing for you."

"Well, Richard—" his mother's smile was again quite plastic "—you can show yourselves to the bar. Come along, dear. The Prestons are waiting to discuss that trip to London. Georgia, it was very *interesting* meeting you."

*Interesting.*

After they were out of earshot, I looked over at Rick. "Very warm."

"I told you they were awful."

"How do you stand it?"

"Alcohol. Let's hit the bar."

Walking through the party, I felt all eyes upon me. Everyone was blond and bland, it seemed. Suddenly my vintage clothes that had felt so elegant when I was with Dominique felt like castoffs—attention-getting castoffs.

At the bar I asked for a glass of champagne, and Rick ordered a scotch. We took our drinks and headed toward the gardens. They were truly breathtaking. They reminded me of pictures of the gardens of Versailles.

"My mother likes to take all the credit for this—" Rick swept an arm out "—but it takes an entire team of gardeners. She really just throws this shindig once a year to get all the credit, have it photographed and bask in the adulation of their wealthy friends."

I looked at the gardens, the scent of jasmine intoxicating. A hedge of azaleas was in full pink-colored bloom. I spun around and looked at the house—mansion, actually. People might drive by a big fancy house like this and wonder about the fancy lives of the fancy people who lived inside, but I would take my rather unusual house with its most unusual residents over this place any day.

"Oh God," he murmured under his breath.

"What?"

"Catherine. My sister. And her fiancé. Greg. He's a partner in the accounting firm of Harris, Harris, Smith and Dunbar. Deadly boring guy."

"How can you stand all this fun?"

Catherine, a younger replica of her mother, complete with a blond do helmeted into place with hair spray, approached and immediately linked her arm through mine.

"Georgia…Rick told me he was bringing you to this

little soiree," she purred. "Let's leave the men to discuss the stock market. You and I will walk the garden."

I eyed Rick helplessly. He shrugged.

Catherine and I took a stroll. She wore an ivory-colored Chanel suit and simple pearl earrings.

"So, I hear you went to high school with Rick."

"Mmm, hmm."

"But you weren't really part of his social circle. Our social circle. I would certainly remember you."

"Right. We didn't know each other well."

"And now you're a what? A nightclub act? Did I hear that correctly?"

"I'm a wedding singer."

"I see. How interesting."

"Funny. That's just what your mother said." I could barely stand it.

"Mom said that? How amusing. Well…we tend to think alike. So tell me…where did you *ever* get that dress?"

"It's vintage."

"Vintage. How charming…." We came to a rosebush with opened yellow blooms dotting it. She stopped, unlinked our arms, and took one to her nose and smelled it. "Divine. This garden is just divine. I don't know how my mother does it." She turned to face me. "Can I tell you something, Georgia?"

I stiffened. "Sure, Catherine."

"My brother has a way of prancing in here with his *flavor* of the season. Last year it was a stripper named Margot. This year, it's you. He picks women who will infuriate my parents. It's like a little *game*. So I hope you don't get your hopes up about *having* a wedding instead of singing at one."

"It's way too early for that."

"Good. Because frankly, we don't…how shall I put this…no matter what the more liberal citizens of New Orleans do… They can fling the beads at Mardi Gras all they want…but here on River Road, things have been a certain way for a long, long time…. You understand? We stay with our own." She reached a hand out to touch one of my curls, which was quite Afro-like in the heat.

Without thinking, I slapped her hand.

She gasped. I gasped.

"I'm not going to tell Rick you did that." She spoke evenly.

"Well, I *am* going to tell him about our conversation. Now, if you'll excuse me, I'm going to find your brother, leave this tremendously boring garden party and give him a blow job in the car on the way back to New Orleans."

I turned around, leaving her shocked face in my wake, and found Rick.

"I need to go," I whispered in his ear, fighting back tears of rage.

He took one look and nodded. "Greg…we have to head back. Something's come up." They shook hands, and Rick again pulled me to his side, protecting me as we left the party.

We walked rapidly through the garden. I tried to avoid looking at the faces of the rich and stuffy as we moved, instead focusing on not crying, even staring up at the hazy sky in an effort to stop the tears that were uncontrollably springing to my eyes even as I willed them away.

He unlocked the car, and we both climbed in. He

started up the engine and blasted the air-conditioning and then turned to look at me.

"What happened, Georgia?"

"Am I this season's attempt to piss off the establishment, Rick? Is that what I am?"

"What did Catherine say to you?"

"You told me she was a piece of work. You neglected to say she was racist. Or maybe you are, too. Am I the flavor of the month? Of the summer?"

He faced the steering wheel, gripping it intensely, and inhaled.

"Georgia," he whispered. "I don't think you'd find too many of the old families out here on River Road who aren't set in their ways."

"Does that include you?"

"No."

"Why…because you don't *mind* dating a woman who's 'not one of your own'?"

"What? Old white Southern guard? Date a woman who's more interested in my bloodline and bank account than me? You know, I don't give a shit who your family is. Fuck my sister, Georgia. I don't care if you are half-black, all black, Spanish…Creole… Let's see… Jewish… Native American… I can keep tossing out examples, Georgia, but none of it matters. I'm falling for you—in this present date and time. Regardless of my family's plantation. Who they are. Regardless of color. Background. You could tell me you're a voodoo priestess who sacrifices chickens and goats in your backyard and visits Marie Laveau's tombstone at midnight. I might be freaked out, but I still wouldn't let you go."

"How'd you find out about the chickens and goats?"

He laughed. "That's my girl."

"Listen, I have to ask. Are you dating me to piss off your family?"

"No. I do that pretty well all on my own without bringing home my girlfriends."

"What about the stripper from *last* 'season'?"

His hand slammed the steering wheel—hard. "God, she's a bitch. Is that what she said?"

"Yes."

"Margot wasn't a stripper. She was a dancer. A real dancer. A ballet dancer. She also happened to wait tables in a pretty rough bar to pay for dance lessons."

He put the car in reverse and backed off of his parents' property.

"Let's get outta here. Where to?"

"The convention center."

On the road, he said softly, "I'm so sorry about Catherine, Georgia. And my parents. But you are not the flavor of the month. I'm crazy about you." He reached over and took my hand and pressed it to his lips.

"I slapped your sister's hand."

He laughed. "She probably deserved it."

"No…she *definitely* deserved it. I told her I was going to blow you on the car ride back to the city."

"Is this my lucky day or what?" He grinned.

"We'll see about that."

"Tell you what…why don't we make plans to go out with *your* friends this week some night. Introduce me to all the residents of the…what's it called? The Heartbreak Hotel."

I thought back to Dominique. How she wanted to

meet the orgasmic Casanova Jones. But then again, she also wanted me to wear plumage to the garden party.

I turned to him and smiled.

"You're on."

But as I watched him steer, my eyes caught sight of his initials embroidered on the cuff of his shirtsleeve, and a diamond cuff link glinted as the sun streamed in from the windshield. His universe was a little far from plumage-wearing queens. I wondered if he was really ready to meet the people I called my family.

## chapter 21

March 3, 1939

*Today Myra and I took a nice long walk. A cool breeze had come up, and we were just strolling. Talking, not talking. Just bein' together. I had on a pretty dress. The wind would catch it, and it would flutter just so. The air would tickle my legs.*

*We ran into a woman Myra knows. All high and mighty acting. She asked Myra, "Is that your girl?" Your maid. Your servant. I am sick to death of it. Sick. I was so mad I wanted to slap her. Myra, she was terribly embarrassed and explained how we were sisters. Then the woman looks very puzzled-like at Myra. Like…you have a colored sister so you must be colored, too.*

*Tonight, I sang the blues. I sang songs that came out of my heart, like I was bleeding. I sang for my love. I sang for me. I sang for Myra. I melted into the words of my song.*

*I'm gonna fly like a bird on outta here
I'm gonna fly 'til my heart hurts no more
I'm gonna fly 'til you're just a memory
I'm gonna fly 'til you learn to love me more.*

*I'm a bird, I'm a bird
But my wings are broken here
I'm a bird, I'm a bird
Gonna fly on outta here.*

*Why do you suppose the Lord made us all this way? Why can't we all just be one color? Makes no sense.*

*Makes no sense.*

*I don't want to write no more tonight. When my lover's lips go down there…I will fly on outta here.*

chapter

22

On Thursday night, Dominique, Angelica, Lady Brett, Maggie, Tony and Rick and I met at Rock 'n' Bowl. Zydeco played as we took lane six and ordered several pitchers of beer. I had asked Jack to come, but he declined, as I thought he would. When I called Maggie to invite her, she said that he had phoned her and apologized for rushing to her on the rebound from Sara. Again, I thought of telling her that we had slept together, but I hoped we were all past it now. Why dredge up the event and hurt her more?

Everyone else was already in the lane when Rick and I arrived. He shook hands with everyone, but I noticed he stiffened ever so slightly as he met the queens. Angelica, Lady Brett and Dominique had apparently gone thrift-store hunting. This was one of their favorite pastimes, and they loved to find oddities like fuzzy dice, plastic snow globes and wonderful outfits they could piece together. They had found three identical bowling shirts, black, with red dice on the breast pocket and the name Shirley embroidered over them. Each of the ladies had on capris and bowling shoes, though as we sat down, Lady Brett, who always wears a blond bouffant wig, was complaining about them.

"Is it so fucking hard to make an attractive bowling shoe? Would it kill them to make something in black leather?"

"Tell me about it," Dominique whined. "I mean... look at mine. They're like clown shoes. *Clown* shoes."

"And who knows who wore them last." Angelica shuddered. She whipped out a small bottle of Elizabeth Arden's Red Door and sprayed the inside of each shoe before inserting her feet.

"A little stacked heel is all I ask," whined Lady Brett.

While the "Three Shirleys," as we christened them for the night, clucked and bitched, Maggie offered Rick a seat and made small talk. Tony was tying his shoes.

"I've never bowled before," he said to me as I sat down next to him and started putting on mine—which had snappy Velcro closures.

"Really? Well, it's not too complicated."

"I'm more a football man myself," he said in the singsong way his lilt rose and fell. "Soccer." He finished tying his shoes and watched a bowler in the next lane. "Doesn't look too hard. Care to make it interestin', Georgie?"

"Such as?"

"Brunch at House of Blues. Loser pays."

This was a bet of unprecedented monetary proportions. "I hate to steal from you, Tony. Sure you don't want to wager a roll of Neccos?"

"You don't scare me, little girl."

"You're on," I said, and we shook on it.

We bowled several frames. Rick was actually a very good bowler. I sucked. Tony was worse. The queens were all about prancing to the line and wiggling their asses as they flung the ball down the lane like a bastardized version of shot put. Style over substance, you might say. Plus they didn't like putting their fingers in the holes—might damage their acrylic nails. They were all terrible. However, they could make a lot of noise.

"Shake that 'thang,' Angelica," Dominique cheered as she sipped her beer. The music was playing full blast, a Buckwheat Zydeco song called "Walking to New Orleans." I was swept up in the fun and laughing until tears ran down my face. Maggie and Lady Brett had climbed onto their chairs and were dancing go-go style. Rick looked as if he was having a good time, too. Until he spotted someone in lane eleven.

"Jesus Christ," he muttered to me after he got a spare.

"What?"

He slid down on the bench. "See that guy over there? The one with the white golf shirt and khakis?"

"Yeah."

"A client of mine. A *big* client of mine. I do all his estate planning."

"So?"

He eyed me incredulously. "So? *So?* Have you looked at the crew we're here with?"

I looked at our party. Three Shirleys in matching bowling shirts, an Irishman in a Hawaiian shirt so bright it was blinding and a porkpie hat he wore sometimes, a now-violet-headed Maggie in a black Ozzy Osbourne T-shirt and a leather miniskirt. And me. In a black vintage baby-doll dress, white bobby socks and red-white-and-blue bowling shoes with Velcro closures. Considering that one time we came to Mid-City Bowling Lanes the queens wore matching 1960s airline stewardess uniforms they found in another thrift-store run, complete with pillbox hats and patent-leather clutch purses, I thought we looked pretty tame.

"We're out having fun, Rick. This isn't a business dinner."

"You wouldn't understand, Georgia. Much as I'm having a ball with you, my life isn't all fun and games."

"Mine isn't either."

"Well, look, there's no point arguing…we should go."

"*Go?* We still have five frames left to bowl. I have brunch riding on this."

"Brunch? Can we grow up a bit here? Or can you tell your friends not to be so loud? Maybe he won't see me."

Angelica had scored a strike through sheer luck, and everyone else was jumping up and down with excitement.

"No. I can't. We're here to have fun. This was *your* idea. I didn't ask you to meet my friends. You made it seem like you could handle being out and about with the denizens of the Heartbreak Hotel instead of the River Road crowd."

"I can. I'm just not going to risk losing Hiram Crawford as a client. Can you do me this one favor…can we just leave? We'll go out with all of them again some other time."

"Where can we go in this city without risking you being seen with us?"

"I'm asking you nicely, Georgia. I can't let this guy see me here."

"You know, Rick…you told me that you were jealous that I lived in a crazy house with my nutty grandmother. But you're not. You don't fit in my world. I don't fit in yours. Worse, you don't approve of my world, or you wouldn't give a flying *fuck* what that guy thought of you."

"Don't make this into something bigger than it really is."

"You can leave," I snapped, hearing my own heartbeat as my anger rose. "But I'm staying and finishing the game."

"Fine. I'm leaving," he said tersely. "I'll call you tomorrow." He bent down to change his shoes. By now, the gang had caught on that we were having a fight.

He stood and nodded to all of them. "I've got a big workday tomorrow. You all finish the game. It was great to meet you."

He leaned down and kissed my cheek as I turned my head away from him. I watched him stride out of the alley, and I didn't know whether to cry or stay angry.

Tony sat down next to me. "If you think your guy gettin' angry with you is going to make me ease up on my punishing game of bowling, you have another thing comin', Georgia Ray."

I smiled. "It was nothing. He just can't handle being seen out and about with the Three Shirleys over there."

"They actually look conservative tonight. Has he seen them in their tiaras?"

"No."

"Or remember the time they wore matching poodle skirts?"

"They were into the rerelease of *Grease.*"

"I kind of like their bowling shirts."

"Tony...no offense, but this is from a man who wears shirts that look like someone threw up in Technicolor on them. Do they wear Hawaiian shirts in Ireland?"

"No...and it's a pity, too."

"I worry about you."

"I worry about you, too, Georgia Ray."

"I'll be okay. This is just what I get for dating a rich lawyer. We'll work it out."

I glanced over at the man on lane eleven. He bowled a perfect strike. Then he strode back to the bench, sat down next to the well-dressed man next to him and promptly kissed him on the mouth. I started to laugh uproariously.

"What's so funny?" Tony asked me.

"You know, I couldn't even explain it. Just one of God's colossal mind-fucks." I leaned over and kissed him on the cheek, rested my head on his shoulder. With Tony, the world made sense. It was about blues, and finding that place that was mine alone.

With Rick gone, I felt myself relax. Maybe I hadn't realized myself how I had been tense, wondering if Dominique might slip and call him Casanova, or her new nickname for him—Dick. I wasn't embarrassed by Dominique. Yes, she was occasionally high maintenance. Occasionally, as when urging me to wear a thong, or plumage, or to buy a twelve-inch vibrator, she was a shade to the left of vulgar. But I realized something.

Maybe, just maybe, I had more of my aunt Irene and Nan in me than I thought. Yes, my friends were unconventional. But they were family. Bowling shirts, bouffants, the fuckable scale, trash talk and all.

"Ladies...Tony..." I stood and went over to pick up my bowling ball. "Prepare to be amazed."

I approached the lane, swung my arm back...and promptly made a gutter ball.

I still needed to work on my approach.

*chapter* 23

Friday morning at ten o'clock, my phone rang. It could only be:

1) a telemarketer; or
2) Rick,

because everyone else I knew was as nocturnal as I was, or lived in the same damn house as I did. I groped for the receiver from beneath my comforter.

"Hello?" I groaned.

"Tell me you're not angry at me."

"Why?"

"Are you?"

"Yes."

"What if I told you I was wrong?"

I longed to tell him how wrong he really was. Ol' Hiram had engaged in some serious lip-lock with his companion all night. But outing Hiram to his lawyer wasn't my intention or style.

"I don't need you to tell me you were wrong."

"Why?"

"Because I know how wrong you were."

"Harsh, Georgia."

"*You* were harsh." I slid up higher on my pillow. "My friends are really terrific people. If you can't handle it, that's your problem. Just like it's your sister Catherine's problem if she doesn't like someone with a mixed racial heritage blending in with the River Road set. You know…I was reading my aunt's diary. Your sister's attitude isn't far off how bad it was in 1939."

He exhaled loudly. "What about when it's just me and you? I've never had this kind of connection with anyone before. So if we need to iron out how your world and mine fit together, that's not an insurmountable problem as long as when it's just us things are the way they have been. I'm sorry, Georgia. Really sorry."

I thought about how I stuck up for Terrence to Dominique. I was always for giving people second chances. Rick sounded completely sincere…maybe the Shirleys were a little hard for a lawyer to get used to the first time out.

"Apology accepted."

"Can you have dinner with me tonight?"

"Wedding."

"What if you came over after the wedding and slept over? I can't sleep without you there. I'm afraid of the dark."

"Chicken."

"Come on, Georgia."

"I can't. It'll be way too late, and I get a ride with Jack. How about tomorrow we have breakfast together."

"What time? Nine o'clock?"

"I was thinking about one."

"That's lunch."

"Not to me."

"Okay, to show you that I *can* get used to your life and your friends, I will make you breakfast tomorrow *after-noon*. I'll pick you up at twelve-thirty."

"Deal."

I hung up the phone and leaned back in bed and smiled. Make-up sex is always the best.

The next morning, aka afternoon, Rick did not disappoint. When he picked me up, he had a red rose as a "peace offering." Back at his place, warm beignets, the Creole version of doughnuts, waited with a fresh pot of coffee and a pitcher of Bloody Marys with bits of horseradish and black pepper swirling around.

"I realize that maybe the Bloodies don't go with the beignets, but you're a New Orleans woman. Spicy and sweet can go together."

He slid up behind me and began nuzzling my neck. I spun around, and we kissed.

"I've missed you," he breathed. "You're spicy and sweet. Makes me think about tasting you."

"I've missed you, too," I murmured.

He knelt down on the floor and lifted my dress. He slid his hands up to my panties and then slowly pulled them down. I slipped out of my shoes, and then out of my panties. Lifting my dress still more, he put his tongue on me, licking me until I shuddered.

Slyly looking up at me, he whispered, "Does that make up for how naughty I've been?"

Still breathless, I said softly, "Not quite."

He led me to the bedroom, and I came again, harder than I ever had before with him. Each time we were together, I felt the subtle barriers of mistrust I had after years of dating disappointments fall away. Each time I straddled him, my breasts in his mouth, or him begging me to let him finally come, we seemed to move as one.

After we made love, we had breakfast around two-thirty. We reheated the beignets in the oven and drank several Bloody Marys. Then we went back to bed, and he curled around me as we napped. The last thing I remember before the heaviness of sleep fell over me was a soft whisper of a kiss and the words, "I'm falling for you, Georgia."

The next week, Rick took me to dinner at a French restaurant. We ordered a bottle of white wine and talked about his week at work, and then the various bookings I'd sung at, including a marriage between a seventy-year-old man and a twenty-something former stripper with double-Ds to put the drag queens to shame.

"That's a hell of a lot more interesting than settling the Morgan account."

"Exactly. His children are all *way* older than she is, and I thought when they took to the dance floor for their first dance as man and wife that one of them would trip her."

"How do you keep a straight face through all that?"

"I've seen it all. Fistfights at the reception. Sides of the family who won't speak to each other. Even—*even*—saw

a groom making out with the maid of honor in an upstairs hallway."

"Holy shit!"

"My thoughts exactly."

"Can I ask you something?" He looked at me, his face
illuminated by the candle on the table.

"Sure."

"All this is fascinating, but do you ever think you
want to live a more normal life? You going to sing in
this band of yours forever?"

"No. I'm working on my blues act. Eventually, I want
to make a CD. Sing in small clubs."

"You don't feel any pull to have a real job?"

I looked across the table. "I have a real job."

"But I mean a more conventional life…. The reason
I ask is a friend of mine is the headmaster at St. Andrew's
Episcopal School. Very exclusive school. They're look-
ing for a music teacher. I told him about you."

"A teacher?"

He picked up a piece of bread and started buttering
it. "Summers off. Benefits. Day hours. It's not a bad idea.
You have a college degree in music."

"In music *performance*. Maybe to you it's not a bad
idea, but I don't want to be a teacher."

"You don't feel at some point it's time to…I don't
know…?"

"To what? Give up on a dream? End up like the rest
of the world, sleepwalking?"

He put his hands up. "It was just a thought."

"A bad thought." Tony, Red, they'd never think of me
giving up. Giving in.

"I'm sorry. I think like a suit. I thought you were

going to break me of that." He smiled at me. That smile of his had gotten him out of trouble his whole life, I guessed.

"And I think like a woman who lives in a haunted house."

"With a drag queen."

"You have a problem with Dominique?"

"No. You have to admit, he's not a typical roommate."

"*She* is a wonderful roommate. I just have to safeguard my lipstick. And my favorite eyeshadow. My tampons are safe, though."

He laughed. "I'm sorry, Georgia. I don't want you to change."

"Good. Because I think you're pretty well stuck with me the way I am."

We ate the rest of our meal, drinking wine and laughing. But later that night, as I listened to the heavy, rhythmic breathing of his sleep, I got up and padded around his apartment, looking at all the art on the walls. I had been different all my life. Even before my father left, he was always out late playing, and his friends used to jam in our living room, moving the furniture (and annoying my mother), the music traveling upstairs to my room. All my friends' fathers when I was growing up were nine-to-fivers.

I thought about the teaching job. I had sometimes contemplated a life without drag queens and narrow bedrooms filled with the brokenhearted. But I couldn't quite picture myself in a house like this, part of the day world. My lineage was, as evidenced by Honey Walker's diary, filled with the blues and the night. It was a moon-and-stars world, not a sunshine world. My mother, I realized now, who had grown up with a gambling, boot-legger father, later a scion of a legitimate liquor com-pany who routinely hosted illegal casino nights, and a mother who didn't mind dancing and a few scuff marks on the dining-room table, had tried to shoehorn both her and me into the day world. I had no idea how it was she even thought she could stay married to my father. But she had never ignited in me a desire for this life.

I ran my finger along Rick's dining-room table. Not a scratch on it. I turned on the dining-room light, the chandelier reflected in the sheen of the wood. What Dominique could do to that table with her size twelves.

chapter

24

General note to the male population: *If your girlfriend is a wedding singer, don't show up at weddings in the same city with another woman.*

Six weeks of bliss had gone by. Rick and I saw each other every minute we could schedule it. I even—albeit with a groan—met him for an early—as in eight o'clock in the fucking morning—breakfast before his first appointment of the day.

Then a Saturday night had arrived and the band and I were playing a big wedding at Louis XVI Restaurant Français. I had almost forgotten about it. Rick had even asked me if we were playing a wedding that Saturday. I told him no, we were playing a podiatrists' convention, but I had gotten my weekends confused. It's all the same to me. Electric slide with foot doctors. Electric slide with grandmas in sequins and bridesmaids in pink tulle. Does it really matter?

The restaurant has a beautiful courtyard with fountains, and people can stare up at the stars while saying their vows. The bride, a raven-haired beauty in a Vera Wang gown, and the well-built groom had chosen a Frank Sinatra standard, "I've Got You Under My Skin," as their first song as man and wife. I was singing my heart out, feeling a little teary as I always do, looking at the happy couple take to the floor, her arms around his neck. He kissing her on the forehead, then on the lips. I pictured Rick and I dancing to the same song. Maybe not at our wedding but at *a* wedding. I secretly longed for Friday and Saturday dates with the man I was so very seriously falling for.

As I sang the words "deep in the heart of me," out of the corner of my eye, I saw Rick trying to manipulate a tall, elegant blonde in a Versace—I'd seen it in *Vogue*—dress to the back of the crowd.

I felt as if the wind had been knocked out of me, like when Andy Franklin punched me in the stomach in third grade. I missed a line in my song, recovered and finished. The crowd applauded. I walked over to Gary and told him I needed to take a break.

"What? You've only done one song."

"Rick is here with another woman."

"Shit. Georgie…don't make a scene. I'm begging you."

"I won't. But I can't sing right now." A lump rose in my throat—more than a lump, it felt like a stone the size of a lemon. "I need to pull myself together.

You sing a couple of tunes, and I'll be back as soon as I can."

Gary, with all his heart, I'm sure, wanted to yell at me. Beads of sweat gathered on his forehead. But then I watched sympathy slide down his face, first misting into his eyes, then softening his mouth.

"Okay, Georgia. And if you need one of us to punch his lights out, ask Tony. He's beaten the rest of us in arm wrestling."

I walked off and out of the lights, and made my way to where I'd last seen Rick. He must have hustled the lovely lady to one of the bars. I walked from one, to the other, as Gary sang "New York, New York." It was supposed to be a very "Liza Minnelli" number—the groom was a Manhattanite. But now it was a very Frank Sinatra version with a male singer, which I guessed they wouldn't mind, since they had chosen Ol' Blue Eyes for their first song.

I finally caught sight of Ms. Versace, as she towered above the crowd in superslim, model-like fashion, in a plunging neckline showing off perfectly balanced, perfectly tight-globed breasts. The fucking bastard had rhapsodized poetic about my real ones, but maybe he actually liked breasts that didn't fall slightly to the side when you lay flat on your back. Perhaps he wanted them to sit up there, perched like hard melons.

My eyes caught his. There was no hiding now.

"Hello, Rick," I said evenly, determined not to cry. "Who's this?"

"Carrie." She smiled and held on to his arm tighter.

She leaned her head to one side and gave a toss of her mane, a very practiced move.

"Hi, Carrie… You know, I'm an old friend of Rick's from high school. My name's Georgia."

"Hi, Georgia." She smiled but didn't extend her hand.

"I wonder, how long have you and Rick been dating?"

She gazed lovingly at Rick. "*Richard* and I have been dating for a while now. My father does a lot of legal work with Richard."

"Richard, is it? Let me guess. Is your father Hiram Crawford?"

"How did you know?"

"Lucky guess. I've seen your dad. You look a lot like him."

She giggled. "People usually say I look like my mom."

"Georgia," Rick whispered, face very pale, "let me walk you back to the stage. I want to talk to you about something."

"What could we ever have to talk about? Could it be about how when we FUCKED, when was the last time? Oh… Thursday night…could it be you didn't really mean all the things you said?"

Carrie's mouth opened in shock, revealing perfectly capped, superwhite teeth. Her lower lip trembled.

"Georgia, please lower your voice. Don't make a scene." He gripped my elbow. "I can explain."

"Don't bother." I yanked my elbow away. "And you know, I've got to go sing for the happy couple. *God, I give up.* Who can believe in love anymore, you know? Toss the rice, then scoop it up and recycle it because chances are you'll need it again at their second weddings.

Rick…keep the fuck away from me. Carrie…good fuckin' luck, honey."

I made my way through the crowd of wedding revelers back to my band. They all looked at me with concern. Jack mouthed, "Are you okay?" I shook my head. No, I wasn't, but I had to go on.

I sang love songs when I wanted to sing the blues.

I sang "Crazy for You," by Madonna. "All the Way" (the Celine Dion song), "Can't Help Falling in Love," (Elvis!) and "Fly Me to the Moon" (Frank Sinatra again). I sang them though I felt as if I wanted to curl into a ball onstage.

At our break, the four guys clustered around me. I'd lost sight of Rick in the crowd. Either he took Carrie home, or he'd sweet-talked her into staying, but they were steering clear of my line of sight, and most especially the dance floor.

"Georgie?" Mike spoke first. Mike never spoke first. Of course, Mike the Cynic would likely tell me I was an idiot. I braced myself.

"Go ahead, Mike. Let me have it. I was a jerk. I fell for him hook, line and sinker. Go ahead. Tell me."

"Nah. We just want you to know we nominated Tony to deck him in the parking lot."

"That's sweet, guys, but…"

"We're not kidding. No one hurts our Georgia and gets away with it," Gary said.

Jack made a move to open his mouth.

"If you do the I-told-you-so-routine, I'll kill you, Jack."

"No. Just say the word, and he's history."

"What are you, the wedding-band mafia?"

They laughed and gathered around me, each rubbing my back or kissing my cheek.

"He's not worth it, lass," Tony said. "You're too good for him." His arm was around my waist. Tony was built solid as a rock. I leaned into him for strength, but at this outpouring of affection, I fell apart. Gary went over to a waiter and got me a linen napkin to blow my nose in.

Jack joked, "They're not gonna want that napkin back now, you know."

"Shut up…. Damn, I can't *believe* it…" I cried. "I thought he really loved me. It was fast, but we had a connection. I thought. What an idiot I am. I thought he cared about me. And did you *see* her?"

Tony patted my arm with his free hand. "She wasn't anything great, Georgie."

I looked at him and rolled my tear-filled eyes. "She is everything I am not. Blond. Tall. Stick-thin. With breasts that stay put when she lies down."

"Breasts like those are overrated, Georgia," Mike offered.

They all nodded in agreement.

"I can't believe you guys are comforting me over implants." I tried to smile.

"Let's all take a walk," Gary suggested. It looked as though we were having a love-in by the stage.

The five of us went outside to the sidewalk, and I inhaled deeply. "Was I blind? What is it about me? What is it that sends me these *losers?* Can one of you tell me that?"

The four of them stared at me blankly.

"Where is Dominique when I need her? She would

know the answer to that." I smiled wanly, and they seemed relieved that I wasn't going entirely off the deep end. We did have a wedding to play, and I tried to make myself laugh a little. Tony dashed down the street and around the corner and returned with a box of Junior Mints.

"I had this in the van."

"Thanks." I took the box from him and opened it. Chocolate can heal the human heart, so I ate my chocolate-and-mint medicine and declared myself together enough to sing "When a Man Loves a Woman" at the beginning of the next set.

En masse, we marched back to the courtyard to begin playing. Tony held my hand. I looked at him from the side. He kept clenching and unclenching his jaw. A small vein on the side of his head bulged.

"I'll be okay," I whispered.

"The bloody fookin' bastard," he said, with the funny way he pronounced "fucking." "I'll bloody well kill him."

I squeezed his hand and moved up on the bandstand. With my heart limping along, I sang the song with a rich, bluesy voice. If Red had been there, he would have said, "You got it, sugar." I was in that place, that place where my mother and father took up a room in my heart. If the human heart is a mansion with many rooms, I was in their room, the room that belonged to an orphan girl. An orphan with a shattered heart. I was shocked, when I was finished, to see people giving me an impromptu standing ovation—at a wedding.

True, indeed—heartbreak is good for a blues singer.

As torn apart as I was, I had found that spot. That blues goddess spot. Maybe that was what my aunt Irene had been trying to tell me in my dream. I had the same lonely heart she did.

*chapter* 25

After the wedding, at which Rick was never spotted again, we helped Gary and Mike pack up Gary's old van. As we packed it up, Tony pulled out a suitcase from the back.

"What's that?"

"Didn't Nan tell you?"

"Tell me what?"

"I dropped by to see her today. They raised my rent two weeks ago, and I just can't afford it. That and I can't take the damn palmetto bugs in that place. God, they're like my bloody roommates, Georgie."

I got the heebie-jeebies. Palmetto bugs are like New Orleans cockroaches. Some of them are big enough to saddle up and take for a ride. I had never even seen where Tony lived. Never even heard him mention the neighborhood. And I was shocked that he'd want to move in to the Heartbreak Hotel. The Heartbreak is long on love but short on privacy. There's no hiding anything from anyone.

"You're moving in?"

"Until I figure something else out. I insisted on paying her the same rent as my old place."

"She must have refused."

"She did. So we made a deal. I'm going to tear up her old garden in the courtyard and put in one that'll look like a regular English garden. And I'm even going to have a butterfly garden in one corner. She can sit out there and watch them."

"Tony?"

"Yeah, Georgia?"

"You are a man of mystery."

"I am. But I'm a bloody good gardener." He grinned in the darkness of the street. I was grateful he was there.

We loaded Tony's bass in the back of Jack's car, and then put his suitcase in the trunk. Gary and Mike came over and kissed me. Mike actually pressed his lips to my cheek. Underneath that gruff exterior, he was an old softie. Albeit an inebriated one. I smelled Wild Turkey on his breath.

"Is Sunday Saints still on…in light of the turn of your romantic fortunes?" Gary asked.

"Yes. If I canceled Sunday Saints for every broken heart I suffered, we'd never have them. I'll see you guys tomorrow." I leaned down to kiss Gary and up on my tiptoes to kiss Mike. "Thanks. I really mean it."

I climbed into Jack's car, and he and I crossed ourselves out of habit as he started the engine. Tony followed our lead, and as we pulled out from the curb and headed home, I nestled between them. Jack kept patting my knee, and Tony held my hand in a show of solidarity. We drove through the city and back to the Heartbreak. As we pulled up, we saw Rick sitting on the front steps, his head in his hands.

"That asshole has a lot of fucking nerve showing up here," Jack snapped, his hands tightening on the wheel as he parked the car.

My teeth started chattering involuntarily.

"Are you cold, Georgia?" Tony asked.

"No…nervous."

"Don't be," Jack said sternly. "Don't let this guy twist your head all up. Remember his high-school nickname."

Tony hopped out of the car, then held out a hand to me.

Rick stood up. "Georgia…you have to listen to what I have to say."

"No." Tony slipped an arm around my waist. "She doesn't."

Jack came around from the street and stood on my other side.

"Rick," I spoke, "I'm honestly not interested. It all makes sense now. You freaking out at the bowling alley. You asking me if I was playing a wedding tonight…"

"Georgia…" Rick's voice was strong, convincing. "You have to believe me. I was dating Carrie right up until two months ago. I haven't called her since we ran into each other. Since our first date. We planned to go to this wedding together ages ago. I felt like I had to escort her. After the evening was over, I planned on telling her I couldn't see her anymore. But…our little scene

pretty much took care of that." He smiled weakly, test-
ing my sense of humor.

I felt a surge in my heart. Could he have faked how
we were when we were together? Faked how he felt?
Wasn't I involved with Jack when Rick arrived on the
scene? It had all been happening so fast.

Tony spoke for me, reminding me what I had seen at
the wedding. "That girl was hanging all over you. It
didn't look like anything was winding down." I watched
him change his stance, looking like a tiger about to
pounce. His jaw clenched.

"Look, pal, I think Georgia can speak for herself.
Georgia…I love you."

"Don't…" I felt myself weakening. "Come on, guys,
let's go inside."

"We'll walk you in," Jack said. "Then come out for
the instruments."

The three of us crossed the sidewalk and moved toward the steps. Rick reached out to grab my arm.

"Georgia…I am begging you. I am *begging* you to listen to what I'm saying. Don't you remember last Saturday? How good it was?"

"Don't, Rick…I'm tired."

He kept holding on to my arm.

"Please, Rick…don't do this."

Still he didn't budge. "Look at me and tell me you
don't feel the same."

I looked at him, but I didn't have to say a thing. Tony
tossed one good right hand to Rick's jaw and knocked
him down. Rick grunted and rolled onto his side.

I screamed and stared at Tony.

"No one fucks with Georgia Ray," he said, shaking

out his hand and escorting me up the steps. I looked down at Rick, now rubbing the red spot on his jaw. My insides were shredded like coleslaw.

I wanted to believe Rick. I really did. But now I replayed other scenes in my mind. The blonde from the wedding, the Winthrop wedding. It wasn't Carrie. It had been another tall blonde. With more Nordic features, but most definitely not the same woman. Jack was right. He had lived up to his high-school nickname. And I suddenly remembered what Damon used to call me every once in a while.

Gullible Georgia.

# chapter 26

We walked inside. Dominique, Angelica and Nan were standing in the front foyer with bathrobes on. Dominique was already in tears.

"Gary already called," she sniffed. "Then we saw Tony deck lover boy. Good for you, muscles." She patted his bicep.

"It was a pleasure," Tony said gruffly, his brogue thick as ever. "Fookin' bastard."

"Come on, honey," Nan soothed. "We have a hot toddy waiting for you in the kitchen."

This was Nan's "cures what ails you" recipe.

## FOR A BROKEN HEART

1 oz. peppermint schnapps
1/2 oz. white crème de cacao

*Fill favorite giant-size mug with steaming milk and top
with a Hershey's Kiss. Drink up with a good friend and
feel better. Good for heartbreak, job loss, significant others who cheat, financial woes and just plain old bad days.*

I allowed myself to be led to the kitchen, which has
ancient black-and-white tile and an oak-door table big
enough for eight. Milk was brewing in a big saucepan,
and Nan started making our toddies.

Dominique patted my hand. "Tell Mama all about it."

And that was it. Those five simple words, and the dam
of emotions I'd held in check all night so I didn't let Gary
down, so I didn't make a fool of myself, gushed forward
and I started sobbing. Mama. Every motherless girl,
motherless woman, whether she is eight or eighty, when
she faces a heartbreak, longs to reach out and be com-
forted by her mother. I couldn't explain it, because we'd
fought so much when she was alive, but I longed for her.
I wanted her to hug me and tell me I was going to be all
right. That I wasn't always going to be singing the electric slide and lonely in a city whose very personality
changes every weekend. I would eventually find the love
I wanted. I looked at the rainbow of hands patting my
arm. Black, white, soft cocoa-colored. Maybe I had love
here, with them. But I still wanted, quite simply, my
mother.

Dominique handed me a tissue. "It's okay, Georgia.
We all love you."

"I know." I blew my nose in the tissue, knowing it was
serious because she'd called me by my real name. "But
you know how it goes…" I took a ragged breath. "You

have to wait for your heart to catch up to what your head already knows. He's a cheat. A liar and a cheat. And I let sex muddle up my head."

Nan kept handing out hot toddies, then sat down opposite me. "Drink up, dear."

I sipped at the drink, which was soothing. A numbness settled over me.

"I feel like such an idiot." My eyes welled up anew.

"You're no idiot, Georgia," Tony said, his face still grim, as if he was taking all that had happened to me personally. Very personally.

"I am."

"Why?" Angelica asked. "Because you believe what people tell you? Honey, I'd rather still believe in love than miss the ride. I'll chance walking in on guys like Frankie caught in the act than be a bitter old soul with no faith in love anymore."

"Yeah, yeah. 'Better to have loved and lost than never to have loved at all.'" I shuddered. "But Tennyson never said how to mend a broken heart."

"Well, for God's sake," Dominique sighed. "Listen to me, not that old guy. The best way to mend a broken heart is to get right back out there again."

"Sure. Is that why we sit in bed in the afternoons watching *Steel Magnolias?*"

"I didn't say I followed my own advice. Besides, I like Julia Roberts."

I laughed and took another big sip of my hot toddy. I was feeling more and more sleepy.

"How about you, Nan?" Jack asked. "You're just a tiny bit older than all of us. You must have some advice for Georgia."

"I've lived a *long* time. And I've had my heart broke too many times to count," she sighed. "And best as I can tell you all, you just have to hurt till the hurtin's done."

"That's the best you've got?" Dominique asked incredulously. "*That's* the best you've got?"

She shook her head. "Afraid so. The heart figures matters out on its own watch. You can't *think* a heartbreak away. You can't wish it away. You just muddle along until you wake up one day and realize you didn't cry yourself to sleep the night before. Then maybe a day or two later, you realize you went a whole hour or more without thinkin' about the pain.

"I only had one daughter. And my daughter only loved one man. Georgia's father. And try as she might, she couldn't make him stop drinkin', and she couldn't stop him from going to New York to seek his fortune in the music business, any more than Georgia's mother could have stopped Georgia from bein' a singer. And when my daughter's heart was broke, I would have laid down my life to make the pain go away. I would have."

She leaned back and shut her eyes. We had an unspoken code between us. We didn't talk about my mother's death. She opened up more. "And then when she got the cancer, I prayed to God to take me instead. I begged God. I said, 'I can't take it, Lord.' I was afraid. Me. Fearless Nan. Tough ol' bird Nan. I was afraid I would just die of a broken heart. But if God brings you to it, God's gonna bring you through it."

She opened her eyes and looked around at all of us. "And yes, that's the best I got."

Nan stood up and went over to the stove to make another batch of toddies. As she stirred the milk over the flame, I told Dominique and Angelica exactly what had happened. From the Versace dress to remembering that Carrie wasn't the blonde from the other wedding—right down to Tony's perfectly executed right hook.

"I love a man who knows how to defend a woman." Angelica batted her eyelashes. Tony blushed.

I laughed, admittedly feebly. I'd hurt for a long while, but I hoped Nan was right, and I'd get through it. She poured us all a second hot toddy. I felt downright woozy. I was tired from emotional exhaustion, plus I think she was socking in some extra schnapps in mine.

"I'm ready to go on up to bed." I stretched. Everyone else stood. Jack and Tony went out to the car to get their instruments, and I waited for them while Angelica and Dominique kissed me good-night and climbed upstairs to their bedrooms.

I faced Nan. "I'll give Tony the room overlooking the courtyard. He'll like watching his garden grow from there…. I never knew you wanted to redo the garden."

"I don't really. But it's something he needs to do, I think." She kissed my cheek. "I love you, Georgia. You saved my life, really. When you came to live with me, when you and your mother came to live with me, it was you who saved me from the grief after she died."

"Funny, Nan. I always felt the same way about you."

She turned from me, smiling, and slowly climbed the stairs. The guys came in with Tony's bass, Jack's guitar and Tony's suitcase, a hard-sided Samsonite with decals and stickers of all the places he had traveled, most of them European cities.

"Come on upstairs. I'll show you to your room."

We left the instruments in the foyer and went up to the second floor. Jack kissed me good-night on the landing.

"Thanks for not saying 'I told you so,'" I said.

"You didn't say it after Sara."

"I thought it, though."

"Yeah...well, I thought it, too." He winked at me and said good-night to Tony.

I walked down the hallway with Tony and opened the door to the room overlooking the garden. I flicked on the light and stepped inside. A set of French doors opened to a tiny balcony.

"You could eat breakfast out there, Tony."

"This is really lovely. Really grand of your nan to let me stay here."

"She likes this place best when it's a full house."

"She's very wise."

I nodded. "Is that why you're so fond of her?"

He nodded shyly.

"Well, I better let you unpack and get to sleep. Your bathroom's two doors down on the right. You'll have to share with Jack. And the closet's empty. The drawers in the dresser are empty. Just use them like this is your home. This *is* your home. And in that trunk over there you'll find extra blankets and some towels and wash-cloths."

"Thank you, Georgia Ray."

I looked him squarely in the eyes. "No, Tony, thank you. If you hadn't punched him, I swear I was going to cave."

"I meant it."

"What?"

"No one fucks with Georgia Ray."

I shook my head. "I guess I really have the blues now."

"I can't stand to see you hurtin' like this, Georgia." He actually winced.

"I'll be okay."

"I wish I could make it all better."

"Like Nan said, you just have to hurt until the hurtin's done."

"That bloody sucks."

"Yes, Tony, it does." I reached up to touch his jaw. "Stop tensing, you're so angry."

"I'll try," he whispered, then moved away from my touch.

I left his room and went down the hall to my bedroom. I opened Honey's diary. I wanted to be transported to another time and place.

*chapter*  27

*June 1, 1939*

*I haven't written in a while.*

*I haven't had the strength to even lift my pen. I'm dressed in mourning.*

*Black is my color. The blues are my song.*

*I can't sleep. I can't eat. I can't sing nothin' but the blues. My heart is broken, and I just might as well die.*

*My precious, precious, adored, loved Sadie is dead.*

*Lord, if we had just made that man go away. If we had turned him back at the door. He gave me a chill. As he chose Sadie to go on upstairs with him, I just wanted to run across the room and beg her to stay. I wanted to tell everyone she was my secret love. But instead I sang. When I could have been protecting her, I sang.*

*Myra held Sadie's head in her lap as she took her last breath. I held her hand, praying. Then Myra and I cried. We held each other in grief, and paid for the funeral. I wanted Sadie buried right here in the St. Louis Cemetery so I can visit her grave every day.*

*So I grieve. But Myra doesn't know. No one knows. They think I'm just sad because she was my friend. We were so careful. So quiet.*

*I loved her. Now I wake up most mornings thinking it was just a bad dream. It didn't really happen. I wake up, then I remember and I feel pain. The pain feels bigger than me most days.*

*She made me feel beautiful. She made me less tired. I stopped feeling restless, stopped wanting to go back out on the road.*

*I spend my nights drinking too much now. I spend the days in bed. I sing, but only the blues.*

*Sadie made me want to sing songs about love. Now I wear mourning clothes and sing songs about death.*

chapter

28

The next day, when Red opened the door for me, he already had a full glass of Chivas in his hand.

"Sugar, I'm breakin' doctor's orders today. We'll have a nice full glass of this stuff today. Maybe two."

"Good news travels fast, I see."

"Well…you could say a little bird told me."

"This little bird wouldn't happen to stand about this tall—" I held out my hand "—and cook a mean pot of jambalaya?"

"Now, I wouldn't want to give away my sources." He winked at me.

Inside his living room, we sat and sipped our drinks. I knew I looked bedraggled and depressed. I hadn't slept all night, just kept tossing and turning. And when I read about my aunt loving Sadie, I was too saddened about the secret love affair to even attempt to sleep. I kept thinking about our resident spirit, Sadie, and her finding true love, then dying. And I thought *I* had problems.

"Red…why do you love the blues so much?"

"Well…I suppose it's 'cause I feel it here." He tapped his chest over his heart. "You know, Georgia, some of the fellows I played with over the years, they were cool cats, but they acted like the only way they could *feel* the blues enough to play them was by doing morphine or heroin. Now, I never could understand that. I was blessed, 'cause I didn't need nothin' artificial to play the blues. You don't either. You just store away this man who broke your heart. You store him away and then bring him out again when you have to sing a song. That's how you'll do it, sugar."

And I did. The same quality of emotion and song that I sang at the wedding came out again. When I was done, Red had two words for me. "You're ready." The Mississippi Mudslide. Deep inside, I knew that, too. It was time.

When I got back home from Red's, Nan was cooking crawfish bisque and a recipe that called for angel-hair pasta and tasso.

"Nan…you're a regular Emeril."

"Hush…but taste the bisque."

It was a sip of heaven.

"Delicious."

"How are you feeling today, honey?"

"Worn-out."

I kissed her and went upstairs to change for Sunday

Saints Supper. I had turned off the ringer the night before. I checked my messages. Eleven from Rick. Each more desperate than the last. Again, I felt my resolve weakening. Only one cure—Maggie.

I dialed her number and she answered on the first ring. "I heard."

"I assumed as much. Telephone. Telegraph. Tell-a-drag-queen."

She laughed, then turned more serious. "I'm so sorry. I really am. It sounded too good to be true."

"Next time someone seems too good to be true, I'll know to run for the nearest exit."

"I hear Tony moved in."

"He's down the hall."

"So, is this like a new record for the Heartbreak Hotel?"

"No. Mardi Gras. Remember? The year *everyone* moved in?"

"Do I remember? Do I remember? How can I forget? Dominique was so heartbroken she locked herself in a room with *Steel Magnolias* and *Titanic* for two days."

"Mags…I'm weakening. Casanova Jones called eleven times. *Eleven* times."

"If you even *think* of going back to him, I'll color your hair green."

"Maggie, I think I'm a sex addict. God…you have no idea. That man literally drove me wild. We would do it three times a night. And I miss him. I miss it."

"You'd lose all self-respect, Georgia."

"But…"

"But you caught him with a beautiful blonde. In a Versace dress. With silicone tits."

"Dominique doesn't leave out any details, does she?"

"No. There are no secrets between best friends."

That should have been the moment when I told her about Jack. But I let the moment pass.

"I'm going to take a nap. Coming to Sunday Saints?"

"No…I still feel weird about Jack."

"Okay. Call me tomorrow?"

"Sure, sweetie. But remember, if you feel weakness coming on, call me not Casanova."

"You got it."

I rolled over and sighed. The heart heals in its own time. There was only one thing to help it limp along: a pitcher of New Orleans Hurricanes.

chapter

29

Forget Sunday Saints. By the third pitcher of Hurricanes, we should have called ourselves the Sloppy Saints. Dominique, Angelica and Mike got so hammered on Hurricanes, they talked Mike into taking them out on the town. Jack decided to join them.

"Come on, Georgie," Dominique pleaded. "Slap on a little lipstick and kick up your heels. You'll be over that bastard in no time."

"Dominique, lipstick does not solve everything."

"What lipstick can't, a vibrator can," she cackled. Thank God Nan had gone up to bed. Gary and Annie had left an hour before.

"Yeah, and that and ten bucks will get you a blow job down in the park."

"Oh…you are being spiteful!"

"I'm not. You guys go. Besides—" I toyed with Jack and Mike "—it seems like you have a perfect foursome. Two boys and two queens."

"Fuck you," growled Mike. But off they went, leaving Tony and I with a very messy kitchen.

"Come on," he said. "Let's do the dishes."

We washed and dried in companionable silence. I put the dishes away in the breakfront and was sort of grateful not to have to fend off Dominique's well-intentioned meddling.

"I want to show you something," Tony said after we were done drying. He pulled a bottle of champagne out of the refrigerator and led me toward the garden. It was a dark night, the sort of night New Orleans is famous for. Moody and silent, with humidity as thick as pea soup.

Tony lit a small candle inside a lantern. He had two lawn chairs set up.

"When I'm done with this garden, you won't be able to recognize it."

"What are you going to do?"

"It'll look like an English garden, overgrown and wild. I'm even going to give lilies of the valley a try. Your nan and I spent the mornin' sketching and planning. Over there—" he pointed off into the darkness "—I ripped out the hedges already. Too…architectural. Boring. Doesn't suit the place at all."

We sat down. He opened the champagne and passed me the bottle. "Best thing to cure what ails you tonight, Georgie. Actually, Guinness is, but we're in bloody fookin' New Orleans. So champagne it is."

I took a swig and passed the bottle back to him. His face was impassive and difficult to read.

"Why do you like flowers so much? Doesn't seem to fit."

"Tough Irish street urchin?" He flexed his biceps and laughed. His upper arm had a four-leaf clover tattooed on it, and an Irish flag. "My mother loved flowers. Had a green thumb. Little pots of flowers in the window. Rest of the house was falling to pieces. But she had flowers."

He looked over at me. "When the garden is done, I'm leavin' the band, Georgie."

"What? That soon? You can't."

"Gary'll replace me. I just can't take ABBA anymore. I'm going off to New York. I know some blokes who can set me up with regular gigs. Then I'll head over to Ireland. I've been saving every penny I can since I came to America. My brother and I are going to open a pub. I want to play the blues in my own place."

"But leave…now?"

"I want to be makin' real music, not the crap we play. We play it well. We're damn good. But this Irish wanderer has been stayin' in New Orleans too long."

"I noticed you travel light. One suitcase. If I left, I'd need ten steamer trunks."

"You'd learn to travel light, too."

"I can't imagine that. My records. My pictures. My room!"

"Well, I'm off. When the garden's done."

I took a swig from the champagne bottle. Georgia's Saints was going to be going through changes. It occurred to me perhaps what it really needed to be doing was becoming someone else's Saints.

"Maybe I'll go, too."

"Really?"

"I want to. I truly do, Tony. I want to be a blues singer. I have it in me, but I'm afraid of leaving home. Can you believe it? Twenty-eight years old—almost— and what would I do without Dominique and Nan and Jack and Gary…and you…and even crabby Mike?"

"Life can't stay the same forever."

"I know…" I leaned back and looked up at the sky. No stars tonight. "But I guess I thought I could stay in this haunted house forever. Just doing what I'm doing."

"You could," he mused, leaning back in his own chair. "But you'd always have that feeling. That maybe you could have done something really grand. I figure if you don't reach for it now, when you're young enough to take a pounding in the music business, you'll never do it. I have to go. This isn't why I came to America."

"Why did you come?"

"All I've ever wanted was to play American jazz. I got into the band as a way to make money until I could make the music I really wanted to make. I used to go to this secondhand record shop in Dublin and buy, trade, beg and steal anything I could get my hands on. But I told myself I would make it here. And I'm going to. Then I'm going to go back to Ireland and show my countrymen what the blues are all about."

"You're pretty confident."

"When it comes to music, I am."

"We've been in the band together for a few years but I really don't know much about you except that you're Irish. You love the blues—you know more than I do about them. And you can garden. And you hate roaches… So come on…tell me. Are you a fugitive gun-runner for the IRA?"

He laughed. "No. No…just a starving Irish musician."

"If you go to New York…maybe I could stay with you if I went there, too. Red has got this friend, and his singer is getting married and moving to Madrid with her new husband. Red's been bragging about me to this guy—not quite as old as Red, but still an old-timer—for a while. Been trying to lure me into auditioning for him. Think I'm crazy?"

"Stark raving mad. But then, so am I. You know I ended up coming to New Orleans on a coin toss?"

"What?"

"It was here or Chicago. Decided at Grand Central Station in New York. Girl broke my heart, and I decided to leave New York."

"So, will you flip a coin when you leave?"

"Depends on whether my heart's broken or not."

I let his comment hang in the air. I felt a surge of determination, steeled by alcohol and a lonely heart. I would leave. If I didn't do it now, I never would—I knew that. Sometimes we have little truths in our hearts, in dark corners where we never shine a light. Then someone comes along with a candle and lights up that corner with something he says or something she does…and we know we can't ignore the truth that's hiding in the dark. Even if we blow the candle out, we know. The truth is there. And it will haunt us as much as Sadie haunts the Heartbreak Hotel.

"When the garden is done, then?" I said, drinking champagne and passing him the bottle.

"When the garden is done."

"New York."

"New York."

"Shake on it?"

He stuck a hand out, and we shook. I looked at the piles of dirt, old hedges in a pile, new plants and seedlings in pots. I had time. The garden looked like shit.

*chapter*

30

The following Sunday, Tony had to pay up for his lost bowling bet with brunch at the House of Blues. Like everyone with a new boyfriend, I had sort of disappeared off the radar for a while. So after the break with Rick I finally surfaced and Tony and I planned it for noon. Admittedly, the place is a chain. The entertainment is sort of luck of the draw. One weekend you can see a phenomenal New Orleans local talent, the next some middling national singer on the road, or star on the way down after a single one-hit wonder.

We got a great table and listened to a gospel singer with a killer set of pipes.

"You're as good as she is," Tony said, smothering his eggs with ketchup. Drowning them in it.

"New York, here I come." My confidence was growing. In the week since the night in the garden, it had rained almost every day, so that meant very little planting had been done. It basically looked as if a tornado had ripped through the yard. However, this had given me time to adjust to the fact that I was certain I was ready to leave. But first, I would sing at the Mississippi Mudslide to honor my mentor, Red. I planned to tell him that afternoon.

"The city that never sleeps. And are you ready to fess up to the fact that you are destined to be a jazz singer."

"Red and I use the term blues goddess."

"Ahhh…you're a goddess now."

"As Dominique would say, a sexy young blues goddess."

"I better pay my respects then." Tony had dressed in a black silk T-shirt and dress pants. He had freshly shaved. I noticed the waitress eyeing him. I felt a surge of protectiveness.

We sat and enjoyed the music, eating eggs and slinging back beers. Since I said I would go to New York after he did, neither of us had mentioned it again. I had no idea where he was going to live. What he was going to do when he got there. I got the sense that Tony was a man who didn't make many plans. He had arrived at the Heartbreak Hotel with a single suitcase and a box of gardening tools. The next day he came over with more plants than I'd even seen in a nursery. I had no idea if he rented space somewhere or grew them all in his bathtub. Plants aside, he traveled so light, I assumed one day he would simply disappear and send a postcard. Not unlike my father.

I liked watching him as he listened to the music. Most guys I knew hadn't really a clue about good music. If it was on the radio, it was good enough for them. Tony's eyes shut at times when the singer's voice took him away somewhere else. For someone so tough-looking, with his eyes closed he looked, for a moment, like an innocent boy. When he opened his eyes again, I was struck by how handsome he was.

We drank beer all afternoon, then headed back home.

"Next time, double or nothing on the bowling." I smiled and kissed his cheek.

"I'm changing my clothes and then off to try the garden. It's likely to be all mud, but I'll give it a shot."

I headed over to Red's.


"Sugar, you look happy today." He smiled as he opened the door. "You over that bad man?"

In fact, I had cried over Rick several times, and screened all my calls. Dominique and Maggie had taken turns sitting on my bed with me, old movies on the television, passing me tissues. Dominique listened patiently as I went over *each* and *every* nuance of everything, every word, every movement of Rick's. At the end of the week, I was still missing him, but I was aching a little bit less. I would do something and realize a whole hour had gone by in which I hadn't thought of him. That was progress.

"Not over him yet. Something else… Red…I'm ready for the Mississippi Mudslide."

"Ye-oowwwwwwwwwwwwwwwwww!" he screamed. Then he started doing a little jig right in front of me.

"Then after that, Red, I think I'm going to go audition for your friend Charlie."

"Oh…he will snatch you up in a New York minute.

Wait until I call him. Man, this is good news. Now, we got to celebrate."

"Chivas?"

"No…something extra special."

He went into the kitchen and returned with a bottle of Dom Perignon.

"Red…that's way too expensive. Where the heck did you get that?"

"Why don't you ask me *when* I got it."

"Okay, when?"

"The first Sunday you came here. After you and Tony came to the club and you sang Etta. Not many people can sing that song right. That week I went out and bought it. I just knew, in my heart, that you were the one I'd been waitin' for. I been sittin' here kind of lonely all these years. Kind of retired. Livin' off piano lessons and some money my brother left me. And when you and Tony kept coming to the 'Slide, I figured you were just a starstruck kid. Till I heard you sing, of course. I said to myself, 'Red, here comes the one. The blues goddess you been waitin' for all your life. The one that'll put all the others to shame.' And so I bought this and been saving it in my fridge, waiting until you said these very words."

I didn't know what to say. I never knew he had that kind of faith in me.

"I got one more bottle of Dom Perignon in there, too."

"What for?" I asked, expecting him to say it was for when I got a recording contract.

"For when I ask your nan to marry me and she says yes."

"Red!" I squealed. "When are you going to ask her?"

"I don't rightly know. She's a very independent-minded woman, your nan."

"That she is." That and then some. I thought of how she said she'd never marry again. But I also knew if I left New Orleans, I would feel infinitely happier knowing she was in that haunted house of ours with Red.

"But I love her very much. And I know she loves me."

"I know that, too, Red. Have you given thought to that crazy house? You know, it's a bit...noisy. It's a little different from this place." *Different* wasn't the word. You haven't lived until you've fought with two drag queens over a shower schedule. I knew she'd never leave it. She wanted to die in that house and come back and haunt me.

"You know, I been set in my ways a while, but when I'm over at that house, I suppose I'm always laughing, and there's always a commotion. And that keeps us all young. As long as I could have my piano. Besides, I got to convince her to say yes, first."

Red popped the cork on the champagne, and we toasted my future. Then we decided on which songs we would do at the Mississippi Mudslide.

"You really don't need an audition. I just have to tell Hugh what night we want to play there."

"In four weeks, a Friday, I don't have a wedding. We had one, but the bride unexpectedly broke her engagement. So...we could do it then. Besides, I have to do it before Tony finishes the garden."

"The garden?"

"He's redoing Nan's garden, and when he's done, he's leaving for New York, and I'm going to follow him. But I want him to be at the Mudslide when I sing."

"Tony and I have had a few talks about jazz. He's one cool number."

"Well, at least I would have some company. I don't have a plan, and I don't know what the hell I'm doing, Red. But for the first time, I don't care. Am I nuts?"

"Nah, you ain't crazy…it's just what the doctor ordered. In a month then. I'll check with Hugh. Man…he's going to be excited. I've been talking you up for over a year now."

Fear hit me in my gut. "What if I don't live up to his expectations."

Red raised his champagne glass. "Impossible, sugar. All you've got to do is sing."

chapter 31

Tony spent the week furiously working on the garden. I spent the week working on my repertoire and listening to my father's old albums. Now that I had started down the path toward leaving, even though it was still just Tony's and my secret—and Red's—I felt a surging freedom inside. When I had to sing "Dancing Queen" by ABBA it didn't bother me the way it used to.

I also told myself that though I would pack a suitcase and leave New Orleans, the Big Easy would always be my home. I was off on an adventure, to shake the complacency out of my life. In a way, I owed some of it to Casanova Jones, cheating bastard that he was. By hurting me, he had forced me to look around. It was as if all the pieces were falling into place.

At night, I would read my aunt Irene's diary. She had

the blues but bad. I didn't know whether to tell Nan what I had read, but I found myself urging Irene to leave New Orleans, to get out of the house, away from the ghost of Sadie. It was her only chance to move on and to live, but I already knew the ending; like seeing a movie before reading the novel.

The following Sunday after a spectacular practice at Red's, I came home singing the blues but feeling happy inside. Dominique greeted me at the door.

"Terrence called me."

"And?"

"And we're having dinner. Is this eat-your-heart-out-yes-I-still-love-you outfit material?"

I stepped back. Dominique was wearing a black, backless dress.

"Halston?"

"Yes? Thrift store. How'd you guess?"

"Had that look. I love it. Understated makeup. Pearl earrings…nice touch. Pearl choker…a tad Barbara Bush."

"No choker." She undid the clasp and handed me the necklace. "Cheap pearls anyway."

"Okay. I would say this is eat-your-heart-out material."

"I've tried to not love him. I've tried to hate him. I've tried to champagne him away. Hurricane him away. Laugh him away. Cry him away. But I still love him, sugarcakes."

"Then have a good time, baby."

She air-kissed me so as to not mess up her lipstick.

"Oh…your grandmother has someone in the garden. Tony's there, too. They're talking. I think they want you to meet them out there."

"Who is it?"

She shrugged. "I've been running around getting ready. I don't know."

"Good luck." I squeezed her hand. I went into the kitchen and opened the refrigerator. Nan had a freshly uncorked bottle of champagne, the bubbles still rising. I poured myself a glass and headed out to the garden. A male voice murmured. First I heard Tony's deep voice, with the brogue. Then Nan's. Then another voice. Smooth. Soft. Unfamiliar.

I stepped out in the garden in the dusk of late summer. Tony's efforts were starting to pay off. Honeysuckle scents greeted me. Nan and Tony stood talking to a tall gentleman. I approached, and all three turned to face me.

I stopped dead in my tracks and dropped my champagne glass, shattering it on the stone pathway. My soul left me in a great gasp. I could only utter one word.

"Daddy?"

chapter 32

He smiled awkwardly and started crying.

"Georgia Ray." He held open his arms.

I had often thought about what I would do if I found him. Would I yell at him, berate him, hate him? What would I do? I had pictured a dozen different reactions, but when I saw him there, older, grayer, tired-looking, lean and yet arms outstretched to me, I reacted with pure instinct. I ran into his arms as I used to when he came home from the clubs, filled with his music and self-content. He would lift me in the air and twirl me around, maybe hum a few bars of some tune he had in his mind. And though he didn't lift me up now, I no less felt the pureness of his embrace. I buried my face in his chest and tears started coming from somewhere, nowhere. I had been an orphan for so long, and here he was.

"Georgia, you are beautiful."

He held me fiercely. I was still unable to speak, and his voice was thick as well.

Finally, I stepped back

"How? I…what are you *doing* here?"

"Oh…I've been keeping tabs on you, Georgia Ray Miller. I've even visited the Web site for your band. I downloaded a song to hear you sing. Now if that isn't the voice of a diva… And then Tony here got ahold of me."

My eyes snapped open, and I looked over at Tony for an explanation. He shrugged.

"What do you mean *Tony* got in touch with you?"

Tony looked to the ground. "I recognized your dad from the picture in your room. I played with him a couple of times, maybe three or four years ago, in New York. I called some old musician blokes I used to play with and tracked him down."

"Why didn't you say something?" I demanded.

He shrugged again. "I wanted to do it for you. A surprise."

"Tony, I didn't know if he was dead or alive. And you let me continue wondering. You're a bastard!"

My father looked at Nan and Tony. "Georgia…I'm sure Tony only meant to help."

"That's no help." I glared at Tony, who refused to look at me.

"Come on, Tony. We should go," Nan said. "These two have some catching up to do, alone. And then Sunday Saints Supper. I'm behind on cooking as it is."

I felt betrayed. How could Tony have come in my room, shared the blues with me, and not tell me he knew where my father was? I stared at him as he walked behind Nan, my heart beating with rage.

I turned to face my father. All I had in my mind were mental snapshots of moments that had faded. It was like memories of my mother. I kept her alive by thinking of her in photographic moments in time. But like photographs, the memories were now sepia-tinged, not in full color. My father was the same way. I remembered Saturday mornings with him, Sundays spent with his records. I remembered how he helped me practice my spelling words, and I remember laughing with him as I tried to learn how to do a cartwheel. But, as with my mother, I couldn't really recall his voice. Not its timbre or tone. I couldn't recall what he smelled like or the touch of his hand to whether his hands were callused or soft. I couldn't even recall meals with him or the day-in, day-out ordinary moments of family time. In short, he was stored like photos in plastic sheaths, not flesh and blood. Yet here he was.

"Ah, Georgia Ray…" He took out a handkerchief. Who even carried them anymore? Then I remembered how gentlemanly he was. It was one part of him that made my mother love him, she said. He blotted at his eyes. "I promised myself I wouldn't do this. Cry, I mean."

The two lawn chairs Tony had set up were at the edge of the evolving garden. Each sundown Tony sat there and took in his handiwork. More often than not, I would bring him a beer or a pitcher of Hurricanes and we would sit in the late evening together in the quiet.

"Can we sit down?" my father asked.

"Sure." We sat facing each other, and he took my hand.

"Georgia…I would not be the least bit surprised if

you hated me. I left your mother and you…and I feel very ashamed for that. Since then I've been through a lot. Not the least of it is…" He sighed, and his hand trembled in mine.

"Georgia…I'm in AA now. And I am truthfully very sorry for some of the things I've done. Before I got sober, every time I thought of coming back to win your mother over again, I would just chicken out. I got in touch with her…she was sick by then. And I came back one weekend and saw her. Damn near tore me up."

"But you didn't see me."

"I did. From a distance. Your mother wanted you to live with your nan. And that was the right thing. I guess we both thought if I showed up temporarily it would just confuse matters. Of course, then I kept telling myself I would come here and talk to you after college. And I kept putting it off until…I couldn't anymore."

"Why not?" I asked warily.

He looked away and dropped my hand. "I just can't live with it no more. I've been in an' out of AA for ten years now. I always fall off the wagon. Only this time…this time I've been doing everything they say. I got a good sponsor. I've been working my steps. And when I got to the step—you see, there's a step where you have to make amends for all you've done—I knew I'd never get a minute of rest unless I came and made it right with you."

I stared at him. "So you've come here now because you want to make yourself feel better? Or is it because Tony called you? If he hadn't, would you have bothered, or would you just go on like you have, leaving me to wonder?" I was surprised at myself, surprised at how close to the surface my grief was. The hurt was as raw as it ever was, but in a different way. Sort of like the way wine ferments. If you leave it long enough, the flavors may mellow, but it's still the same wine, same grapes. I felt a flash of anger.

"I got a call from Tony. Tracked me down through a friend of ours, Slim Johnson, plays the piano. Your friend there is a mean bass player—almost as good as me." He smiled, hoping that I would soften.

"But if he hadn't called, you wouldn't be here, would you? You would just let me sit and wonder. Wonder if you were dead. Wonder what was wrong with me. Why I wasn't important enough to you to make you come back. Why—" I fought to keep my voice from cracking. A singer whose voice was betraying her.

"You were always important enough. I was just too messed up to see you most times. I wanted you to be proud of me. I didn't want you to pity me."

"You know, Dad…" The word *Dad* sounded foreign to me, felt strange as it moved over my tongue. "I've been singing hoping to make you proud of me, wherever you were. Do you remember when I was maybe twelve? I sang an old Billie Holiday song. You were sick, which was…now I realize, a hangover. And you told me to be quiet. You said no one would ever sing like her. That I could never sing like her. To be quiet… You told me to be quiet." I had never told anyone that memory. Yet I replayed it over and over in my mind.

My father's skin was tan, still unlined. His eyes were black, his hair, instead of dark black, was now flecked with white. He looked away. "I couldn't have said that. I know I did, if you say I did, but I swear I don't remember, Georgia Ray, which is no excuse."

I was silent for a long time. I was the girl they used to whisper about. Her father left them. Her mother's dying. Whispers had swirled around me like autumn leaves for so long that I realized now I sought out safety. A cocoon to protect me. My cocoon had been Dominique and Nan and Georgia's Saints.

"I understand if you don't want to have anything to do with me. I understand. I really do."

"Let me see your wallet."

"My wallet?" His expression was confused. He reached back and pulled it out of the pocket of his well-worn khakis and cautiously handed it to me.

I flipped it open. There, in the picture section, was my infant baby picture, fresh from the hospital—one of those ugly pictures with me scowling at the flash of the camera. I flipped to the picture on the reverse side. It was my mother in her wedding gown, in black and white. The next snapshot was one of me as a little girl with big hair and two missing front teeth. And the final one was one of me from the band's Web site. Cut out on a piece of printer paper.

I handed him back his wallet. He *had* loved me all these years. I was old enough now to understand a few things, not the least of which is when love comes to find you, in whatever form, you don't shut the door on it. "We've got to get to know each other, Dad. You don't even know me. And I sure as hell don't know you."

"I realize that. I'm willing to do whatever it takes to

be even a friend. You don't have to treat me like a daddy, but we could start as friends."

"Just so long as you don't think you're getting your record collection back." I smiled.

"You still have them?"

"Yes. They're mine." I winked at him. "But I just might let you listen to them."

chapter 33

Hours later, as the summer sun started to fall lower in the sky, everyone arrived for Sunday Saints. I had the strange and foreign task of introducing my father to my friends. Each time I said, "This is my father," and he extended his hand to someone, I felt as if I were dreaming. Even the word *Father,* or *Dad,* stuck in my throat. It was an unknown feeling to use that word. Sort of like the first time I used the word *fuck* in order to feel grown-up. At first, it tripped over my tongue, sending a thrill through me. After a while, I used it liberally, and it wasn't so different from using any other word.

After introducing my father all around, to which everyone tried to pretend not to be shocked—except for Dominique, who squealed and hugged him and started crying—I told everyone to be quiet and that their presence was requested at the Mudslide in four weeks for my debut as a blues goddess—at least I hoped that would be how I sang. Jack looked genuinely pleased for me. Even Gary, I think, was coming to some sort of grudging acceptance that sequins and ABBA were not my destiny.

Red had a brainstorm.

"Teddy…don't you play the bass?"

My father, who seemed rather shy suddenly thrust in with our boisterous group, looked happy to be discussing music. "Sure do." He nodded.

"Well, then, why don't you play bass, Mike the drums, and I'll tickle the ivories and we'll be Georgia's trio?"

My father, sitting next to me as Nan ladled out gumbo into bowls, looked sidelong at me. "That's up to Georgia. Tony's been playing the bass with her for much longer."

"That's okay," I said icily. "I'd love for you to play with me, Dad."

I didn't even look down the table to see Tony's reaction.

That night, late, after settling my father into yet another spare bedroom, I knocked gently on Tony's door.

"It's open."

I walked into his bedroom. He was standing looking out over the garden.

"I was waiting for you to come yell at me," he said without turning. "Before you start in, understand I thought it was a good idea at the time."

"You had no right to call him."

"I didn't mean to upset you, Georgia Ray. I didn't

even know if he would come… I didn't want to get your hopes up." He turned to face me.

"What were you thinking? How could you do that without even asking me? Without even telling me you *knew* he was alive? I barely know him, Tony."

"I…wanted to do something to show you I cared. And when I saw his picture, I thought that I could do something really great. I don't have a fancy law practice like your last boyfriend, Georgia. I had one thing special I could give you that no one else could."

"I don't understand…"

"You do. You just don't want to. When I called your father, Georgia, he was so ready to come here. So wanting to be a part of your life…just didn't know how to open the door and walk through it."

"You still had no right."

"I know." He turned his back to me.

"Typical, Tony. You're done talking so that's it. I'm stuck talking into nothingness." I left his room, trembling as I shut the door.


We threw ourselves into rehearsing. My father and I spent hours talking in between rehearsals and at moments when we found ourselves alone. He was a stranger to me. He was also a wonderful listener. And he wanted to hear about every little detail of my life from the moment he left.

I talked to him about my mother. About how I was certain I had hurt her before she died. I told him about the men in my life right up to Casanova Jones.

In turn, I listened to him tell me about how he'd found sobriety, about his AA friends, and about the var-

ious jazz gigs he'd had in New York. Turns out as a sober
musician, he'd discovered even more layers to his own
talent. Going back further in his memories, he told me
about his courtship of my mother. It was as if my life
had been colored in shades of gray but now it was getting threads of color through it.

But what I liked best were evenings when, after rehearsing, he and I would listen to the old records I'd kept.

"My God," he said when he first saw them. "I just assumed someone would have put them in an attic somewhere and they'd have gotten rained on or something.
New Orleans heat woulda melted 'em."

He pulled out a Kid Ory record. The Kid played "tail-
gate"-style jazz—where the trombone takes an important role in the music. Kid is true New Orleans jazz, and
my dad loved him.

"Look at this, my Kid Ory." He looked over at me.
"Can we play it?"

"Hell yeah," I said and put it on. The ebullient music
filled my room, and my father grabbed me and did a silly
two-step.

Never one to miss a party, however small, Dominique
came flying into my room—without knocking, champagne bottle in hand—and joined us. My father stuck
to his Canada Dry ginger ale, which was now his "drink
of choice," he told me.

I'd spent my whole life longing for this moment, I
thought, looking around. All right…I hadn't *exactly* pictured a drag queen in the mix. But the feeling of family, of being with my father, of knowing being a blues
goddess was within my grasp, there, like a distant melody.
Everything was perfect.

Okay, not perfect. Tony and I avoided each other. We didn't even speak when we played together. I was aware of a greater vacuum than I had thought. No one left me Junior Mints at the microphone. Or sang me Irish drinking songs. Or found me rare blues records and told me stories about the Delta blues that even I didn't know. Most of all, there was no quiet listener who patiently heard all my fears and worries. All those Sundays we had sat and talked. The days we had listened to the rain, the blues playing on the turntable.

Still, I felt very ready to finally step into the spotlight on my own. So if being a blues goddess was my destiny, why on earth—or heaven—was Sadie so angry? For as soon as my father arrived, she was slamming doors like a New Orleans hurricane coming in off the gulf.

*chapter*

34

"Everyone—" Nan said, smiling as she escorted a tall, elegant woman with dark hair peeking from beneath a turban, and black eyes, into the dining room "—this is Madame Ravel. She's going to conduct the séance."

After three sleepless nights of door-slamming and footsteps, Nan had definitely had enough. It was either find a priest who would cleanse the spirit out of our house (and we discovered that they weren't too keen on messing with the "other side"—in fact, I think both priests we called thought we were crazy) or find a voodoo priestess. In New Orleans, trust me, they're plentiful.

Nan contacted her old friend, Madame Ravel. They had known each other for years, and Madame Ravel had been to a couple of our Mardi Gras parties. She spoke with a faint French accent. I always assumed her to be a big fake, but Nan believed she could speak to the dead.

Madame Ravel wore a turquoise turban, big earrings, a black sleeveless turtleneck and a long, flowing black skirt. Her eye makeup was dramatic—big smoky eyes. I looked at Dominique, who seemed enchanted. I guessed she would be copying this look as soon as possible. Basically, Madame Ravel looked like a walking, talking ad for Psychics-R-Us.

Madame Ravel swept into the room with a smile and took a seat at the head of the table. Seated around, their faces flickering in the candlelight, were Dominique (who was wearing, not one, not two, not three, but FOUR large crucifixes around her neck from her "Madonna" period; she wasn't taking any chances, she told me), Tony (no crucifix, but bemused by the entire thing, though now admitting the slamming doors were a bit "peculiar"—and still avoiding looking at me), Jack (dying to do a séance since he moved in), my father (opinion on Sadie unknown; he found it all "odd" but after all he'd seen in life, odd didn't surprise him anymore), Nan, Angelica (dressed in a Psychics-R-Us outfit to rival Madame Ravel's), and Maggie (who, after all the years she'd known me, besides being into wearing black and "loving" psychic stuff, was no way missing a real séance).

Madame Ravel asked us all to hold hands. Jack sat next to Maggie, and they seemed to be over their awkwardness. He took her hand immediately. I sat between Tony and my father. This was accidental. Dominique had insisted at the last minute on changing her seat because she wanted to hold Nan's hand on one side and Tony's on the other. She was chicken.

"Now," Madame Ravel spoke, "if anyone here is a nonbeliever, they need to leave their doubts out of the room. They need to be fully present. I will call the spirit into the room, and the spirit will speak to me, we hope. We all need to concentrate our energies toward welcoming the spirit. We don't need to be afraid." She looked at Dominique. "This seems, from what Myra tells me, to be a mischievous spirit, not a malevolent one."

Dominique looked up at the ceiling. "You hear that?" she asked, speaking to Sadie. "We want friendly ghosts here."

"Yeah," Maggie muttered. "Casper."

Madame Ravel stared icily at Maggie and then took a deep breath.

"Concentrate on the candle flames, and I will call up the spirit."

Needing a good night's sleep, I figured I had nothing to lose. I stared into the candle flame and held tight to my dad and Tony—despite my lingering anger.

"We invite the spirit of this house to come forward and speak. We invite her to this room with us. Reveal to us whatever it is you wish to say."

I sat and wondered just how it was Sadie would communicate. I mean, what? Would she just start talking? Would we see an apparition? Or would she be pissed off that we were having a séance and simply slam a door.

Instead…she blew out a candle.

Dominique gasped. "Who did that? If one of you blew that out, I'm going to kill you. Stop freaking me out."

I looked around. No one had done it. I was certain I had felt a burst of cold air, like a rare cool breeze in New Orleans, sweep over me and blow out the candle. I felt goose bumps on my arms.

"If that is our spirit, give us another sign," Madame Ravel intoned.

Another breeze, another candle.

I've seen enough scary movies in my life to know a real ghost when I feel one. This was the real deal. And though I'd lived in a haunted house for most of my life, I was frightened, and held still tighter to Tony and my dad. Looking around the table, I could see that all nonbelievers had tossed out their doubt. We were all spooked.

Madame Ravel inhaled deeply, as if putting herself in a trance. "The spirit is speaking to me," Madame Ravel said. Her eyes were shut. "She says she is not alone."

"Great," Dominique whispered. "What is this, a ghost hotel?"

"Who is with her?" Nan asked.

"The spirits are trying to communicate with me. Sometimes it's not clear…. There are three women present. I see them as a triumvirate."

"Three?" I asked.

"Yes. There is the one you call Sadie. She has lived here the longest. She is the one with great authority among them."

"Who else?" Jack asked.

"There is one who loves her."

"My aunt Irene!" I said excitedly.

Nan looked up.

"It was in the diary, Nan. Irene didn't leave because she was mad at you. She left because she was heartbroken after Sadie died."

"Well, I'll be…" Nan shook her head back and forth, her mouth slightly open in shock.

"The spirits say yes. She is the one they call Honey. Does that make sense to those present?"

Nan nodded.

"Who's the third spirit?" Angelica asked, her eyes wide and shining in the glow of candlelight.

"There is one more. You have to understand it's not always so clear. With this one, I am getting symbols. Many symbols. She is showing me symbols for mother, daughter…and a bridal gown. For wife."

"My sister never married," Nan said.

Madame Ravel nodded. "No. Not your sister. Not Sadie. Another."

"Nan, who else died here?" I asked. "Think back to the time of Sadie and Honey."

Nan looked confused. "No one. Maybe it was before I came here. From my grandfather's time."

But my father's hand had gone cold in mine. I looked over at him. My father whispered, "My wife."

Madame Ravel was silent. Then she nodded. "Yes."

Tears stung my eyes, and I forced myself to look upward, to try to contain them. If this was a parlor trick, if this woman was a fake, she was doing a damn good job of it. My mother had been the door-slammer of New Orleans?

"My mother? My mother is in this room?"

Madame Ravel nodded.

"What does my daughter have to say?" Nan asked.

"She speaks directly to her daughter."

My father squeezed my hand.

"Yes?" I asked.

"She says…maybe this makes sense to you. She is showing me symbols that mean a journey. Are you leaving home?"

This time Tony squeezed my hand. "I was thinking about it," I whispered, to which Dominique inhaled loudly enough for us all to hear.

"Your mother…she says it's time for you to go."

"That doesn't sound very much like my mother. You don't know her like we do. She would never want me to leave."

Madame Ravel laughed. "In the spirit world, you'd be surprised. There is no fear. The spirits come to see that obstacles we see in our path in life are only an illusion. So are all the false faces we show to the world. What we should have done in life, they learn, is follow our heart's desire."

"So is that what heaven is?" I asked aloud to my mother…to Madame Ravel. "Is it believing in yourself? Being true to yourself? Is that heaven, Mom?"

Madame Ravel seemed to be listening to someone. "Yes. She says yes, that is what heaven is."

In the flickering light, I saw tears falling down Nan's face. She had always urged my mother to be fearless. In death, she was.

"So is that why she's slamming doors?" I asked. "Is she the one? She seems angry. They all do this week."

"She wants you to know it's your time to leave this house. The three of them say it's your time."

"My mother is saying that?"

Madame Ravel laughed. "She also says she always loved you." She looked at my father.

My father smiled bashfully. "I'm sure she knows how I feel."

"That is part of heaven, too." Madame Ravel smiled. "Knowing true feelings. And to you—" she nodded at Nan "—she says she feels most at home here."

She looked around the table. "Whose name begins with a T?"

Tony's eyes widened and he said, "Mine does, ma'am."

"All three say they love the garden. Does that make sense to you?"

He nodded. I shook my head in amazement. Madame Ravel *had* to be real.

Spent, Madame Ravel fell back in her chair. Another cool breeze swept through the room and blew out a third candle.

"They've left. They've stopped communicating. The house is at peace now."

Though we could stop holding hands, we didn't. We all sat around the table looking at each other. Quiet. I didn't know what to say. I felt a longing to see my mother in the flesh. Not as a breeze. Not as a door-slam. At the same time, I knew she was with me… In this house.

And true to her word, my mother stopped slamming doors. We all were allowed to rest. Except me. All I could think about was the Mississippi Mudslide…and the garden that was transforming outside.

This was my moment. And I needed to be goddess enough to grab it.

chapter 35

September 9, 1939

*It's time to leave. I promise that I will come back. I'll come back and tell Myra why I just cannot stay here where every breath I take in this house reminds me of my beloved Sadie.*

*She is in the air. At night, I wake up and see her sitting in the chair in my room. She's combing her hair, staring at the moon. But as soon as I reach for her, she disappears.*

*I swear I smell her. The scent of jasmine. A perfume that was hers.*

*And the greatest torment. I touch her. I do. I know it sounds crazy, but I have dreams that are so real. I dream that we are making love. She is there. I feel her. And then I wake up and my arms are empty, it just reawakens the heartache. I can't sleep.*

*I can barely move through the day. It is as if my legs and arms, my very heart and head are made of stone.*

*Yet, I cannot shake the feeling that perhaps she is here. Crazy, I know. But I feel it. She IS here. And yet if I stay here, I know I will die. I can't take the fog of mourning that shrouds this house.*

*It's this house. It was always too big. It always frightened me. I remember being a little girl and my daddy sending me up to the attic. Ooooh, I just knew there were bad things in the attic. Whether it was spiders or spirits, I don't know.*

*I know when I leave here I will breathe better. But I also know how much it will hurt Myra. Still…I feel like she cannot understand my blues. She keeps asking me what's wrong, Irene. What's wrong? What can I say? That my heart is broken for good? That I'll never get over the love I have for Sadie? That I cannot even bear another night here?*

*I have to go. I have to leave this city. I will go to New York or Chicago. I'll sing my way from town to town. And I'll become someone. People will remember hearing Honey Walker sing. That will be my way of honoring my love. My Sadie.*

*chapter*

36

The night before I was scheduled to go on at the Mississippi Mudslide, Maggie called.

"When were you going to tell me?"

I uttered the words, "Tell you what?" But I knew.

"That you slept with Jack. My Jack. The Jack I have been in love with from the moment I saw him."

"Oh…that Jack," I tried to joke with her.

Dead silence.

"Maggie…it was a stupid thing to do that… just…happened one night. And what's with him telling you all this? It's over. It was over before it started. Before Rick. And I knew it was wrong. So why is he bringing it up?"

"Because we've been seeing each other. And last night we were supposed to sleep together. After the séance.

We'd been planning it. It was supposed to be our first time—sober. I was going to tell you, but after I made an idiot of myself sleeping with Jack when we were drunk, I decided to just keep quiet about it."

"Wow…this is so great. I'm so happy for you."

"Well don't be. Because thanks to you, it didn't happen. We got in a big fight. He told me about you and him because he wanted to be honest, but I…I couldn't handle it. And I was so shocked you'd kept it from me. I mean…that is what really blew me away. That you didn't tell me."

"I would have. But when you guys slept together that night he got drunk, it was all such a mess, I didn't even know what to do."

"What I don't understand—" her voice cracked "—is how you could sleep with him, knowing how I feel about him?"

"Maggie, it was a huge mistake."

"You never have trouble meeting men. Me? I am always the friend. This was the one guy. My one guy."

"What do you mean, 'the friend'?"

"You know what I mean. The sidekick. The friend next to the beautiful Georgie."

"That's not true."

"Isn't it? You need to look around." Her voice was angry. "When we go out, you're the one who gets the attention. Half the time I think I color my hair just so someone will look at me."

I sighed. "How long have you felt this way?"

"Forever. Since the day we met."

"Maggie…I don't even know what to say. What I did was wrong. But you can't mean this."

"Of course I mean it." The anger in her voice subsided, and now I could hear a quiver.

"Mags…and please, please whatever you're feeling, however you're angry at me, please don't let it stop you and Jack from starting a relationship."

"I don't know."

"Are you coming to Mississippi Mudslide?"

"I don't think so."

I felt a chill come over me. "Maggie…please. You're my best female friend 'with estrogen,' as you always point out."

"Which you wouldn't know from what you've done."

"I know. But please, please come."

"I can't. Listen…I'll call you next week."

"But—"

"I've got to go."

And as I started to respond, I realized, with a click, that I was speaking to dead air.

So that was it. I had done the unforgivable to someone I loved. Forgiveness was in short supply around this place. I still hadn't spoken to Tony.

Sleep eluded me. Nerves settled into my stomach like an entire flock of geese (forget butterflies). I got up and put on my robe and headed down to the kitchen, where I took a bottle of champagne to drown my sorrows and headed into the garden. I settled into a chair and inhaled all the night fragrances. By day, Tony was slowly transforming the patch of earth plant by plant into an overgrown careless English garden that, of course, belied its truly careful planning. I sat alone and breathed in the jasmine.

"Penny for your thoughts."

I let out something that was a cross between a gasp and a scream. "Jesus Christ, you scared me."

"Didn't mean to frighten you." Tony emerged from the shadows and sat down in the dim light filtering into the garden from the kitchen.

"That's okay. I can get a heart transplant."

"Checkin' on the progress, are you?" He sat down in a chair, his Levi's grass-stained and faded, his white T-shirt covered in mud.

"Just wanted to think about things…. Listen…I understand, I think, why you looked up my father. I'm sorry I've been such a bitch."

"I never meant to upset you."

"I know. I find myself wrestling with leaving the past in the past. It's great to have him here, but it's not perfect. I want to ask him a hundred times a day, when we have a laugh, or we sit and talk, 'Why'd you leave?'"

"So ask 'im."

"But the answer is in the bottle. So I either move on or miss out on knowing him now."

"Do you watch him when he plays the bass? He's somewhere else. Just like when you sing, you're someplace else."

"Think I got it from him?"

He nodded.

"I always related to you, Georgia. You not having a mother and father. I never really had anyone to watch out for me. Always had to make it alone. But you've got this grand house. With all these people who care about you. And even if you go off to New York to make music, you'll still have them. As alone as I was, I knew that what I had in here—" he pointed to his chest "—was all I had learned from the people I loved. So…it's not like they'll leave you really."

"I…I know this sounds like a wimpy bullshit cop-out, but part of me really wants to go onstage at the Mississippi Mudslide, and part of me wants to chicken out."

"Makes sense to me. You know, Georgia…you're the only one of us who has to think about becoming a star. What if that happened? What if you didn't just leave New Orleans, but you left us *all* behind?"

"I wouldn't change."

"Everyone says that."

"But I wouldn't. Really I wouldn't. I've been singing since I could first talk. I always craved being the center of attention, from my father. From my mother even. Dance lessons. Singing lessons. If it all came together, I think I'd look at my watch and say, 'Well, it's about time.'"

I took a swig of champagne and held out the bottle. "Want a sip?"

"Nah…" He held up a cold beer. "I have this."

"So do you think I'm ready? For the Mudslide?"

"You always were."

"Anyone ever tell you how mysterious you are? The blues. The way you're obsessed with them. Like the other night, with my father, I came downstairs and you guys were talking about T-Bone Walker, and you knew more than he did."

"So what do you want to know about me, Georgia?"

He spoke in a low rumble. Rough. I found myself taking another sip of champagne. I'd made a mess of things with Jack, Maggie…I'd let myself fall for Casanova Jones. I didn't need to be noticing Tony's T-shirt was bunched up, and he had this thin line of black hair on his belly, and a set of abs that looked hard as the stones he'd cast aside while digging the garden.

"The blues thing. Why?"

He put the cold beer up to his temple, as if he had a headache. Exhaling, he spoke quietly. "I cannot tell you, Georgia, what growing up poor in Ireland is like. It was brutal. And I lost my mother very young."

"How?"

"Don't know. My father was always off, at the pubs, doing a few illegal activities. He never even told me or my brothers what happened. We buried her with the simple thought in our minds that she'd been 'sick.' Of what, that I cannot tell you."

"I'm sorry."

He shrugged. "When you can't talk about what's inside…can't…give it a voice…sometimes a kid turns to music. Or drugs. Or drink. My oldest brother did that. And petty crime. But for me, it was music. Instead of rock 'n' roll, and most especially, instead of British rock 'n' roll, I liked American music. I actually really got into Elvis."

"Like Elvis? Our old guitarist?"

He laughed. "He took it a little more seriously than I did. I don't think you'll see me wearin' a polyester jumpsuit, now, lass."

"There's always sequins."

"No, you've got that department covered."

"Not anymore. I get to wear what I want now."

He smiled. "I think you look fine in sequins…. I think you look fine in anything…. Anyway, how did I get into the blues? Well, I had this one friend. A dear old guy, kind of like your Red. He owned a record shop. I would beg him to let me sweep out the back of the store, unload records, categorize them. Just pay me in records. And what I picked, what I wanted, was the blues."

"So why so closemouthed?"

"Don't know. I've been alone my whole life, really. My brothers are at least ten years older than I am. And they all left as soon as they could. My father was really just a bastard. And I guess...I'm not used to talking. I've lived up here—" he pointed to his temple "—for so long. I need to start living from here." He patted his chest again.

"You know," I said, "we all love you. You don't have to play your cards so close to your chest."

"I know. I was kind of hoping that the garden here would express what I feel. That's why I like plants, you know. They say what I can't. Come on." He held out his hand.

"It's pretty dark."

"I know, but come see this one corner."

I took his hand, and we walked over to a little patch filled with tiny little flowers that looked like little bells. He lit a small candle in a lantern.

"Lilies of the valley?" I asked.

He nodded in the dark. I was keenly aware of his hand, as I had been at the séance, too. It was a strong hand. A hand, I guessed, that had worked hard. That dug in the earth and moved stone and got cut and bled. A hand as unique as Tony. Scarred and rough. But gentle enough to lead me.

"I always used to think that fairies rang them." I smiled, though I knew he couldn't see my face. Lilies of the valley have always been my favorite flower. My mother's, too. That must have been why the spirits said they liked the garden. My mother had had lilies of the valley in her bridal bouquet.

Tony and I both squatted down to make them out in the flicker of candlelight.

"This is your corner," he said. "When I am working on it, I call it Georgia's Corner. When you come here, you can know I did this for you. And over here is Nan's. I'm growing her jasmine."

"It's beautiful."

I stood up again. We looked at each other awkwardly, but I didn't trust myself.

"I should go inside."

I turned quickly, before he could say anything, and I let go of his hand. Walking away, I felt a great pang of loneliness. We seemed to communicate without saying a lot. I told myself that wasn't enough. But upstairs as I took a shower, I started crying. It's Maggie, I thought. But looking down at my hand, thinking of holding his in the garden, I knew that wasn't the only reason I was crying.

chapter 37

Early the next morning, Red knocked on my bedroom door. Early as in eleven o'clock. Early for a musician.

"What's up?" I asked groggily as I opened my door.

"Shh," he whispered and walked into my room. "Tony let me in downstairs." He handed me a tiny velvet box.

"Oh my *God,*" I squealed.

"Shh," he urged me again. I shut the door, and he sat down on the edge of my unmade bed. I opened the box. Inside, nestled in the velvet cushion, was an antique ring, platinum, set with a small diamond, and then surrounded by little diamonds in an old-fashioned setting.

"Where did you get it?"

"A friend of mine. He's got a fancy antique store. I've

played at his Christmas party five years in a row, and his family's kind of fond of me. Got me a deal."

"It's beautiful."

"You really think so, Georgia?" He took out a crisp, white handkerchief and mopped his forehead. "I'm nervous."

Suddenly, I had intense panic that Nan might say no. What would *that* do for our night at the Mudslide? A woman going crazy over the men in her life, a recovering alcoholic bass player, a brokenhearted piano player and a drunken drummer. What a motley crew. I'd name us that, but that name was already taken. Actually, we took the name Georgia and the Whorehouse Blues in honor of the séance and that haunted house of ours.

As if he could read my mind, Red said, "I know it sounds crazy, me askin' her today of all days, but you know, I feel like you've given me some courage."

"Me?"

"Sure. You leavin' the Crescent City to make some *real* music. I haven't been this excited in years, sugar. So I figure it's time to get up the nerve. Who knows how much time any of us have left? Might as well spend it makin' the music we love, with the people we love."

Nan and Red were made for each other, and I just hoped she could see that. Funny how I could see how other people were meant for each other, but could never figure it out on my own.

"Good luck." I leaned down to kiss him. "If she says yes, can I call you Grandpa Red?" I winked at him. I had asked him once if he had any children and he said he had a daughter once, out of wedlock, but she had died when she was fourteen in a traffic accident. Another bit of pain he brought out at the piano. Her name had been Celia, and he wrote a song about her that I often heard him playing as I walked up the path to his front door.

"Nothing would make me prouder. You're my family anyway."

He stood up and took out his handkerchief again, mopping at the beads of sweat forming on his forehead. "Is it hot in here?"

"No. I have my fan on high, plus the air-conditioning. You're just nervous."

He stuck the handkerchief back into his pocket. "Suppose I am…"

I handed him back the ring box. "Good luck."

He smiled and opened the door and marched down the hall to Nan's room. He tapped gently on her door, and she opened it and invited him in. As soon as they shut the door, I ran down the hall to Dominique's room, which stood on the same side of the hall. One of her walls shared the wall of Nan's sitting room. I knocked softly.

"Come in," she answered.

"Got a glass?" I asked hurriedly as I walked in. Dominique was sewing a lost button on a Dior blouse.

"Over on the table there." She stopped sewing.

"I'm eavesdropping."

"What?"

"On Nan."

"Now *this* I have to see. What is that old glass thing, a James Bond trick? And why are you eavesdropping?"

"Can't say."

"You come in here with crazy bed-head hair, in a T-shirt with no underwear on…I can see your ass cheeks poking out, honey. And you want to listen in on your poor almost-eighty grandma and you won't tell me why?"

I tugged my T-shirt down farther. "Red is asking Nan to marry him."

"Holy shit!" she said, flinging the blouse aside and leaping up, grabbing a glass and coming next to me. We held our glasses to the wall, but the voices on the other side, despite our nifty "spying" technique, were muffled.

"Can you hear anything?" she whispered.

"No, Mata Hari, I can't…." I walked over to her bed and sat down on it. "I guess we'll have to wait until they tell us."

She sat down next to me. "Borrow my robe, Pussy Galore," she handed me a pink chiffon number. "You look terrible. Still sad about Rick the Prick?"

"Not really. Maggie and Jack." I slid an arm into the robe, then the other arm. "Did you know they were seeing each other?"

"Uh-huh. But I figured after the Casanova thing, you didn't need to hear about it. Certainly an attack of the crazies around here."

I nodded. "Maggie is pissed off at yours truly. She knows about Jack and me. And I don't blame her for being mad. I really don't. But she says she's not coming tonight."

Dominique wrapped an arm around my shoulders. "I'm sorry. She'll come. I'll talk to her."

"Don't. The whole thing is messy enough."

"So what does that mean? That I can't fix it? I'll have you know I'm very good at fixing relationships."

I rolled my eyes. "What about the Lady Brett fiasco?"

One time Dominique tried to repair things between Lady Brett and her boyfriend, an Italian who called himself Fabio. Before the whole thing was over, thanks to Dominique, three cop cars were called to break up a dish-breaking scream-fest of epic and histrionic proportions.

"All right. But what about the time I helped Maggie with her boyfriend the fireman?"

"Sure…you got them back together for a whole twenty-four hours, but before the week was out, she needed a restraining order on him."

Dominique held up her hands. "Fine. I'll butt out…. So what else is bothering you? You nervous about tonight? Things okay with your dad?"

"Yes and yes…. Look…what do you think of Tony?"

"I'd do him in a heartbeat if I thought he was gay."

"Really? Like him more than Clooney?"

"I just may. You *know* a woman can't resist the charms of a brogue. He's been in the band for years now, but he's quiet. He's not the flashy lead singer, or the dreamboat guitarist. He's the bassist who holds you all together."

"Gary holds us together."

"No, Gary tries to control you."

Sometimes a queen can make a lot of sense.

She continued. "Tony is the quiet one, the one who is there to make sure you all get along smoothly. He's the one who runs out and buys you chocolate when you've had a bad day. He's the one who sleeps on a deck chair on the riverboat when Jack has a girl, even though Tony's bed is nice and warm and has a pillow. He's easy to overlook, but underneath that quietness I would bet is one very intense, very fuckable guy."

"You think?" I arched an eyebrow.

"Oh yeah…haven't you *noticed* those biceps of his? Those hands? That delicious ass?"

"I hadn't…until he came to stay here. Dominique…I'm a mess. I don't know *what* I want."

"Oh yes you do."

I looked at her. She was so confident. "You do," she said firmly.

"You think?"

She nodded. "So you sing your heart out tonight, sister, and then you go for what you want. It's your time. It's just your time."

We heard a loud whoop and holler from the next room. Next we heard pretty spry footsteps from Red, who stuck his head out in the hall and called me, "Georgia!"

"Come on." I grabbed Dominique's hand. We ran into the hall. Red gave us a big thumbs-up.

"Champagne coming up!" Dominique ran down the stairs, and I hugged Red and went in to see Nan admiring her hand with her new engagement ring on it.

"Isn't it beautiful, Georgia?" She held her hand out.

"Wonderful." I leaned down to kiss her. "I am so happy for you. You deserve it, Nan."

Red just paced the room, beaming. "This is the best day of my life."

Dominique returned with the champagne and four flutes expertly balanced from her bartending days, and she popped the cork and filled our glasses.

"To Nan and Red," I said. "Two beautiful people with a beautiful life ahead of them."

"Cheers, darlings," Dominique said, and her eyes were welled up. She cries at happy occasions. She cries at sad occasions. She's an equal-opportunity crier.

"Cheers!" Red toasted me in turn. "And to our blues goddess, Georgia Ray, may she blow away the citizens of New Orleans tonight."

We drank our champagne. Nan held on to Red's hand. After we finished our bottle, Dominique said, "I'm still repairing my outfit for tonight. Off I go, darlings. See you at the 'Slide tonight."

"See you tonight, Dominique." I smiled.

"Well…I hate to say goodbye so soon to my fiancée, the soon-to-be Mrs. Watson, but I've got to warm up for tonight." He leaned down and kissed her goodbye tenderly. "I love you, Myra."

"I love you, too, Red."

He kissed my cheek. "See you at the 'Slide."

"See you tonight." I held up my hand, and he high-fived me. "Love conquers all," I said.

"Spoken like one who knows." He winked.

Nan and I were alone, and I lifted my glass again. "You know, I don't know if I've ever thanked you for all you've done for me. You've given me a home, and you've taught me the real meaning of family."

"Georgia…you are my *raison d'être*."

"I'm very happy for you and Red. Thrilled, really."

"So why didn't you tell me that you were going to leave us when the garden is finished?"

"Red told you, huh?"

"Yes. And he and your father are cookin' to go off and make some music together, too. There's some club owner from Chicago who wants him to play there for a few weeks…. The last of the great bluesmen." She sighed. "When did we get old?"

"You're not old. Just wise. How do you feel about him doing that?"

"I feel like I'll miss him and your father…and you. Feel like it's about time you spread your wings."

"Yeah, but—"

"Georgia, we all like to think the rest of the world would stop if we left. That we're the only one shouldering all the burdens, all the blues. I know you. What you think. That the Saints would perish without you. That I would fall apart. That Dominique and I wouldn't be able to go on. But you know, the most freeing thing in the world can be to discover that, indeed, life goes on without us. It can be humbling and freeing both at once."

"So how'd you get so smart?"

"Many years. Many heartaches. Many joys. Perhaps I am a Buddhist at heart. But the wheel goes around. It turns, with us or without us."

"Like Honey Walker?"

"Like Honey Walker."

"She didn't leave because she hated you. She didn't leave because of the way this city treated her. That pained her, but she left because she was Sadie's lover and staying in this house made her too sad."

"I carried a pain in my insides for so long that maybe I had made her leave, but I didn't. She just had to go. And in the end, all these years she's been wandering these halls, reunited with Sadie…and your mother."

I nodded.

"Life sure is strange, Georgia. Just when you think you've got it all figured out, it puzzles you."

"Does it make you feel weird, thinking about them being here in the house? Mom here?"

"No. It makes me feel very content. And I suppose when Red and I die, we'll come back here and haunt you, too. We'll just all be here until then it's your children, and your children's children. Our lineage will stretch out like an endless thread. And we'll all be together. Now, isn't that a nice thought?"

I watched her, silent for a while. I could see her mind piecing together bits of scraps like a quilt, putting it all together until she had the entire picture. Finally, she nodded decisively. "Yes. I think that's how it will be. You know, if I had maybe had half a brain, I would have figured it out. About Sadie and Irene. It was there in front of me all along."

Which made me think of Tony.

"Nan…speaking of something right there in front of you…"

"Tony."

I stopped marveling at her powers of intuition. She knew me better than I knew myself.

"Yes," I said. "It seems so obvious now. To me. We've been so close all this time. But at the same time, kind of quiet, you know?"

"Maybe that's it. Not that you can't talk to each other, but that you don't need to. That you understand the spaces in between the words. The silences. The music."

"It is in the silences that I feel like I know him best. We just seem to understand. Yet, when we do talk, it's very nice, too. But it's so strange that now, after all this time, we've connected in this way."

"Sometimes you just have to wait for the music to move you." She smiled, sounding an awful lot like Red.

"Maybe…let's talk about you and Red. When's the wedding?"

"Before you all leave. In the garden."

"But then I'll be off to New York. Will you be okay?"

"Don't I have a suitcase? Dominique can hold down the fort here. I won't come right away, but I'll head up to the Big Apple this fall. Red and I can take it as an extended honeymoon."

"Were you surprised? By the ring?"

She clasped her hands, "Yes, I was. And if a man can surprise you at *my* age, then it's a good idea to keep him. Does Tony surprise you?"

"Yes. But I am starting to question whether I have the slightest idea what I'm doing. I thought I loved Rick, too, you know."

"Sweetheart, if we had it all figured out, life wouldn't be very interesting."

I stood up. "If I'm going to sing tonight, I better try to do something with this hair of mine. I can't believe I'm actually going on. With my father."

"He's a good man, Georgia. He's had some hard times, but he sees now he needs his family."

"You're not angry with him?"

"If we stayed angry at every person who hurt us, we'd be mad at the world, Georgia. Loving people means getting hurt. That simple."

"Thanks, Nan."

"What are you wearing?"

"The black Valentino dress Dominique found for me in New York. She said the guy running the thrift store had no idea what he had. It was just in a box in a corner. She bought it so fast her hands were shaking when she pulled the money out. Too small for her, but just right for me. And not a sequin in sight."

"I'm very proud of you."

"I love you, future-Mrs. Watson." I kissed her and went to my room.

I was wrapped in a towel and ready to jump in the shower when Jack knocked on the door and poked his head in.

"You ready for tonight?"

"No. Musically…yes. But I'm nervous and have a lot to do yet."

"Can I talk to you?"

"About Maggie?"

"How'd you guess?"

"Not many secrets between us all. This house is pretty much like living your life on the front page of the *Enquirer.*"

"Which is why I told her. We can't have secrets between us. Not if we're going to make a go of it."

"Which is why she hates me and won't be at the Mudslide tonight."

"I'm going over to the salon. I'll talk her into it."

"Good luck. Underneath her purple hair she's a natural-born redhead. Good luck talking her into anything when she's mad."

He laughed.

"Can I ask you something, Jack?"

"Shoot."

"You've known her for years. Why are you seeing her now?"

"Ever look at somebody in one way for a long time, and then they do something, say something, touch you in a certain way, and suddenly, you can't believe you'd never noticed them before. Her eyes are pale blue, and she has this little scattering of freckles across the bridge of her nose. It reminds me of the Milky Way. And she has this spot right here." He pointed to the hollow of his clavicle. "It's so beautiful. And when she laughs, I just go crazy."

"You're making me gag."

"But you're not upset?"

"Not if you don't fuck this up. And not if she forgives me."

"She will… I'll let you shower." He turned to go.

"Jack?"

"Yeah, Gorgeous Georgia?"

"Are we okay? Me and you?"

"Yeah. We're A-OK. You know…I think I was looking for someone I could rely on after Sara. And that's a stupid reason to be with someone."

"Jack…you know I'm leaving, don't you?"

He nodded slowly. "When I heard you that night at the Sunday Saints Supper, I knew. You need to go. You takin' Tony with you?"

"Why do you say that?"

"Look at him with a new set of eyes, Georgia. You just might be surprised at what you see. I've known him as long as you, but you know, sometimes when it's just the guys, we get to talking."

"And?"

"And he always kind of amazes me. He's a really deep person. And he's got a lot of integrity."

"Jack…promise me we'll always be friends."

He smiled. "Can't get rid of me, even if you go touring through Europe. Just promise *me* you'll invite me when you play Carnegie Hall."

"Sure." I rolled my eyes.

"I'll miss you, Georgie. But break a leg tonight."

"Thanks."

He shut the door quietly, and I walked into the bathroom and looked in the mirror. As long as I was looking at Tony in new ways, maybe I had better start looking at myself in new ways, too.

The face that stared back at me had a broad nose, brown eyes that were shaped like a cat's, high cheekbones. Full lips. A tiny scar over my left eye where Joey Dunn stabbed me with a pencil in third grade. I'd managed to swing a textbook at him and gave him a shiner. My mother made me write him a note saying I was sorry. He never said he was sorry to me, and I had a scar to remind me of the incident. From my scar, my eyes shifted to my big hair. Inescapable big hair. But it was growing on me. Hell, that had taken long enough. But my hair was me.

The face in the mirror, I finally accepted, was pretty. She was sexy.

And she was a blues goddess.

*chapter* 38

Just before we were scheduled to go on, I felt as if I was going to throw up. Then two things happened that made me want to hurl right into the laps of those closest to the stage.

1) Tony told me he loved me. Thirty seconds before I was scheduled to go on. So there was no time to discuss, dissect or deny.

2) I spotted Casanova Jones at a table by the stage. Alone. With a single long-stemmed rose. And looking as fuckable as he always had. Was it right to go back to a man just because he introduced you to multiple orgasms?

★ ★ ★

I looked at Red. I looked at my dad. I looked at Mike.

"I can't do this."

My father came over to me and put his hand on my trembling one. "Georgia, I was the coward. I ran out on your mother and you. You stayed to nurse her through being sick. You stayed with your nan, and you've sung in this city all these years. You can do this."

"Dad…my ex-boyfriend is sitting in row one. You know…the one I told you about."

"Then you make him realize what he lost."

We were introduced. The spotlight shone on me, and I forgot about Casanova Jones. I became the Blues Goddess. I don't know whether I was channeling Honey Walker or just shining a candle on the dark places in my heart, but I found a voice that was between a growl and moan, a blues voice that rang true, and I sang from my soul.

Instead of Casanova Jones, I sang to myself. I imagined myself in the front row. Not me now, but the me at that high-school lunch table. And I sang to her. I sang about loss and love and grief. I sang for that girl who loved a boy from afar. I sang for how lonely she was. I sang for her the way death invaded her home. For her mother.

Out of the corner of my eye, despite the spotlight, I glimpsed Jack holding Maggie's hand. I turned to face their section of the audience. I sang for a carrot-topped girl who never believed a man she loved would love her the same in return. I sang for her caught in the crossfire of her father's rages and her mother's tirades. I sang for the way her best friend had hurt her because she was too cowardly to tell her the truth.

I sang for Red and Nan. I sang for a woman who had never backed down from life. I sang for a man who found the place in his heart that was about the blues and played the piano for a daughter long gone.

I sang for my mother who had haunted our house. I sang for the way she had loved a willful young daughter and saw in her the potential to love. I sang for the way we hadn't been able to connect in life, but had somehow shared love in death.

I sang for Sadie, selling herself despite wanting to be with the woman she loved.

I sang for Honey Walker, who inspired me to understand the blues in a deeper way and to leave this city I called home for the call of somewhere else.

I sang for my father who was missing from my life, then found. I sang for the way he had discovered a peace he hadn't known was possible. I sang for the courage it took for him to come back to a daughter he barely knew.

I sang for the boy Damon, who became the woman Dominique. I sang for the pain he had, not being accepted in his own home. I sang for the love she found with her new family. I sang for the vulnerability that lies beneath the false eyelashes. I sang for her friendship, as it had buoyed me and made me believe in myself.

I sang for all of them, the rainbow in my life. I sang for a family that was anything but normal, yet loved more fiercely than the one I glimpsed on River Road in its fancy facade.

Finally, I sang for an Irishman who had seemed to be

a quiet rock in my life, but turned out to be burning beneath, like lava. I sang for the space between the notes. For finding someone to share the silences with. I sang for the way he moved me. I sang for going off to the unknown.

I sang "Good Rockin' Tonight," "Goin' to Chicago" and "If I Could Be with You." Finally, I sang for Casanova Jones. For the man who took me to the moon and back again, but showed me by hurting me, that perhaps the best love was in my own garden with a man from Ireland. I sang of forgiveness.

I sang from the place where I felt old grief and old wounds. And when I was done, and spent, when I'd looked at my father and Red on the keys and Mike at the drums and seen them become one with me, I looked out at the crowd, all on their feet. They understood that I sang from a special place. They had seen the birth of a new blues goddess.

The crowd gave me a standing ovation, and we performed three encores.

I took my bows and introduced my band. I took Mike's hand and we both stood with Red and my dad in a joint embrace.

Finally, we played one last song, "I Didn't Know About You." How true that was. I didn't know about Casanova.

My father.

And most of all…Tony.

I took a bow and left the stage. No, most of all, the one I didn't know was myself. But now I had laid bare my soul on the stage and in my song. I knew all about myself. And finally, I liked what I knew.

# chapter

39

I was mobbed as soon as I hit the floor of the Mud-slide. I was congratulated by strangers, and someone asked if he could take his photo with me. A reporter approached me and asked if he could call me the next day for an interview. I soaked it all up, feeling like Cinderella at the ball.

Then I saw Dominique.

I rushed forward. "What the hell happened to you?" I asked. She was dressed in a conservative Dior blouse, the one I'd seen her repairing that morning. She wore a plain black skirt and sensible heels.

"Where are your fuck-me pumps? Where is your hat? Your feather boa? Your fishnets? Your red nail polish?" I turned her hand over. Her nails were in an elegant French manicure. I put my hand to her forehead. "Are you okay?"

She giggled. "I am. I decided that maybe, just maybe, Terrence deserved another chance. This is my 'wife of a computer analyst' outfit."

"You're not fooling anyone. The Adam's apple gives you away. That and your size-twelve shoes."

She hugged me. "Enough about that. You were terrific. I love you."

"Love you, too."

"You were beyond fantastic." She gave me a squeeze.

"Is that skirt made of tweed?"

"Yes."

"It's so unlike you."

"Terrence said so, too. He met me here. Said he loved me just the way I am. Platinum wig and purple shoes and all."

Terrence approached with a snifter of Baileys Irish Cream for Dominique and a Canadian Club and soda for himself. He kissed her on the cheek (having to stand on tiptoe to do so; as I said, Dominique wasn't fooling anyone), and then leaned over and kissed me.

"Great show, Georgia."

"Thanks, Terrence."

"Did Dominique show you the ring I bought her?"

"No."

Dominique waved her hand. A rather conspicuous diamond in a gold setting.

"Is that an engagement ring?"

"Yes." Terrence beamed. "She was right. I'm not hiding us anymore. I don't even like her in this getup. She deserves to wear what she wants."

"Congratulations."

"We're going to have a commitment ceremony. I want you to be maid of honor," Dominique said.

"Thank you. Just no ugly bridesmaid dresses."

"For sure. Something you can wear again," Terrence said, pushing his glasses up the bridge of his nose.

Dominique and I looked at him.

"What?" He blushed.

"Don't you realize that is the biggest hoax foisted onto innocent women everywhere? Such an outfit does not exist. Besides, I would venture to guess you'll have three bridesmaids all wearing shirts that say 'Shirley' on them," I said.

"We don't know any Shirleys."

Dominique and I laughed. "She'll explain. In the meantime, welcome to the family."

I looked at Dominique. She beamed. "I was actually thinking a whole *Gone With the Wind* theme."

"No hoop skirts."

"Not even for me?" She pouted.

"You're about the only one I would agree to wear one for."

I moved over to Jack and Maggie and enveloped her in a hug. "Thank you," I whispered into her ear.

"I couldn't stay mad at you." She hugged me fiercely, then released me. Jack wrapped his arm around her waist. She leaned her head on his shoulder.

"You two look so cute together."

"Don't they?" Gary came over and pecked me on the cheek. "You were great, Georgia."

"Thanks, Gary. We've come a long way from our days when we first learned 'Celebration.' Remember Elvis and his hip swivels?"

Gary grinned. "But all good things must come to an end."

"What's that supposed to mean?"

"That I know it's time for you to go. That I took out an ad for auditions for a new lead singer."

"But—"

"Georgie, I may like ABBA, but that doesn't mean I don't know good blues when I hear them. You were re-born up there. Just promise me when you're famous you won't forget your old band. Thank us at the Grammys."

"Please. Blues singers starve as much as wedding bands."

"Not when they sing like that. So what do you want to drink? I'm buying."

"I'll take a champagne cocktail."

Nan kissed me. My father came over to embrace me again. Feeling him wrap his arms around me was so strange, to have my cheek on his shoulder. He had been a ghost all my life, and now he was flesh and blood. Tony stood to one side, sipping "a pint" as he called it, and waiting for me. Red had his arms around Nan. And out of the corner of my eye, I spotted Casanova Jones making his way toward me. Tony stiffened, and everyone else sort of took a step closer to me on impulse.

As he stood in front of me, I stepped away from my friends so Rick and I could speak alone.

"I saw you from onstage."

"This is for you." He handed me the rose. "You were

unbelievable." He reached out a hand to touch one of my curls. The scent of his cologne made me feel weak.

"Thanks."

"So, are you going to give me another chance? Don't you know how crazy I am about you?"

"Me and the female population of New Orleans."

"Georgie, we happened so fast. But I miss you like mad. Don't you miss me?"

"You know, Rick, I do. I miss your touch. But in the end, I think I'm looking for the silences."

"What?" He leaned in closer to me, a guy ever aware of how beautiful he was. He was used to his good looks being a substitute for honesty.

"The silences. The spaces between the notes."

I could see Tony drinking his beer silently, staring at Rick and me, his gaze drifting, almost as if he couldn't stop himself, back and forth.

"Sorry, Rick." I turned and walked toward Tony. Rick followed me and put his hand on my arm.

"Wait!"

"Don't do this. Not here. Not tonight."

"Then let me take you to breakfast tomorrow. To brunch. We can talk about it then. Let me make you eggs and bacon."

"Rick…I'm leaving for New York. I'm going to audition for a band there."

"Let me talk you out of it."

I handed him back the rose. "You know, the fact that you would try means you don't know me all that well. Don't know what's important."

"Then teach me."

"No. I shouldn't have to, Rick. Look…I don't hate

you. All the years since high school, you were my great, unrequited love. But the fantasy of you was better than the reality. Being with you taught me a lot about myself…and it somehow inspired me to do what I did tonight."

"I wish you'd give me a second chance."

"Our whole affair was a second chance."

I turned my back to him and walked over to the queens.

"What's with the tiaras, ladies?" I asked of Lady Brett, Angelica, Monica and Desiree.

"We usually celebrate Tiara Tuesdays," Angelica said.

"We drink tequila. We're into a whole alliteration thing," Monica added.

"But if ever there was a reason for non-Tuesday tiara-wearing, this was it." Angelica said, "You rock."

"Well, I'm honored."

"We have one for you." Angelica smiled and pushed a funky rhinestone-encrusted tiara on my head.

"To the Blues Goddess!" Red lifted his glass. We all drank, and I felt up to my head where the tiara perched in some curls. I'd never won anything before. And any thoughts of being homecoming queen down here were banished by the bottled blondes. But tonight, I was belle of the ball.

# chapter 40

Tony was gone.

One minute he was there, the next, he wasn't. I took off my tiara and frantically combed the crowd. How had he slipped away?

I looked around the bar. "Anyone seen Tony?"

But no one had. Maybe he had gone to the men's room. I sent Jack to look for him. He wasn't there. Did Tony misinterpret Rick's rose? I stayed for one more round, then headed home with Angelica.

"Stay for another drink," Terrence urged me as I collected my things. "I'm buying."

"I need to go. I need to talk to Tony."

Once in Angelica's Miata, I turned to her. "Honey, if you can floor it, I'd be eternally grateful."

"Let's fly," she said, put the car into drive, and we hurtled down the street.

Arriving back at the Heartbreak Hotel, the light over the front door was lit. I let myself in. "Tony! Tony!"

I ran up the stairs and knocked on his bedroom door. No answer. I let myself in. The place had been cleaned out. His suitcase was gone. I rushed over to the French doors and opened them, praying he would be in the garden. I looked down at the flowers, but he wasn't there.

Shutting the door, I felt the tears come. This wasn't like when Rick hurt me. This was a sense that part of me had been ripped out, forever.

I left Tony's room and started down the hall to my own. Angelica was just coming to the top of the landing.

"He's gone. I finally wake up and he's left."

"He'll be back."

I shook my head. "You don't know him. This is it. Done. Off to New York, then Ireland. Gone."

"Let me tell you something."

"Hmm?"

"You see me and the other Shirleys? Dominique, Lady Brett?"

I nodded, cursing myself inside.

"We're all about having a good time, but you think it's easy to pick this life? Would I *choose* it? This is my destiny, but it's full of hard times. Lonely times. And if I loved someone, if I knew it, wouldn't nothin' stop me from gettin' *my* man."

"I hear you."

She put a manicured finger to my chin and tilted it up.

"New York ain't so big you can't find a person who probably wants to be found anyway."

"Thanks." I walked into my room and stared at the records. Every Sunday he had come here to my altar of all things blues, and he had loved me all along.

I picked out Etta James. I put the record on my turntable. I put the needle down and listened to the hiss as the needle moved to the first song. Then I sat down with a box of tissues and cried the blues.

*chapter*

41

Dominique was three hankies into the wedding ceremony. They weren't even on the "I dos" yet.

Nan looked like a vision in an ivory silk dress she had bought in Paris when she was younger—it still fit. Red was quite handsome in a dark blue suit. The Unitarian minister stood in the garden, and our family, as motley and odd as we were, sat in white chairs we rented for the occasion, in several rows.

As Nan and Red spoke their vows, I could only think of Tony.

Aching, I looked over at my father. He felt my mother in the garden. I did, too. It was as if the ghosts had all along been there, urging us to piece back together our lives. They knew all the broken parts. The ghosts heard our cries and prayers in the middle of the night. They had been there as we knelt by our bedsides and searched for answers in thoughts lifted to God. They had been there in the tears and the laughter. In the loneliness. They saw the shards of grief only voiced by the blues. Then they worked their voodoo to make sure we all came together.

I looked around. The garden was a vision. The corner that Tony had planted for me, in daylight, was delicate and precious. He had coaxed violet morning glories and tea roses, jasmine and honeysuckle, and two fragrant lemon trees that framed Nan and Red at the outdoor cupola we used as an altar. A pale white butterfly drifted on a breeze that Tony must have bought with some magic. The garden spoke in the silences.

When at last the happy couple said "I do," we threw up a cheer in unison and tossed birdseed and then engulfed them in hugs and kisses.

Dominique and I had been bridesmaids, and my dad a groomsman. And Terrence, who finally decided living without Dominique was more painful than even the closet, was there looking at her adoringly in her little hat with a baby-blue veil.

In three days, I was to leave for New York. Red also heard from a record producer who wanted to see me play live in Manhattan. How all the pieces fell together... And then I remembered my mother. How she only wanted stories with happy endings. I didn't believe in them. But she had somehow seen to it that the Heartbreak Hotel would, with whispers and footsteps and slammed doors, make us all believe that might just be possible. All I needed to do was find a tough Irishman who, I prayed to Sadie and all things blues, really did want to be found.

chapter 42

Saying goodbye was sloppy.

Dominique sobbed and clung to me.

"Promise me you'll call every day."

"Yes, Dominique."

"And you'll be careful."

"Yes, Dominique."

"And you won't change."

"Dominique, when you went to New York, you left as a preppie and came back as a queen."

She sniffled. "I was a queen inside since I was five. I was just making the outside match the inside."

"I left you that red scarf you like."

She put her crumpled tissue to her nose. "Well, I stuck a sequin halter top in your suitcase."

I hugged her and then went to Nan's room to say goodbye.

"I'll be back."

"Oh…don't you be feelin' sorry for me, Georgia Ray," Nan said. "I've been wishing this for you for a long time."

"I love you."

"I love you, too. Now scoot or you'll miss your plane."

"Goodbye, Mrs. Watson."

I shut her door, then went to my room one last time. I was traveling light. I had already said goodbye to Maggie and Jack, Gary and Mike. All that was left was saying goodbye to the ghosts.

I looked around the room. Most of my pictures still hung on the wall. I whispered a thank-you. Somehow my aunt's diary had shaken the dust from my dreams. Like blowing the dust off an old record before putting it on the turntable.

My father and I flew together. We arrived in New York, and I stayed with him for a few days until my sublet was ready. We laughed together a lot now. And he was starting to really know me.

"You're laughing, but it's not reaching your eyes, Georgia," he said to me over breakfast one day around noon—I really *was* his daughter.

"What if I don't find him?"

"You will."

"How do you know?"

"I seen the way he looked at you. I heard it in his voice when he called me. Say he thought I should come to meet my daughter. How she was a blues singer. I heard it in his voice."

I rode the subways and went to blues clubs, ate Chinese takeout and listened to the traffic outside my window.

I auditioned for Red's friend, Hugh. His quartet was tight. On a rainy Tuesday afternoon, in an empty club, I sang the blues for him and his musicians and was hired. We worked on our sets, and if I thought occasionally Red was a taskmaster, he was nothing compared to Hugh.

But I knew the first time I sang in New York City that I had somehow been waiting for that moment since I was five years old and first saw my parents dancing to "At Last" in the living room, me hiding on the stairs, seeing something between them I couldn't quite define yet. I stepped into the spotlight and was transported back to the time of Honey Walker.

My life in New York was a blur. It was about singing and coming home at night with an ache that made even breathing hurt. Every musician, every person in the music business I could ask, I did. But no one had heard of an Irish bluesman looking for a band, looking for work. I even called some limousine companies. Most of the dispatchers hung up on me. One told me, "This ain't a fucking baby-sitting service, lady."

"Come on, just tell me if you have an Irish limo driver."

"This is fucking New York. You know how many O'Malleys, O'Brien's, O'Somethings we got?"

"But this one is off the boat. Irish accent and all."

"Give it a rest. I don't fucking know."

My father and I ate together often. I called Dominique every day. But I had the blues. Where were the ghosts when I needed them?

After three months in New York, as the weather turned bitter, my father called me one Monday.

"I think I found him."

"Tony?"

"Think so. Sittin' in for a friend of mine tonight at a place in SoHo."

I scribbled down the address. My sublet studio was tiny. Dominique was right. My old room was the size of a Manhattan apartment. Roaches congregated in the sink. There was a drag queen on the second floor, but all in all it wasn't home. And that was okay. I found, despite the pain, I liked moving forward to someplace unknown.

I looked at the club address on the slip of paper. Out of habit, I talked to Sadie. Let him be there, I whispered.

I spent the day pacing and listening to music, waiting for the time to go to the club. As soon as I walked in and slipped into the crowd at the bar, people in sophisticated New York fashions—most of it black, not a queen in the bunch, I heard the bass and knew it was him.

I looked at Tony. I thought of all the times he had been there, quietly nursing his own blues, yet totally in tune with me. I remembered my garden corner.

I saw him on the stage, in black, intense. As if he could hone in on me, he lifted his face to the bar area. I inched forward, squeezing through spaces between people. Feeling pressed-in, claustrophobic.

We stared at each other, and I felt a shiver. In the spaces between the notes, I knew we understood each other.

On break, he came over to me. His face was etched with dark circles under his eyes. I touched his cheek.

"Hey, lass."

I just rushed forward and hugged him tightly. At first he kept his arms down by his sides, but eventually he encircled me.

"I love you." I said it first.

"I love you, too."

"I've missed you. More than I ever thought I could."

"Baby," he growled in my ear, "I've missed you since the moment I met you. I need you."

We stood in our embrace until it was time for him to go on again.

Taking his hand somewhere near three in the morning, when the band was done, in the city that never sleeps, we walked long blocks until we got a cab, and went back to my studio. I showed him in, and I lit two candles and then turned to face him. His was a face that mirrored my own. He knew loss. He knew the blues. We'd had each other all along.

I took a step closer to him. He put his hands on my waist and drew me still closer.

And because he understood me, he simply kissed me. And I knew, though Rick had made me feel crazy and insatiable, in love and in lust, though Rick's kisses had made me forget all men before him, it was this love that took a kiss to another level entirely. Casanova Jones was a myth of my own making. This was real.

I breathed him in and let him envelop me, finding a place in his arms that felt like home, like my old house with its ghosts, I felt a sense of belonging. I kissed him again, more hungrily. He undressed me slowly, then took off his shirt and jeans. He moved toward me again, breathing ragged and we touched each other, holding on to each other like survivors, two souls who almost drowned.

"Wait," I urged him. I went over to the CDs I had brought with me. I found Etta James. I put it into my boom box and started to play "At Last." Tony was lying in my bed, and I went to him and slid into the space he created for me in the crook of his arm. The music said it all.

At last.

# chapter 43

*Dear Diary,*

*So if my aunt Irene, the original Blues Goddess, had a diary, why not me?*

*I'm writing this at a desk, in a rather drafty cottage in Ireland. I took a walk today and saw sheep. Sheep! This is a long way from queens and magnolias.*

*We played well last night. Tony and I and the band of blues lovers he's dug up here. He and his brother opened a pub, and we play for the tourists and the locals and anyone who loves the blues. After this, we're going to Chicago. Then L.A. Or maybe vice versa, depending on a toss of a coin. In L.A., I've got a pretty good shot at making a recording. Final touches on the deal.*

*Tony and I still play poker to kill the time. But not for candy. First it's strip poker. Then when we're out of clothes, we play* for sexual favors. Then we just say fuck the cards and let's make love. We're not so quiet anymore. We talk incessantly—I guess finally sure this is it. Each other. We heal all the heartache we each carried with us. The blues place.

My father is still sober. One day at a time, he tells me. We speak on the phone every week.

Nan is happy. She and Red are like any honeymooners, here in Ireland to visit. Including leaving a Do Not Disturb sign on their hotel door until well into the afternoon. Anyone who thinks old age can't be sexy ought to get a load of those two. And Red is finally, even legally, my grandpa. He had been all along, I suppose, but this just cements it.

Dominique and Terrence are running the Heartbreak Hotel. Dominique hasn't given up her go-go boots.

Maggie and Jack didn't make it. Not for lack of trying. He's moved on to a magnolia queen, a Southern girl, without the tattoos. I don't even know that Maggie is sad anymore. Sometimes you find those unrequited loves aren't all they're cracked up to be.

The Heartbreak Hotel will always be full, I think. Right now, it's Dominique and Terrence, and Lady Brett. The Heartbreak is a house that craves people. It welcomes the broken-hearted until they can figure out their broken parts and off they go, like doves being set free. But as Angelica says, as long as there's love, there's the risk of heartbreak. It's just fighting your fears so that you can live life.

Like Dorothy in The Wizard of Oz, I thought I had to escape to become a great blues goddess, but now I find myself looking forward to going home. The Mississippi Mudslide wants me for a guaranteed gig nearly every Friday. So after Ireland and Chicago and L.A., we'll go back to our house and the garden.

*We'll go back to the triumvirate of spirits: Sadie, Honey and my mother. We'll show them how we've changed. We'll show them the new love in the old empty spaces.*

*Now that I am happy, everyone wonders if I still love the blues.*

*The answer is yes.*

*Because it wasn't just about the notes, but about the silences, and about what the notes could say.*

*The notes could speak the things I couldn't. They're a part of me.*

*Like New Orleans.*

*And Dominique.*

*And the queens and the three Shirleys.*

*The blues are my family and my father.*

*The blues are Tony. The way, when we make love, he knows just what to do, and as I sink to his cock, as I touch him, there's a familiarity. And when we press our chests together, heart to heart, we speak the same rhythm.*

*The blues are the Heartbreak Hotel.*

*They are my mother.*

*They are death and they are life.*

*And they whispered to me all the time.*

*"Georgia Ray," the blues said to me, "you are a blues goddess."*

*And now I say back to them, "I am."*

*I am the Blues Goddess.*

On sale in September from Red Dress Ink

# Lucy's Launderette

### Betsy Burke

Ever had the feeling that your life is spinning
out of control? Lucy has! Despite her degree in
fine arts, she is working as a professional gofer
for an intolerable art gallery owner, her
free-spirited grandfather has just passed away,
leaving behind his pregnant girlfriend, and she is
the only sane member in her eccentric family.
Read LUCY'S LAUNDERETTE to find out what
finally puts Lucy back on the road to happiness.

**RED
DRESS
INK**
™

Visit us at www.reddressink.com          RDI09031-TR

Also on sale from Red Dress Ink

# Milkrun

## Sarah Mlynowski

MILKRUN is a fun and crazy novel about drinks, dates and other distractions, as twenty-five-year-old Jackie Norris tries to find love in Boston—that is, if she can find a decent single man living in Boston!

**"Just wonderful—funny and heartbreaking and true, true, true."**
**—*New York Times* bestselling author Jennifer Weiner on MILKRUN**

**"Mlynowski is acutely aware of the plight of the 20-something single woman—she offers funny dialogue and several slices of reality."**
**—*Publishers Weekly***

Visit us at www.reddressink.com          RDI09032-TR

Also by Erica Orloff

# Spanish Disco

Prescription for heartburn:
Avoid spicy foods, alcohol, coffee and stress.

Prescription for heartache:
Avoid feeling sorry for yourself.

Too bad for editor Cassie Hayes, she's got a bad case of
both. And now that her publishing company is in dire
straits, she's stuck on an island with an epic poem that was
supposed to be a long-awaited sequel, a cook who goes
a little heavy on the cayenne, a nasty coffee addiction,
a predilection for tequila and a reclusive author more
than happy to ply her with beer. There's little doubt that
she'll survive the adventure, but will you?

Visit us at www.reddressink.com

RDI0103R1-TR

**Think you're supposed to be married with 2.5 kids by the age of thirty? Think again! Check out these books, and discover the wilder side of life after thirty.**

**With all these options we might just keep you up all night!**

Pick up your favorite titles
at your local bookseller.
For more info on our titles and authors
check out reddressink.com

**RED
DRESS**
I N K
TM

Visit us at www.reddressink.com          RDIBL031-TR

If you liked *Diary of a Blues Goddess,* you'll love...

# Strapless

Leigh Riker

### Australia or Bust!

Darcie Baxter is given a once-in-a-lifetime chance to open a new lingerie shop in Sydney. So she packs up and moves to Australia, leaving New York City, her grandmother and her possessed cat behind. A whirlwind affair with an Australian sheep rancher sends her into panic mode, fleeing Australia with a bad case of the noncommittals. Who wants to be barefoot and pregnant in the Outback? But don't worry— she won't get away that easily!

**RED DRESS INK** ™

Visit us at www.reddressink.com                    RDI0802R1-TR